The
Urban Erotica
Fairy Tale
Collection

The
Urban Erotica
Fairy Tale
Collection

HONEY CUMMINGS

4 Horsemen
Publications, Inc.

4 Horsemen
Publications, Inc.

4 Horsemen Publications, Inc.
1497 Main St. Suite 169
Dunedin, FL 34698
4horsemenpublications.com
info@4horsemenpublications.com

Cover & Typesetting by Autumn Skye
Edited by 4 Horsemen Publications, Inc.

Library of Congress Control Number: 2022952008

Audio ISBN: 978-1-64450-795-7
Ebook ISBN: 978-1-64450-794-0
Print ISBN: 978-1-64450-793-3

Table of Contents

THE URBAN EROTICA
FAIRY TALE COLLECTION

Beau AND Professor Bestialora

HONEY CUMMINGS

B eau loved books.

He also loved games and anything fantasy including movies and the occasional guilty pleasure of erotic fairy tales. Regardless, this semester had been rough. Stopping in front of Professor Bestialora's office door, he took in a deep breath and held it.

She'd been a monster.

Her temper short and he had lost his patience on more than one occasion and the entire class was dismissed the last time. They had fallen into a cold shoulder attitude the last few weeks, and now, she had emailed him to discuss his draft for his final paper. Over the course of the Dark Ages History class, they had been a volatile mix; their opinions on some of histories accuracies had shown how passionate they were on the topic.

That was, until she found his profile on YayLove.

They were matches, at a high percentage and considering they were into a lot of the same fandoms, why wouldn't they match? Worse, she sent an inquiry. Beau hadn't responded and soon after, her temper had faded in class. Looking down at his phone, he pulled the profile up and stared at the smile he never once saw in class.

Does she know this is me? She must know. It's the same picture I use for all my university profiles. I mean, the weight of silence between us in class...

And now he stood at her door for their scheduled meeting.

Swallowing, he glared down at his Game of Thrones shirt with disdain. He was a geek and she was, well, his professor for one more week. Clicking off the profile from his phone, he left it still unanswered as he slid the phone in his pocket. Besides, the woman was just on the other side of this door. The words of her profile whispered into his head since he'd read it repeatedly. They had so much in common, but the way things had been since he entered her classroom had been a complete disaster.

Puffing out his cheeks, he knocked, and the door flew open. She didn't look angry. In fact, she looked nervous, scared even.

"Come in, Beau." She waved him in, and the door shut loud.

The lock slid in place and Beau was now trapped within her castle.

He swallowed down his nerves, "You wanted to see me?"

"You can say that, but..." She walked around and leaned on her desk in front of him, horribly close. "I want an answer."

"Wh-what?" He paled; *she couldn't mean.* "Answer?"

"I know we got off on a bad foot, but after reading your profile on YayLove, I..." She lost her words, a first as her face flushed. "I want to start over, Beau."

"But what about school policy." Her finger hit his lips and her own tickled at Beau's ear.

"Let's not bring school into this. This is about two people looking for sex." Her perfume rolled in his nose, the heat of her body enthralling as her sultry voice whispered. "I've been a bitch. A beast, even. It wasn't my intention, but it's been so long..."

"So long." He echoed as her finger pulled away. "Miss... I mean, Beatrice. I must admit, I didn't think you would have pinged me on YayLove. With how things started, I..."

"I'm sorry." It pained her to say it, but her blue eyes landed on him and something stirred inside him. Her profile echoed, *I love Game of Thrones, D&D, Tolkien, and anything Fantasy.* "What is your favorite lovemaking scene in Game of Thrones?"

The question fell from him and caught them both off guard. Her red lips curved upward. Teeth baring, his heart raced, and his cock grew hard. There it was, the smile he had seen on the profile and at last, it was his now, only for him in this private moment. Her long brown locks framed her face like a lion's mane and a hint of her fantasy-loving side hinted as the long, black nails tapped on the desk.

Does she play as a warlock in DnD?

"When Jon Snow finally gave way to his yearning and the wildling girl pounced him at last." She cooed, unbuttoning her jacket, her chest heaving.

His cock rubbed against his jeans and he groaned, watching the jacket slide off her shoulders to reveal hard nipples and a GoT shirt underneath matching his own. Her breasts were large, stretching and distorting the logo of the Stark House. In this moment, he realized the frustration between them hadn't been disdain, but sexual tension. She had figured it out before him, and she intended to act on it in this private moment between them.

He flew from his chair in reckless abandonment. Locking lips, he wanted more of Beatrice Bestialora. His hand slid under her shirt, a moan escaping her as his fingers discovered a braless breast. Her tongue pushed between his lips only to meet his own as he forced her to retreat. He wanted to explore her first, conquer her and stalk her every move.

Pinching her nipple, twisting, she moaned into his mouth. Her fingers were fumbling with his pants and came to her aid, his freehand quick and they fell to the floor. Hot silky fingers grasping his cock, firmly the rubbed his length and now he moaned. She circled the tip, slick with precum then back to stroking his shaft, her thumb riding the underbelly. His fingers abandoned her breast, unzipping her pencil skirt, feeling hungry to explore more. It fell away revealing black lacy thongs and he pulled away grinning to admire the view.

"Did you wear these just for me, my little warlock?" She laughed hiding her face into his shoulder.

Ha! I knew it!

"How did you know what I play in DnD?" Her fingers tightened their grip on his cock, and he groaned.

"I can't decide." He moaned as she stroked his length more aggressively, her breath hot on his neck. "It was... it was either the black fingernails... or..."

"Or what?" Again, her sultry voice in his ear sent chills across his body and he couldn't stop the shudder in his shoulders. "I want to know, my beloved Beau."

"Or how well you're handling my wand."

She laughed and he throbbed in her hand.

Pushing his hand into the front of her underwear, he found the pink valley and flooding river awaiting him. Two fingers fell into the heated depths of her folds and she collapsed into him, her nipples hard against his chest even through his shirt. He stood firm, her grip waning on his throbbing cock; he was winning. Her moans and shivers only encouraged him further, rubbing in and out ever faster. Nails clawed at him through his shirt before balling into fists.

"No more..." Beatrice huffed, her body on fire and rolling on the edge of an orgasm. "I want, I want you."

"You have me." Beau grinned, pulling his fingers out of her pussy, leaving her throbbing with desire.

They both rushed in the break, shirts dropping to the floor and abandoning what little clothes remained. The last of their walls gone, they stood on even playing fields in their complete naked state. With a wave of an arm, Beau sent half the items on her desk scattering to the floor. A Jon Snow Funko doll rolled and stopped to watch them, unmoved by their actions. Beatrice started to scoot her bare ass onto the desk, but Beau gripped her hips. With skill, he twisted her around, pulling her into him.

Hot hands rolled over her bare skin, chills of anticipation rolling across her body as a shudder now rocked her shoulders. One hand glided to her breast, massaging, and teasing her nipple. The other rolled over her navel and between her thighs. A finger found her clit and began rolling over it. She stiffened, the sensation only adding to the wetness now dripping down her thighs. A whimper escaped her, and she bit her lip, fighting the orgasm he tempted from her.

She wasn't ready to come, not until he entered her. A wicked grin crossed his face, he could tell she was fighting it, holding it back. He wanted her satisfied again and again. He would make her come for him, against her will. They may have come to a stalemate time and time again in the classroom, but she would no longer be the beast between them here in this moment.

With each moan from her, she could feel his cock throb with delight against her thigh. It excited him to see her lose ground with each passing second. A warm tongue licked across her shoulder and up her neck. Beau began sucking, pulling a hard suction as his hands picked up pace, growing aggressive with each passing second. Reaching up, she clawed at his hair, failing to pull him from his work on her neck.

"You'll..." A yelp left her lips. Lunging forward only resulted in feeling the muscles in his arms tighten and pull her back. "You'll leave a mark."

Releasing the suction with a large pop of his mouth, he ran a tongue over the hickie.

"Now they'll know I tamed the beast." He cooed, suckling on her earlobe.

Her body shook and he knew she back on the verge of an orgasm. She had fought so hard and it delighted him to feel her body struggle and react against her will. He switched breasts, her thighs tightened over his hand and he shoved his fingers deep inside.

A wail of ecstasy howled from her.

Nails clawing to pull him out from between her legs as she came. Seizing the opportunity, his hands retreated. Pushing her forward, he let her fall onto the cool desk, wiggling and cooing as she rode out the orgasm. She could feel the heat of his hand riding across the small of her back and up her spine. Before she could recover, he slid inside her, his cock hard, throbbing with each squeeze of her pussy. She hadn't finished her orgasm and now fuel had been added to her fire.

Another shriek escaped and he pushed her firm against the desk, strong fingers wrapped around the back of her neck. He had been slow, pushing inside until he could go no further. Torturous pleasure racked her every fiber of being. He was thick and long, swollen in her tight orgasm. She indulged in the moment of stillness with nothing more than his throbbing cock in response to her squeezing. This was the instant she had wanted and now she had him.

At first, slow, he teased her as he pulled all the way out then pausing before sliding slowly back in, all the way until his hip bones dug into her ass cheeks. Over and over, her pussy dripping down her thighs. Moaning, he leaned over her, he began picking up speed, he was growing closer. His fingers tightened on her neck and hip, their bodies on fire and sprinkled with sweat. She could feel his cock growing harder with each wave, he was nearing his first orgasm and she squeezed her pussy tight.

His hand pulled away from her neck and his body followed, leaving her cold in its wake. Gripping her hips, he spun her around, sliding her far enough on the desk to get the angle he wanted. Arms wrapped around her, arching her back as he entered her again. She whimpered, shuddering as lips wrapped around her nipple. The heat of his lips and the flick of his tongue made her breath catch. His moaning, his thrusting, the very strength of his body sent it over the top once again.

He had made her come again.

Screaming was met with teeth nipping at her nipple. She clung to him, fingernails clawing at the skin of his back. His shoulder blades holding her up and his pace quickened. Moaning turned to grunting. The swollen cock tight against her slick inner walls. Gasping, she gripped the back of his head, tugging his hair and he looked up into her eyes.

"Not there. Cum anywhere you want, but not there." It was a growled plead.

He paused, weighing her blue eyes as he caught his breath. "Anywhere?"

With a toothy smile she echoed, "Anywhere."

She watched his eyes wondering what devious plan she opened the doors to allow him such a wide range of options. His stare trailed downward across her body as he stood straight. First, they lingered on her lips. He slid out, stroking himself as he prepared his answer. They broke free and glided over her breasts, her chest rising and falling, nipples erect with excitement. Once more, their brown glare moved back to between her spread legs and he smirked at how swollen and wet he had managed to make her.

Goosebumps trickled across her skin. He hadn't rushed the decision and it filled her with excitement and fear. Instead he savored every detail and option her body had to offer. Her heart raced as his freehand slid over her clit. Fingers dove in and she hummed as he stroked himself, playing with both. He longed to have released there, but she had denied him. Cruel and teasing, just as he had done to her and he looked pained by the options. She tightened around his two fingers as the strokes grew more aggressive in and out of her pussy. He huffed, squeezing, and stroking his own cock in frustration.

The fingers left her, sliding downward. Her breath caught in her throat. His eyes watched her face, gauging her reaction. She hadn't revealed anything but want as he slid into her ass. Her secret desire to take all of him, in every way a step closer without needing to plead. One finger, then two, and she could feel her pussy dripping wet with anticipation. Her body had given him the hint he was hoping for, she wanted him to find this path. Pulling his hand away, gripping her thighs and pressed the tip of his cock against her anus.

"Anywhere." He repeated, entering just the tip.

She never broke her stare with him. "Anywhere."

He pushed in, the tight fit making both moan by the rush of new sensations. Raising her knees, she gave him all the access he needed. He was slow and steady, watching as she arched, grinned how wet she continued to become with each stroke as he built the momentum up once more. Her hand snaked downward, playing with herself, and he found himself on the edge once more, far quicker than he had anticipated. Grunting, slamming himself in and out of her ass, watching her fingers dive into her pussy as she squealed with another orgasm.

He peaked and she wailed once more.

Vicarious relief washed over him, his cock pushing deep, filling her with cum. He glided his hands over her hips, across her abdomen before squeezing her breasts. Three times she had come for him. She was a beast hungry for sex and he wanted to know how much more could this monstrous appetite could take. How many more times could he make her rise and fall before he won the war in a series of battles?

Breaking away, he squatted between her legs. A thumb circled her clit once and her legs clamped around him like a bear trap. They met his shoulders and he could see her pussy throbbing. With his other hand, he dove into her swollen folds and stroked with uncanny speed. A gasp and shrill filled the room fingers gripping his hair, egging him on now that everything had grown oh so sensitive. She tightened and peaked with alarming ease. His cum dribbled from her anus, her entire body tense.

That's four.

Again, he retreated, rubbing her thighs and body down with the heat of his hands. She couldn't speak. Panting, she shuddered as waves of exhilarating sensations jolted through her. He pursed his lips, blowing hot air across her pink valley. Thighs squeezed his broad shoulders, unable to hide the unbearably sensitive parts from their attacker. Deep down, she didn't want it to end.

Knock knock!

"Dr. Bestialora?" It was Professor Gaston from next door. "Are you alright?'

The doorknob jiggled, but it had been locked in preparation of what she had hoped would unfold between Beau and her.

"I'm fi..." She lost the words as silken lips wrapped around her clit and suckled.

"What's going on in there?" Professor Gaston demanded. "Didn't I see Beau come in?"

Beau released her and replied, "We're discussing my work on relationship practices during the Dark Ages and how they differ from the Age of Antiquity."

She gave Beau a skeptical look, "Yes, Beau and I are in the middle of... ah."

Beau's tongue slid across her pussy, hot and silky before sucking on her clit once more. She was sitting up, her hands tangled in his hair and unable to pull him from his prize.

"In the middle... of impor... important discussions for... for next year!" She knew he was making a game of it; could she talk to Gaston and not give herself away. "C-come. Come back later."

There was silence before Professor Gaston pressed, "You sound breathless. Are you unwell?"

"I'm fine!" She shrieked, Beau's work growing more aggressive.

He slid his tongue inside her, making her legs shake. Biting her lip, she fought the urge to squeal or moan. She had been wailing like a banshee, surely, he had heard that. The suckling grew and teeth nipped at her swollen flower. He was devouring her as if she were a melting ice cream on a hot summer day. And she didn't want it to stop.

"Please go..." She couldn't tell which man it had been meant for.

"Fine." Professor Gaston sounded pissed off. He knew and yet, "Dinner at my place is still open..."

"No!" She wailed as Beau sucked long and hard on her clit. "I can't stand it. Please, stop!"

Beau let go, flipping her over to grasp the chair so they both face the door. His cock was hard again and he had her teetering on the edge for a fifth time. With Professor Gaston's silhouette in the frosted glass of the door, he wanted her to come knowing someone was there. He wanted Gaston to hear what he couldn't have. He rubbed the tip of his cock against her swollen lips, teasing her, entering her just barely only to pull away and rub his shaft against the wet heat.

"Look, I won't stop."

The doorknob wiggled more, and Beau dipped the tip just barely inside her.

"Stop being a tease." She moaned, abandoning their game.

Beau shushed her, shaking his head as he pulled away and rubbed his hard shaft against her thigh.

"Please give it to me." She whimpered, wiggling her ass against his hips. "I want more."

"You can't have it," He began playing with her clit once more. "I want you to scream it, none of this playing nice or using manners. I can't imagine a warlock being such a pushover."

Her face flushed, her grip on the chair tightening.

"Beatrice? Beau?" She glared at the silhouette as Gaston refused to leave.

"Fuck! Fucking do as I told you, welp!" Beatrice had abandoned her composure as Beau rammed in her pussy.

His fingers dug into her hips as he fucked her hard and fast; they were peaking together. He started moaning and it was all she needed to roll over the edge a fifth time. Her pussy tightened, holding his cock and he came. She rocked against him, savoring the elations; waves of pleasure making her tremble over and over.

Professor Gaston had walked away at some point in the peaking seconds of pleasure. Beau pulled away, flopping down on her desk behind him. She stayed there, panting, and bent over the chair. Cum dripped from her, mixing with her own wetness, making its way down her legs. Her body on fire, riding out the never-ending tide of pleasure.

Boy smirked, catching his breath and enjoying the view.

Maybe I can get her to come a sixth time?

END

THE URBAN EROTICA
FAIRY TALE COLLECTION

The
Goat's
Gruff

HONEY CUMMINGS

Table of Contents

Part 1

Sitting in front of his computer, Taylor Rolley stared at the GreetUp website. He heard rumors about those events with certain keywords. The ones with "naughty intentions" and wondered if they really existed. If he wanted to venture out and explore his unspoken sexual side (without judgment), this was the place to start. With a twist of his lips, he registered, then moved the cursor into the search box, first typing in "sex", followed by "intercourse". But no results.

How do you find them? I have no idea which keywords to use!

His phone buzzed, his close friend Lou Brigadier texting him. He scowled at his phone. If it wasn't for Lou's wild stores stories about attending these sexual parties, he wouldn't have found this site. Shaking his head, he unlocked it and text messages appeared.

Lou: [Did you register yet?]

Taylor: [Yes, why?]

Lou: [Sending you an invite to the party.]

In a flash, his phone and computer dinged in unison. There it was. The invitation from Lou titled, *Erotic Masquerade Party*. Taylor scoffed at the title.

Erotic... why didn't I think of that.

Scanning the details, they were very vague. A mask would be presented at arrival to keep all identities a secret before knocking on the door. *No names* and *no garments* were the only listed requirements.

The theme... *fairy tales.* Taylor rolled his eyes. *Invite only and come ready to swing.*

Taylor: [Isn't swinging for couples?]

Lou: [Na man. Just hungry peeps.]

Taylor: [I don't have a mask.]

Lou: [Just wear that art project you made in high school, dude. I'll pick you up at 9.]

Taylor swiveled his chair and stared at the homemade troll mask. It was meant for use in a play, but it creeped everyone out, so the entire production refused to use it, giving it to him as a consolation prize. The play had been called the *Three Billy Goat's Gruff.*

The mask was solid white with warty features and tusks. It was designed so the lower half was missing, keeping the jaw uncovered so it wouldn't interfere with the actor's performance. He had only joined drama for that year, all for a chance to impress his crush, Celeste.

Fate intervened. We just weren't supposed to be together. Yea, I'm still salty even after all the time that's passed...

Taylor shook the memories from his mind. Instead, focusing his imagination at the present situation. He tried picturing himself naked, save for a mask, then shuddered at the possibility.

Taylor: [No one wants to fuck a troll.]

There was no reply.

Lou knew better than to respond to Taylor's excuse. If Lou ignored him now, it would ensure Taylor's attendance at the masquerade.

He sighed. *Nothing ventured, nothing gained*, he thought as he cursed silently into the bathroom, preparing for an evening, completely in the nude.

Part 2

They arrived at the address, passing the security gate without trouble. Good thing since Taylor didn't want the guard to see how ridiculous he looked in a bathrobe and a handmade school mask. As they came around the bend, the house was huge. The only structure at the end of a cul-de-sac of empty multimillion-dollar lots. Still sitting in the car, Taylor watched as plenty of masked people in bathrobes entered the house.

At least I match the trendy crowd this time. Unlike high school...

Music pulsed through the air and the moonless night made him feel like he had been transported into an erotic version of the *Purge*. The question was whether he was the slayer or the slayed. Blowing a puff of air from his nose, he settled on becoming the latter. That's if he could even step out of the car and join the festivities. Shuffling, in his seat, he tugged the robe's belt tighter as if afraid to reveal what lay underneath.

Shit, I don't think I can do this... this is a terrible idea. Curiosity killed the cat and will definitely kill me at this rate.

Knots twisted Taylor's stomach, making himself sick as he looked at his own body, feeling betrayed.

I'm just an average guy without a six pack. At least I don't have a beer gut. Oh man, I can't... I don't have the body to pull this off.

Lou elbowed him, nudging his head towards a unicorn and fairy. They were naked, not a bathrobe in sight. The girls were curvy and beautiful enough to grace the cover or spread in a *Maxim*. Aroused, he remembered he did have one secret weapon.

At least I'm hung like a fucking horse.

He looked at Lou and they shrugged. At least there was eye candy at every turn. Inhaling deep, he gathered his nerves, regaining his lost confidence.

I can do this!

"Ok, so this is the place to be," Taylor declared. "But what do we do now?"

Lou turned off the ignition and twisted to face him. "Some rules. I can't have you fucking this up for me."

"Gee, thanks for the vote of confidence?" Taylor marveled. *Asshole.*

"Seriously, we can't use our names here. It's taboo and you'll get banned." Lou adjusted the polygonal wolf mask on his face. "The moment we step out of the car, my name is the Big Bad Wolf and you're Troll. Got it?"

"There's no way in hell I'm calling you that." Taylor tightened the cord on his own mask, thankful for how it conformed to his face. "Wolf. That's all you get from me, mutt."

"Fine, Troll."

Lou stepped out of the car, assuming his new identity, despite how awkward he felt. Taylor hadn't had a pretend name since online gaming back in grade school.

Troll followed as Wolf continued to lay the rules out. "Whatever you do, don't take off your mask, even if they insist. They'll ban you. If someone says no, leave them alone or they'll ban you. And lastly, don't dare imply you know the person underneath the mask or..."

"They'll ban you. I got it. Secrecy is top priority." Troll and Wolf went through the front door, entering the foyer. "So exactly how does... this... holy fuck."

What the hell am I looking at? So much... skin and moaning and... wow.

Troll's eyes scanned the grand living room. He couldn't tell what furniture filled the room, except the naked masked people filling the space. Masks came in different levels and colors; Furries, full-faced animals, masquerade, and even gimp masks covered the identity of the participants in the room. Blinking, he assessed each cluster as if selecting which porno, he'd beat off to for the night. Sexual orientation had no restrictions as threesomes of all combinations groped each other.

So, this is what an orgy looks like in person.

One mask brought his eyes back to it with each attempt to take inventory of the events unfolding. It was nestled and half hidden behind the sea of bodies. Troll tilted his head, feeling nostalgic as he tried to get a clear view of a familiar mask. Two girls dressed as a bunny and fox were tag teaming at pleasuring a girl in an elaborate goat mask. Distraction took hold, his eyes falling to her lower jaw and exposed deep red lips. She bit them and he swore they locked eyes, a glint of surprise in her deep dark irises.

Does she recognize me? Do I know them?

His eyes lingered, travelling downward to her rosebud nipples and hourglass figure. Her skin had a healthy glow, even in the low lighting. As if alerted, Bunny and Fox looked his way, giving him a clearer view of Goat. Thighs open wide as fingers retracted from their play, the provocative view tantalizing on all levels. Troll could feel himself getting hard. Licking his lips, this was what he'd hope he would find. He refocused back on the mask.

What kind of mask is that? It looks familiar.

"Wolf, how does this..." He turned to find his friend slipping away. "W-wait! What do I do? How does this work?"

"Fuck someone." Wolf waved him towards the room. "I think I found myself a Red Riding Hood to chase... enjoy!"

What does 'fuck someone' even mean?!

Wolf faded into a crowded hall of people drinking and groping. Looking back to the orgy in the room, he lost sight of the three girls that had tickled his fancy. On the far side, a centipede made up of a sexual chain was forming. On tables were fishbowls filled with colorful packages. He walked over to find a variety of condoms, even sample Viagra packs. He was crashing from sensory overload now that he lost his initial focus.

They don't mess around at these things. Granted, they did insist we come naked so... but what are the rules of engagement?

Two people brushed pass him, making him painfully aware he hadn't shed his stolen hotel-room bathrobe yet. He untied it and gripped the edges, his hardon glaring up at him like a dog begging for scraps. He should be naked like the others in the room.

Hung like a horse. Christ, it looks like I'm wielding a fucking broom handle. Then another harrowing thought struck him. *What if I smack someone with it?* He shuddered. *What the fuck have I gotten myself into?*

Closing his eyes, he let the robe fall to the ground, among many others. Even throwing his arms out like some kind of naked showman. He waited for...

What the hell am I doing? Everyone's naked and busy having sex, so why the hell would they be staring at me?

Snapping his eyes back open, the chain of sex had grown longer. His stomach knotted, the unrivaled exploration unfolding before him was too much. He scanned the room again, hoping to spot one of the three girls he had seen, but at last, no signs. Twisting around, he decided to explore the house. He'd never been in a mansion like this, so what did it matter if he took his time? Besides, he wanted to be more comfortable with being nude in the sea of cocks and pussies.

Looking at my competition, I'm in the younger selection as well as the bigger dicks lot. Maybe I'll get to let loose after all.

A smile came to his face. He was comparing himself with every man he passed, and it was enough to grow his confidence. On occasion, he would peek into the various bedrooms, watching what scenes were being played out. The women came in all colors and sizes. The Queen of Hearts was spanking an Alice, while she choked down the Mad Hatter's dick. He wondered if watching other couples while pleasuring themselves was taboo. His hardon was pure arousing agony as he enjoyed the roleplaying unfolding before him.

Wow, those porno parodies ain't got nothing on these people. He looks like a dead ringer for Johnny Depp.

Another room had Snow White being gang banged by all sort of forest animals, and he had to decline an invite as the horse pounding her waved him in.

Apparently, Prince Charming's horse wanted in on that action too.

The people, male and female, came in all shapes from plump and tall, to short and skinny. He'd never thought about what his physical preference would be until now. Granted, this place was the first time he could see the full menu up close and personal. His cock seemed to know, giving a clear sign of who he wanted to touch and those he didn't.

I like hips, subtle breasts, and lips that unfold like flower petals. Dark hair. Long, wavy but not curly... and down and falling over the shoulders. Not sure why, but dammit that's hot. And between the thighs I like... I wonder, maybe try my luck with... dammit, I can't walk around dipping my dick in every vagina I find, can I?

He spotted a girl in a poodle mask and grew hard, his mind checking off his list of wants. She was only a little shorter than him, her hips large and curvy. She was as average as he was, but he liked that, and he wanted that. Unlike Wolf, it didn't take much to snuff out his self-esteem. Her hair was pulled back in a ponytail and she leaned on the wall, a glass of wine in hand. Puffing up, he approached her. He glanced down at his dick which stood at attention.

Here's goes nothing! Don't let me down, buddy!

"Hi there."

She turned, her eyes looking him up and down, lingering on his hardened length. "My, aren't we a big boy."

Score, now for the kill...

"I was wondering if..."

"No thanks. You're not my type." She shot him down fast and hard, his libido deflating some. "Besides, who'd want to fuck a troll."

The laughter from her stung. She pulled off the wall and walked away. Passing a table, she abandoned her wine glass and grabbed the painfully obvious older man in the horse mask. She gave Troll a glance, making sure he was watching. Groping the man's cock, she pulled his hand to her pussy, excited that he would watch her fuck another man.

Anger seeped in, and Troll turned away. *What a Bitch. Well, I didn't want to fuck a gold digger anyhow. Dammit... I knew this mask was a shit idea. Wear that mask from high school, he said. It'll be fine, he said. You fucked me over, Wolf.*

He went upstairs, no longer pleased with the lack of action happening on the first floor. Peeking into the first room, he found Wolf. Indeed, he'd found a petite girl, in nothing but a red hood and plain white masquerade mask. She was on all fours atop a king-sized bed. The headboard banged against the wall and the mattress springs squeaked from their efforts. She panted, moaning with each thrust as her breasts swayed. Her skin was pale, hair blonde, petite—on all fronts, completely Wolf's type.

I swear. The girls he picks could almost pass as sisters. Like cookie cutter people. Blonde, nearly midget height pale thin things every time. I want a woman that I don't have to wonder if she'll break under my touch like a porcelain doll.

Rolling his eyes, Troll continued down the hall. He didn't come here to watch his friend screw, but he needed to find someone to mingle with. *And quick.* Turning a corner, he froze. At the end of the hall he saw Bunny. The long white ears stood erect, covering her face like a superhero's mask. If Wolf had a gander at her, he'd want to hit that. Short blonde hair and a petite body, standing in the dimly lit hall.

Perfect Wolf bait.

Following her line of sight, a few more steps to clear his own view, he saw Fox.

Ok, two out of the three...

Her little top hat and ears complimented the orange and white whiskered animal face obscuring her face, enhancing her alluring black lipstick. She was taller than the majority in the hall. Her arms athletic and a body fit for a kickboxer at best. Even her thighs and calves made it clear she either ran a lot or lifted weights heavier than what he'd ever attempt in this lifetime. Hooking up with a woman like that would make him feel like the porcelain doll.

That's two. Does that mean...

Sidling to the side, shouldering the wall of the hallway, he caught a glimpse of the third girl, the one he was after. Her pink nipples on tan skin, red lips like rose petals; he didn't need to see the mask to know it was her. He grew hard again and cursed under his breath. Shoving pass a fucking couple, he locked eyes with her once more. Brown pools looked on in shock as if frightened by Troll's approach. A smirk filled his face. For the first time in his life, he felt like a hunter chasing prey. His pulse raced as his heart beat against his chest. He leaned to the right, trying to catch a glimpse of her oh-so-familiar mask in full. Spiraling horns and a Y-shaped mouth gave it away at last.

She's the goat! That's what I'm after, I'm the troll. Dammit I want her so bad, I'm blue balling just thinking about what I could do to her. And why does her mask look so familiar? Where have I seen it before? The paint is amazing but...

A hand gripped his shoulder and spun him around. He closed his eyes tight. Goosebumps rolled across Troll's skin at the idea of someone seeking him out. His heart fluttered. This was it, his first invitation to fuck.

Please don't be a dude, please don't be a dude.

Troll opened his eyes and Wolf threw up his hands. "Whoa, watch where you're pointing that thing."

Glad his face was covered by the mask, Troll's cheeks heated with embarrassment and frustration. Looking over Wolf's shoulder, he snorted, seeing no sign of Red Riding Hood.

I don't have time for this...

"Don't tell me you two-pumped-chumped her, Wolf."

"You're such a troll." He crossed his arms as if questioning how much Troll had seen. "Seeing your hardon tells me you still haven't fucked anyone. What the hell are you waiting for? Blue balls? There's plenty of naked people to pick from."

"Shut up." Troll rubbed the back of his neck, his groin aching for something palpable than simple eye candy. "I tried a few times, but no one is interested."

Wolf began to laugh. "Then don't ask permission. Show them the troll love they're missing!"

Troll looked over his shoulder, catching a glimpse of Goat's horns above the crowd of naked bodies. He swallowed, clenching his clammy fists. He didn't want to lose her again, but his confidence faltered as his eyes spotted Poodle. If that failed, what were the chances of him rebuilding his confidence in a matter of minutes? Recalling his past failed relationships, including the time he'd approached his longtime crush, didn't seem likely.

Celeste shot me down. Granted, I didn't know she was dating someone at the time. Ugh, that was high school... She's long gone, and I'm at an orgy standing around with a monster-sized erection like a dumb ass. Use it or lose it!

"Work them over how?" He turned back to Wolf, determined to change his fate. "We both know I suck in real life. How will a mask make a difference?"

"Dude, watch and learn." He shoved Troll to the side as he sashayed to Poodle.

"I tried to hit that, but..." his voice trailed off. Sucking on the side of his cheek, he discouraged himself from stopping Wolf. *I hope this fails. Or it will prove how pathetic I already feel.*

Wolf didn't hold back as he went in for the kill, first licking her collarbone, then carefully tracing the curve of her neck.

Troll cringed. *He can't be serious. No way in hell can this end well. Who fucking approaches a stranger, then licks them without a formal introduction?*

Circling behind her, Wolf slid his hand over her hip and ass cheeks before wandering back to face her. Troll waited for the inevitable face slap, but Wolf continued his attack, relentless and unapologetic. Pinching one erect nipple, then using his other hand to dive between her thighs. The bold move made Troll shift uncomfortably on his feet. Poodle abandoned her wine glass onto the floor, whimpering like a hungry dog as she arched into Wolf, giving him easier access to all the right places. This only made Wolf's hand dive deeper and he leaned down to suckle the other nipple.

What the fuck just happened? What the hell just happened?

Wolf looked his way before tossing his head back and howled into the ceiling. It was the most ridiculous thing Troll had ever witnessed in his life, or even in a cheesy porno.

Debbie Does Dallas made more sense than this!

With that, Poodle bent over, giving him a direct route. Wolf gripped her hips, sliding his cock right into her, hard and fast. She panted and barked with every thrust. The whole event growing wilder and more confusing to Troll as he took it all in, every detail.

I can't believe this. He shook his head. *What happened to the old man dressed as a horse? Did he even get this far?* Anger crept forward. *Goat's missing and now I'm watching this bullshit go down.*

"Poodles are such bitches," Troll muttered, stewing in his bitter thoughts.

Is he out of his mind? What made him think I could be bold enough to approach a naked stranger by sucking a titty or poking my fingers into their pussy?

Scanning the hall again, he locked eyes with Goat once more and grew hard again. Grunting, the sensation was agonizing now. Something about the way she moved, the jawline and hair cascading down her back in long dark waves. The divet down her back, the subtle rise and fall of her shoulder blades, even the dimples on her hips. Every part of her body appealed to him, one way or another.

God, she's gorgeous.

Looking back to Wolf, he had swapped roles, his dick already lodged in Poodle's throat. Wolf gave him a thumbs up before continuing his conquest. Troll cringed. His attraction for Poodle vanished as soon as Goat returned into view. It was then he realized his purpose; time to act out the role he had dressed for.

If everyone here wants to roleplay, then the Troll is after a goat. What was that tale? Oh yea, The Three Billy Goats Gruff. That's the whole reason why I even made this stupid thing for the Drama club. All I wanted was to get closer to Celeste, but they cancelled it and...

Cracking his knuckles, he charged down the hall. Wolf grabbed his arm, his cock still deep in Poodle's mouth. He pointed down and Troll scowled at him. He was making an offer and it sent a chill across his spine.

You can have that...

"Wanna piece?" Wolf grunted as he pulled out, taking a step back, enjoying his domination over her. "C'mon Troll, your part of my pack. Get in here."

Troll looked down at Poodle. On her hands and knees, she moaned and wiggled her ass as if to entice him. He could see the light catching her inner thighs; the woman was beyond wet and ready. Looking back at Wolf, he could see the stupid face his friend Wolf would make under it.

Two mutts deserve each other. Nothing sexy about her at this point.

"I got a goat to chase." A smirk crossed his face, the troll in him cackling.

The Poodle pulled herself off Wolf's cock, scoffing. "Did he just refuse to fuck me?"

"Yea. Apparently, you shouldn't have been a bitch to him earlier." Wolf gripped her ponytail and shoved his dick between her lips, silencing her. "No one fucks with the troll unless he wants to play with you first."

Part 3

It seemed like hours had passed. Troll had lost track of Wolf, even though the front window showed his car still parked under a streetlight. Snorting, Troll searched everywhere for the scrumptious goat. Waves of people had come and gone, new masks appearing to mingle in each new sexual delight. A fairy stopped him, groping his cock. A new constant manner of greeting in this surreal sexual world. Grunting, he scowled down at her, annoyed by the unwanted intrusion. By this point, he had accepted his inner troll and played the part with enthusiasm. It didn't take him long before attendees expected him to be rude, harsh, and a bad boy.

Who knew talking down to people would invoke such priceless reactions!

She whispered promises as she stroked him, "I'll let you suck my sugarplums if I can play with your club, Troll. What say you?"

He laughed. *Ok, I give her credit on the pickup line, but I'm not in the mood.*

Leaning down, he growled. "A fairy will break under my mighty club. Besides, I'm hungry for goat and have no time to be gentle with the likes of you."

Her eyes widened and she knelt before him. "Please, oh please. Gobble me up, Troll! I am much sweeter than any goat. I am sure of it."

Begging... to have me. I don't even know what to do with this.

Troll's heart raced and he swallowed. She was pretty, light brown hair in a pixie cut. Her lips were thin pink lines on her angular face. The masquerade mask was colored like a monarch butterfly, and the wings she wore were a matching set. Shimmer paint and loose glitter decorated her body, making her look surreal in the chaos of the unfolding orgy. Her breath teased the tip of his cock, and it made his blood rush. She wasn't his usual type, but her bold approach had piqued his interest. And arousal.

I wonder... maybe I can just relieve this agony.

Curious, he leaned down and kissed her, deep and passionate, their tongues chasing each other in a dance. She suckled his tongue, refusing to let it go. He hardened in her grip. At last they broke away, her hand stroking his dick. The agonizing throb of his hardon returned to the stiffness he endured from the Goat's stolen glances. Grunting, he locked eyes with the woman under the mask, her mouth opening wide to take his length in.

Oh, sweet release is so close now.

He saw Wolf chasing another girl dressed as a fawn, antlers and full body paint. Following him to the hall, he saw *her*. Goat peeking at him from behind a wall, her eyes falling downward. The heat of the Fairy's breath against his cock startled him, forcing him to pull away. Her look of confusion made him smirked.

I can't. I don't want this. I want her more than a blow job. Wait. Am I losing my mind?

"This isn't the taste you want. Fly free and seek out the Big Bad Wolf." He pointed in the direction Wolf had gone, in a dark hallway full of entangled bodies. "He's in the enchanted forest of moaning trees."

I sound so cheesy...

"Y-yes." She rushed off and down the hallway.

Well that worked a little too well.

Troll scratched his chest, smirking.

You're welcome Wolf.

Sighing, he peered around the living room, the designated *Orgy Centipede Room*. Nothing here enticed him, and he wished he was somewhere else, to join the hunt. But his chest ached. The Bunny or Fox were nowhere in sight, the Goat's closest companions. Perhaps he'd been chasing a lesbian trio, too tired of the party and they left.

No. I know I saw her, but she's gone again.

Troll reached to his back pocket and only managed to pat his bare ass, forgetting he wasn't wearing pants. He wondered, with all these people invited via a GreetUp post, maybe he could find her that way.

He searched the floor for his robe. *Fuck*, he thought, searching frantically for it. *Where is it?* At some point during the orgasmic activity, someone must've removed them. And it wasn't a short trip to the car. His anxiety crested as his eyes locked on the back door.

Surely a million-dollar home has a pool or garden of sorts. I need air.

He stepped into the night, chills crawling the entire length of his body. Cursing under his breath, he took in the pool area, barren and free of bare flesh. Inhaling deep, he calmed his nerves. A bridge cut across the center of the pool, and he smirked at the irony of it. As he walked across, he peered over the railing and frowned. The pool was void of water, the empty span reaching the concrete edge to the far right and left.

Infinity pool? Gotta cross the damn bridge just to reach the garden? Seems like a bad design. Block this, and no one's crossing the bridge and going nowhere.

Leaning on the rail, he glared down at the empty basin. A grin came across his face. At last, the troll had his bridge. Though being naked in the cool night alone seemed pathetic. With no water, at least he didn't have to see his reflection. Nothing killed his self-esteem like catching a glimpse of his reflection, made worse by his troll mask and naked body.

Holy smokes. I just realized there are no mirrors here. Not one room, not any of the bathrooms, nowhere. Even if I wanted to see how ridiculous I looked, I'd have to return to my car and use the side mirror.

He reached under his mask and rubbed his eyes, freeing his mind from the oversaturated sex scene still raging inside. Instead, he redirected his thoughts on the starry sky, even the crickets chirping beyond the trees, where an owl hooted in the dark.

So, does that mean they drained the pool for this event? Christ, the water bill to drain it... no, to fill it back up. Is it worth having your home painted in bodily fluids? Then again, I suppose this keeps them from fucking in the pool until one of them drowns.

Part 4

"Trip, trap, trip, trap." The quaint female voice startled him.

He turned, and there stood Bunny. His heart raced. Once more cute white bunny ears tilted with intrigue. She fit the role well, but she had ventured outside the safety of the mansion and dare cross his bridge alone.

They didn't leave. No. She didn't leave.

A smile crested his face. Unlike Goat, Bunny was short and petite. Her blonde wavy hair skimmed passed her shoulders, brushing against her small pink nipples. *Beautiful.* Sighing, he eased into his role as the troll of the bridge, luring the goat to cross the bridge into greener pastures.

"Who's that tripping over my bridge?" He cooed as he peered around, hoping to catch a glimpse of seeing Fox and Goat. But they were alone.

"Oh, it's only me." She replied, taking a few steps onto the bridge. "The tiniest one. I'm going to the garden to masturbate."

"Oh?" He puffed out his chest, stepping into the center to block her way. "Are you not afraid?"

She tilted her head, the white ears shifting accordingly. "Why? Should I be?"

"Doesn't it scare you that I may gobble you up?" Part of him felt silly for acting in this provocative manner, but he hadn't been the one to trigger the dialogue.

If this worked for the fairy, surely, it'll work now.

"Oh, no! Don't eat me." With her arms behind her back, she giggled. "Wait until the second one comes. She's much bigger."

He looked her over. If she passed, then surely the goat would come this way. Every time he had spotted one of the trio, the other two were close by. Scratching his chin, he wondered exactly how far he could play out the Three Billy Goats Gruff in this manner.

What the hell. Let's go all in.

"Fine." In high school, he had rehearsed the script a billion times since he'd been the understudy for the troll. Here, he'd have to improvise, to make the hunt exciting while he awaited his prize. "Be off with you, after you've kissed me."

Bunny let out a giggle as she skipped along the bridge, stopping at the peak with a big, toothy grin, devouring him with her eyes. He tilted his head, watching as she fingered herself, begging for him to lean closer. He obeyed and she kissed him, deep and passionate. Suckling his tongue while her fingers caressed his cock.

With each of her fingers, he moaned, hardening on command to her touch. *Damn, the rabbit knows how to kiss.*

Unlike the fairy, she was an expert at teasing his tongue with the tip of her own. He chased her, even within his own lips. Her fingers rolled over his swollen flesh, caressing under his shaft with just the right amount of pressure. Fingertips glided across all the right spots, her touch magical and silky. His breath caught as she circled the ridge of his cap. At last she broke free, ending their kiss and releasing his throbbing erection.

"Promise to gobble me up later, Troll."

Before he could come to his senses, she rushed off into the garden. He stared with wonder at how his night would end at this rate. He rubbed his cock, stoking it for a moment. The sensation of how she kissed him was far more tantalizing than the fairy before, he didn't want it to fade just yet. The numbing pleasure of his cock made his shoulders shudder.

To think a woman could have a touch like that.

"Trip, trap… trip, trap." This voice was sultry, pacing each step.

Troll spun back, and there stood Fox. His cock ached, excited at the prospect of seeing Goat. Fox had to be every bit as tall as himself, thick thighs and built like a female MMA fighter. He snorted, imagining how she could pop his head off if she maneuvered him in a headlock. She took a few steps forward and his heartbeat quickened.

I don't think I was well prepared to guard my bridge at this rate. Bunny nearly had me coming in her hand, I can't imagine how I'll defend against a girl this athletic.

"Trip. Trap?" Fox tilted her head.

"Who's tripping over my bridge?" He said in a questioning tone.

"Oh, it's me, Fox." She rubbed herself, her breast bulging out of her hand while the other dipped between her thighs. "I'm going to the garden to help Bunny play with herself. I'm rather in the mood to eat rabbit."

I'm starting to think I may want to eat Bunny too.

Troll's cock hardened further. If the three of them repeated their performance from when he first arrived, he hoped they'd let him watch and stroke to each of their movements. Who knew you could watch porn live? Fox came closer, so close that he could feel heat waving off her body against his torso and cock. She grinned, her painted black lips curving into mischief. The fox mask leered down on him, and he remembered it was his turn to respond.

"I'll gobble you up." He warned, nervous at how close her lips hovered to his.

"Promise?" She cooed.

Before he could reply, she kissed him. Unlike Bunny, she chased his tongue back into his mouth, their tongues rubbing together in a wrestling match. It wasn't the kiss he was reacting to this time. Her breasts pressed into him; nipples hard as she began to grab his ass. His hardened length slid between her soaked thighs, rubbing against her swollen pussy in the heat of her body. She was rougher than Bunny. Predatorial. He throbbed against her and she pulled away.

"Oh no!" She chuckled, making him chase her with his eyes as she crossed the bridge. "Don't take me. Wait a little bit and the Big Billy Goat Gruff will come. She's the one you've been wanting to gobble up."

Laughing, Fox took off into the garden. At this stage, Troll turned to lean on the railing. His heart raced and chest ached, cock aching for more pleasure and more release. Skin against his skin, hot and silken, none of the encounters had been as sufficient as Goat's companions had been. Cravings rattled through him. Feral desire haunted him. He was so hungry now. This was the most foreplay and roleplay he had ever performed in his entire sex life. His nerves rattled him, his throbbing erection a reminder that everything he was experiencing was *real*.

No one will believe me that I trolled a bridge for sex. The high school play may have been cancelled, but shit, the encore performance is...

"Trip, trap, trip, trap." The female's familiar voice shook him.

It couldn't be!

Looking over, Goat had arrived. He froze. Her long wavy hair cascaded down her golden skin. She had ample breasts with rosebuds for nipples, her thighs as thick as Fox's own, but more of an hour-glass figure compared to her companions. Her exposed red lips bloomed like petals underneath the goat mask. Those brown eyes took his breath away before he realized the mask's detailing. The paint had obscured it until he could take a closer look.

The mask! I made that mask in high school!

"Trip, trap," she took a step closer with every word. "Trip, trap."

"I want to gobble you up." The words tumbled from his lips.

"I don't think that's the next line, Troll." She snickered, stopping in front of him, a hand placed on one hip. "Shouldn't you be asking who's tramping across your bridge?"

"I already know who's on my bridge." His heart raced with high school nostalgia, building at his core.

I'd recognize that voice anywhere, but could it be... am I dreaming? I haven't seen her since graduation.

"In that case..." She came in, leaning close until her lips tickled his ear in a whisper. "Come along with your spear, poke me like you wanted that year, curl a finger around my stone, crush me under your body and bone."

"Then, I'll gobble you up, Celeste." He wrapped his arms around her, and she squealed. "I'll gobble up the goat, you're all mine! You stole my mask and I aim to take it back!"

"How'd you know it was me, Taylor?"

He began kissing and biting at her neck, his cock hard with excitement.

"My you're hungry!" She laughed, letting him take his fill.

He laughed into her. "Because I made each mask, but and I could never find the best of the goat ones to take home, so I settled for the troll instead."

He pulled away, Troll staring at Goat. Both smiled and in this imaginary fairy tale, they'd found what they'd missed out on long ago. Goat melted down to her knees. The heat of her hands sliding down his chest sent a shudder through him. Troll had his back against the bridge railing, unable to move. He grunted as the heat of her breath brushed against his throbbing erection. The tip of her tongue circled the head of his cock, making his blood boil. She kissed the tip, and he moaned. Lips hot against the tender flesh, she kissed and suckled on his hardened shaft, from base to tip, repeating the cycle.

How long have I imagined this moment, and never did I think it would unfold like this... wearing my masks!

Gripping the railing, Troll fought the urge to shove his dick inside her mouth. The way she worked his dick, gracing it with her lips before tickling the tip with her tongue, was mind blowing.

He moaned, and she pulled away, leaving him cold. Grunting, he looked down. They locked eyes and she dropped her jaw open, her tongue stretching out like a red carpet. He reached down, a fist full of hair, and shoved himself between her lips at last. Slow, watching one another, he enjoyed letting her take him into the heat of her mouth. Any faster and he just might come too soon.

"I want you to gobble me up..." He muttered, shivering with excitement.

As he crested into the back of her throat, she moaned. Lips sealed tight around him and he throbbed in her wet warmth. She sucked, hard and long, drawing him deeper until the tip of his dick could go no further. Wiggling her head, he fought the urge to collapse forward. Every movement orgasmic and agonizing as she tried to hold back. She pulled and pushed, fast then slow. He fought his desire biting at his core.

Oh, if I knew back in high school, that this moment would be waiting for me, maybe I wouldn't have been such a bitter asshole.

He hummed as her tongue wiggled and stroked the underbelly of his erection. Rocking his hips, he tilted his head back and closed his eyes. Each wave of pleasure made him tighten his grip on her hair. Her breasts rocked into his thighs, soft and hot against his skin, hardening her nipples. Biting his lip, he fought the urge to explode.

There's too much still to gobble up. I'm still hungry for more... not yet. Please not yet!

Looking down, he had swollen until she struggled to hold him in her mouth. He let go, pulling himself from her. She stood confused by the reckless abandonment. He wanted to taste her as she had tasted him. Shoving her back, she stumbled into the opposite railing, the sharp cold metal making her gasp as he launched his attack. Troll suckled at her neck, working over Goat's collarbone until his hungry lips found his favorite spot. A moan escaped her, egging him on. He teased her nipple with his teeth, and she wailed with delight.

I want to hear her scream... I want to taste more of her...

Under him, he could feel her shudder with each taste of her breast. The jealousy of its companion striking him, he shifted to explore the other half of her chest. His erection hungry to have her yet still ignored by its master, the agony drowned out by the arousing sound of coos and hums. Denying his desire, he pleased her to no end, making her scream into the night air as he gobbled her down. Fingers knuckled on the back of his skull, encouraging him to suck her breast harder. A hot thigh glided up on his hip, signaling for him to travel deeper into the oblivion of her shaved pussy, already hot and soaking wet against his cock. Again, he refused to enter her.

I'm still hungry... I'm still tasting her body...

Abandoning his meal, he grew thirsty. A trail of kisses and lingering strokes of his tongue ventured across the valley of her stomach. The skin under his nibbled rippling and quivering with want. He knelt slow and steady much like a setting sun as he sunk between her legs. He shoved the rising thigh over his shoulder, and she parted her red door, allowing him in. He licked her, hungry and needing. Now it was her turn to grip the railing, her body arching into him as she cried out once more. His tongue dove deep in her and her body shook. Never did he think her peach would taste so sweet, be so juicy with each lick and suckle.

This will be a night she'll never forget... I want her to remember me above all others.

The sounds coming from her visceral, calling the attention of other animals from within the garden. Fox was the first to appear to feed on Goat's body. Hungry black-painted lips began suckling on a breast and before long Bunny had latched onto the other. Goat cried into the night, arching against the railing as Troll wrapped his lips around her clit. He teased the swollen jewel with the tip of his tongue. She shuddered, the leg on his shoulder shaking from the electric shock of erogenous pulses in every part of her being.

Oh, how I want to be inside her...

Two fingers slid into the wetness, hot and throbbing. A moan came from her trembling lips. Troll watched Goat's eyes roll back. Sucking and stroking, he demanded she not look away with his own glare from under his mask. She was breathless, breaking down from the exchange as she began to rock her hips, urging him to stroke deeper. Pulling out his fingers, he dove his tongue inside her once more and she cried in ecstasy, gushing with her orgasm.

I could drink for her all night, but...

Glancing at the Rabbit then Fox, he could see how they played with themselves, thighs wet as they moaned into Goat's breasts adding to her own waves of desire.

Do they wish for me to gobble them down too? Or are they hear to enjoy the festivities?

His aching dick only wanted one of them. Satisfied he had made her peak at last, he stood. Raising her leg high on his shoulder, keeping her trapped between him and the railing. He waited, catching all three of their gazes waiting for the next act. Their stares flowed down to his cock as it rubbed on top of her pussy, keeping Goat guessing as to when he might enter her. Fox and Bunny bit their lips in jealousy.

All eyes on me... she's mine and only mine.

He slid slow into Goat, her tight, wet, heat making him tremble. Her breath caught as he dove deeper inside her still. Both his cock and her pussy were swollen and aching. Her wetness allowed him to glide inside her with ease. Flesh rubbing flesh as she tightened and arched. She moaned, unable to retrieve her shaking leg as he hugged it to him. His other hand gripped her hip, keeping her from escaping him. With careful timing, he moved in and out, slow and calculating as he felt her tighten.

I want to be deeper; I want to see her face clearly...

He let her leg down, pushing himself hard into her, gaining more depth. She panted, moaning with each stroke as they rocked into one another. Wrapping his arms around her, she responded with wrapping her legs around him. Fingernails clawed across his back as she clutched him, wild with passion. His skin pimpled with anticipation as he lifted her off the railing and aimed to escape. Much to Fox and Bunny's surprise, Troll walked away with Goat in his arms, cock still in her.

Dammit I want her to myself!

"Where are you taking me?" The heat of her breath against his neck made him throb inside her, and she tightened in echo. "When are you going to come?"

Soon enough, but for now this fairy tale isn't done...

"Come along with me my dear, if you please, I'll poke you all year, crown a finger with a stone, and crush your body with my bone." They laughed as they made it to the garden.

He laid her down gently on the hillside of soft, cool grass. Goosebumps waved over her skin as his body towered over her. He pulled off his mask, shedding his identity. Taylor thumbed her beautiful lips, his hand gliding up her jaw to remove the mask. Celeste laughed, rocking her hips as she began playing with herself, moaning. At last he had his wanton woman.

Her libido is uncanny. She might crush me, body and soul.

"You're so damn beautiful." He searched her eyes, the confession lifting a weight he had been carrying all these years. "I wanted to see your face before this all ended and, and..."

"Stop slowing down," She pulled him down, her breath like hot wax against his shoulder. "And fuck me hard, Taylor. Fuck me like I know you want, until I know nothing else but pleasure that..."

Taylor's arms dove under her, making her arch her back as another primal scream erupted from her. Taking a nipple into his mouth, sucking hard, he rocked his hips ever quicker. Oh, how tight she had become! She was hot and drenched, thighs slick. Their bodies yearning for more. Moaning, her legs widened to give him full access, her fingers gripping his ass. She wanted him to be deeper and he let go of her breast. Freeing his hold, he took both her legs over a shoulder. Leaning forward he pushed in her and she gasped.

That's the first time I girl took me all the way in... my god... to think this whole time...

He would slide nearly out of her pussy before returning, shoving himself harder and faster, earning gasps and shrieks of delight. Slapping against the bottom of her thighs, her fingers dug into the ground now, enjoying the angle he had forced her into. Taylor moaned, tittering on the edge of coming, losing his fight against his body. A visceral cry escaped her; head tilting back as another orgasm shook through her. His cock stiffened. Pulling out he started to cum, the hot liquid slapping against her abdomen. They looked to one another, panting and half laughing.

I can't believe I held out that long despite blue balling all night.

Celeste rolled up to her knees and started kissing him passionately. It was his turn to lay down in the grass. She straddled him, taking him inside her once more. He panicked. He was spent. She caught the glimpse of fear in his eyes and shushed him. A promiscuous look on her face as she caught her breath a moment.

"I want you to watch me play with myself while you rest."

Oh... my... I've opened Pandora's Box.

She rocked atop him, her breast swaying. She ran a finger across the cum on her body and they dove down to her pussy. Humming, her finger dove between them, rolling over her clit. Another hand smeared his cum across her body in the other direction before rising to grope a breast. The whole while he agonized over his throbbing cock in her pussy. Grunting, he thought back to the Viagra and cursed himself for not thinking to use some. She shifted forward, still grinding, still keeping him hard enough to please herself on. Her breasts pressed on his chest as she arched into him, peaking for a third time.

How many times is she going to come? And am I going to keep up with her?

"Oh, I could just keep coming again and again." She kissed him hard and wild. "You feel so damn good inside me, Taylor."

'Goat will crush the Troll, body and bone.' That's how that story ends. Is that how I'm going to end?

Snip. Snap. Snout.

A Bunny and Fox came out.

Panic waved over Taylor. The concept of pleasing all three terrifying at the rate things were going. Celeste sat up and began to place her mask back on. Taylor wondered where his had gone, still trapped under the crush of his life (in more than one way). Heart racing, he waited for what would unfold next.

Maybe I get banned... and I'll be ok. Right?

Bunny picked up the Troll mask. He had flung it out of reach during his declaration of love. Giving it to Celeste, Goat kissed him and placed it back on with delicate care. He wouldn't be banned tonight. This was a secret garden party, and he was the main course.

Oh no, I'm still playing the part of the troll...

"We need one more to join us, Goat." Announced the Fox. "He can't keep up at this rate."

Phew, at least someone acknowledges that much!

Troll looked at the three animals before him, only one thing came to mind. "Go get the Big Bad Wolf."

Bunny and Fox looked at one another and grinned. "Big Bad Wolf?"

"Who?" Goat looked down at him, tilting her head. "You came with a friend?"

"Yea..." He cleared his throat. "Just let him know Troll sent you. He'll come running. Especially if Bunny asks him to."

Bunny giggled. "So, he's a sucker for blondes, hmm?"

"Oh no, he came?" Goat laughed, shaking her head. "Yea, Bunny, go find the Big Bad Wolf, but take Fox with you. She will ensure the chase will lead back into the garden."

Then they were gone.

At last, Goat dismounted and laid beside him, curling into his body as they stared up into the starry sky. He could feel the hum of his body relax, falling into a steady breathing rhythm, ready for another round. She nuzzled against his neck, her body tight against his side. It all seemed so surreal.

"Is this your first time?" Her voice startled him.

"At sex, no." He laughed, looking over at her. "At a masquerade sex party, yes."

She sat up. "To be honest, at first I wasn't sure it was you I spotted in the living room."

His face flushed, making him thankful the mask covered his face's betrayal.

"When we locked eyes, I couldn't see the mask. All I knew, was I wanted a piece of you." He confessed.

"And how was it?" Her lips curled in a coy smile. "Hmm?"

Sitting up, he leaned into his knee, thinking. Her hair was a mess, leaves and grass sticking to their bodies. Under the dim light, their bodies glistened with sweat and glitter. He inhaled deeply, holding it then releasing it slow and steady.

He stared into her eyes. "You're more than I can handle," he admitted. "Like the troll in the story, the goat crushed my body, crushed my bone. It all belongs to you now."

"Oh, does it now?" She looked skyward, hiding her expression from him. "So, the troll has admitted defeat to the goat."

"Yup." Troll marveled over the cloudless night. "My body is yours."

"Prove it." She rose to her feet and stood before him.

"Prove it how?" Again, his heart raced as he sat there taking in her shapely body.

What the fuck did I just step in...

"Lean back." She commanded like a Pagan Goddess.

Swallowing, Troll leaned back, propping onto his elbows.

"Open your legs." Her gruff voice was hungry and full of desire.

He pulled his knees apart. *What the hell is about to happen to me?* "Wider."

All the way, he exposed himself. His mouth ran dry as he felt helpless, his cock throbbing against his will. She dropped to all fours, crawling across the grass as she licked her lips. His blood rushed, his excitement growing. Grunting, his cock hardened, standing at attention for the Goat's hungry lips. Her loose wavy hair slid down his inner thighs, tickling him. He exhaled. A hot tongue licked slow and purposefully from base to tip. Lips cupped the cap and suckled. Moaning, he closed his eyes to savor the sensation.

She took him all the way in, the fleshy wall of her throat squeezing the tip. Some part of him wondered if she truly intended to eat him, to suck him dry. She bopped her head up and down his shaft, her drool trickling over his balls as she stroked them. She purred as she took him deep, repeating the motion. Abandoning the task, she crawled across his body. Lips as soft as rose petals kissed his hip, up into his abdomen. The tip of his throbbing erection rubbed her collarbone, between her breasts and over the swell of her stomach. Her tongue circled his own nipple before she suckled his neck. He didn't care she left marks across his body. He felt alive, on fire as she continued to ascend, his dick falling between her wet thighs, rubbing against her pussy.

My body is hers...

A rustle in the bushes made him jerk his eyes open, spoiling his ecstasy. Bunny burst through the hedges, a set of arms catching her around the waist. She squealed but was soon drowned out by a long howl. Wolf came into full view, nibbling at Bunny's neck, growling like an animal. It ended quickly as an athletic arm locked him into a head lock, pressing into one of Fox's breast.

Yea, there's nothing sexy about that. His head may pop off...

"Holy smokes. Bend me over and fuck me." Wolf howled again, embracing his part full heartedly. "As long as Bunny can play too!"

Goat bit Troll's neck. "Ouch!"

"T-Troll?" Wolf escaped the headlock and looked on with surprise. "Found greener pastures, I see."

Goat started to kiss her way back down his body, making his dick throb. "You gotta help me."

"W-what?" Wolf tilted his head, taking count of the women. "Help you with them?"

Fox wrapped her arms around Lou, kissing at his shoulder and neck. "Yes, he said you would help us."

"They're hungry." Moaning, Troll tensed as Goat pulled his cock into her mouth once more. "I can barely keep up with her."

Bunny leaned onto Wolf, kissing him. It was the same move as before, and Troll knew he would be snared, lost in the rabbit hole. Bunny's talented fingers made Wolf hard in a single stroke, trapping him. Fox circled them, waiting for an opening. Wolf's hands slid down and gripped her ass, threatening to enter her. Bunny sunk to her knees and began suckling on Wolf's dick. Fox dropped on all fours and rolled across the grass, sliding between Bunny's legs. She began eating her out, making her squeal and choke down Wolf's cock even deeper.

"Oh, man. You hit the jack pot, Troll." Wolf hummed as he rocked his hips.

Troll moaned again, Goat's tongue slipping under his swollen shaft. She let go of Troll's cock and stood, his heart leaping into his throat. She paced around him, shooting glances at Wolf and Bunny. A part of Troll grew afraid. He hadn't imagined the prospect of sharing her with anyone else, causing him to sit up in alarm. But, Goat twisted her heel into his shoulder, slamming his back flat on the grass.

"I'm hungry." She laughed. "And you're invited to dinner, Troll. Like you, there's only one thing I want tonight."

In a practiced move, her knees were on either side of his face as fast as her lips were back on his throbbing cock. Her pussy on his lips, he wanted what she was serving. Moaning into each other, he licked and suckled as vigorous as she attempted. They rocked into each other, the pleasure rattling through them both. He knew he had hit a sweet spot as she faltered in her sucking. Tilting his hip, he repeated the flick of his tongue and suckled. Again, she faltered, pressing him to the back of her throat as she collapsed further on him.

She crawled away from him, but he gave chase. Troll gripped her hips, dragging her across the slick grass and entered her. Her breath caught once more. He hadn't taken her yet in doggy style, and the way her body curved out and away added to his rising arousal. He slipped a thumb into her ass and arched and moaned, grinding into him. The way her pussy tightened around his cock told him she was more than willing to submit to his next desire.

"You ready for dessert?" He pulled out and pressed against her back door.

Looking over her shoulder, she licked her lips. "Make it a cream pie."

And this tale is told out.

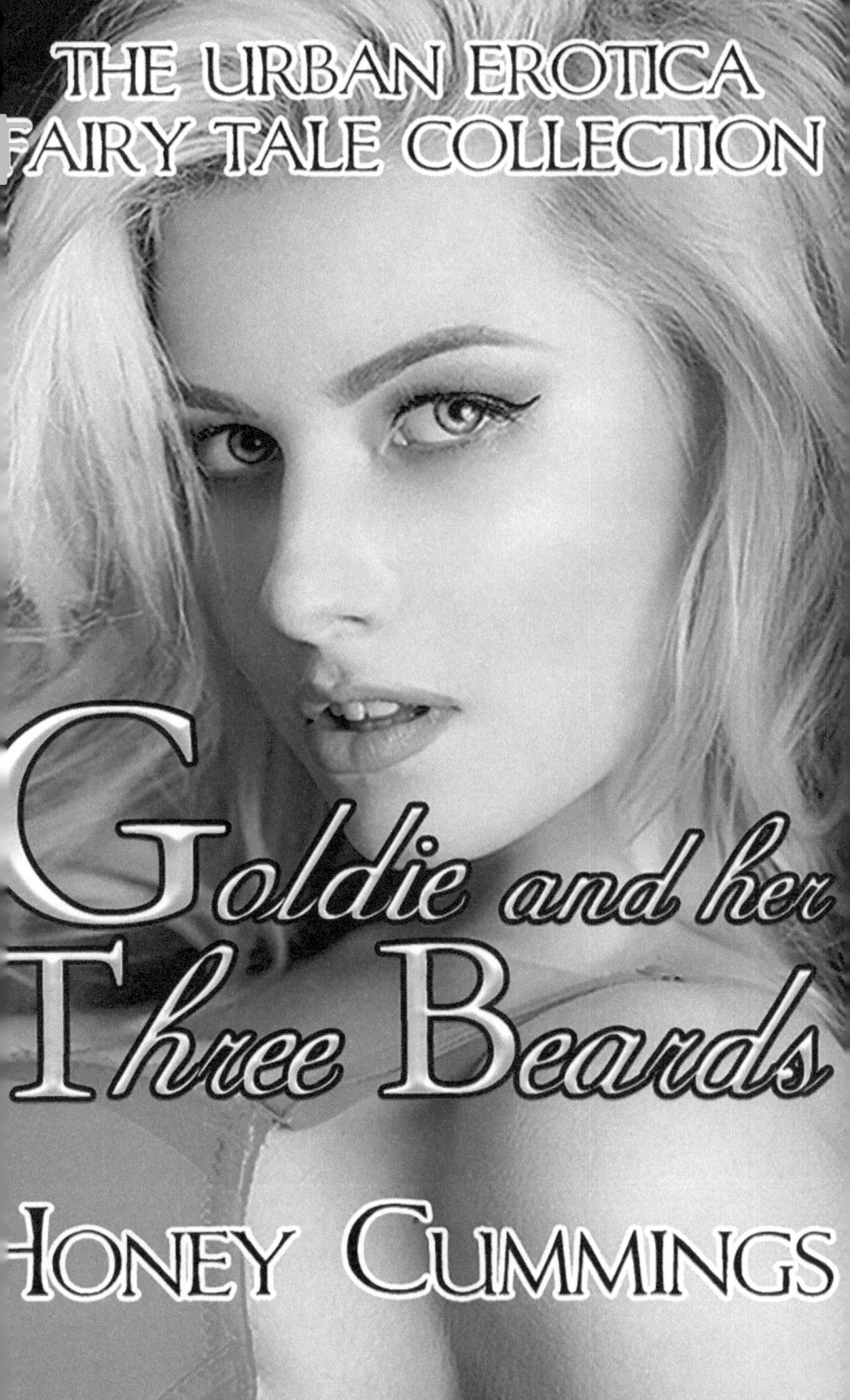

THE URBAN EROTICA FAIRY TALE COLLECTION

Goldie and her Three Beards

HONEY CUMMINGS

Table of Contents

The Dilemma

V alentine's Day was only two days away and Goldie didn't even have a date, let alone a boyfriend.

Pulling a lock of golden hair over her shoulder, she scoffed. The new golden tan and near professional level makeup did nothing, and the sexy lingerie now lay abandoned in her top drawer. Nothing seemed to get her the attention she wanted from the opposite sex. Around the office, her coworkers chattered about their dinner plans, their dates, and their bedroom plans.

She could still hear Kyle's words the week before Christmas. *It's not you, it's me.*

What a lame excuse. Who are you fooling, Kyle? We both know you picked that fight to avoid buying me anything. Guess who now has a new Apple Watch? Merry Christmas to me!

"Goldie." DeeDee, her cubicle mate, popped her head over the partition wall like a noisy neighbor. "What plans do you have for V-day?"

"Nada." Goldie leaned back in her office chair, spinning slow and aimless. "I've no plans nor a no man, DeeDee. This sucks."

She disappeared, then reappeared in the cubicle doorway. "You've had a whole month to figure something out. What's wrong?"

"I don't know. No one feels... just right." She stopped spinning and collapsed onto her desk, hiding her face. "It's like being hungry and not knowing what to eat."

DeeDee laughed. "You know what this means, right?"

Goldie groaned and peeked over her arm. "I don't know, DeeDee." *It couldn't be anything good.*

DeeDee pulled out her phone and wiggled it. "Time to download Sinder and find yourself a date!"

Goldie stared at the drop-down ceiling. DeeDee had recommended the top dating app in the country before she met Kyle, even after Kyle ended their relationship.

She grabbed her cell phone and looked up the app, her finger hovering over the download button. She had made it this far without using this monstrosity of an idea, but her desire for companionship, on Valentine's Day placed too much pressure on her. *Why can't cupid just spare a minute and help me out?*

"It's either the app or BOB." DeeDee leaned over her shoulder. "Take your pick. You're running out of options, girlie."

"Bob?" Goldie furrowed her brow. "Who the hell is that?"

DeeDee's smirked, then her breath tickled Goldie's ear. "Battery Operated Boyfriend."

Groaning, Goldie hit download. "Nope."

"Oh, come on." DeeDee laughed, leaning on the desk. "Don't discredit a night with Bob."

"I wouldn't if he could do it for me." Her face flushed, watching the download bar grow.

Unlike her friends, sex toys like pocket rockets, vibrators, and dildos just didn't satisfy the same. Sure, they worked in a pinch when she couldn't temper her horny desires, but this wasn't how she wanted to spend her Valentine's Day! She wanted the real thing, bent over and pounded until she came. Or a man's lips against her pussy while his beard added pleasure between her thighs.

The app loaded and launched. She created an account and was immediately bombarded with what felt like fifty billion questions in the form of survey-styled questionnaire. Each question designed to impress and attract, to recommend the best match for the type of man (or woman if she wanted) for hooking up and dating. She glared at the profile section, the idea of typing it via her phone was far too annoying.

"I'll finish signing up tonight," Goldie declared, closing the app.

"Boo. I wanted to watch you answer some of those questions." DeeDee twisted her lips, then shrugged. "Remember, swipe left for no and right for... just right."

With that, DeeDee winked and left.

Goldie rolled to her computer to finish her workday. Every so often, she'd glance at the phone, fear and excitement pushing her work task back into her mind. *What on earth have I gotten myself into?*

The Setup

Pouring deep red wine into a glass, Goldie settled on the couch with her laptop. She steeled herself, going through and filling out all the mandatory information. It felt strange creating a sultry bio in hopes of spicing up her dull, ordinary life. Sure, she had hobbies, but the last time she physically visited a beach had been well over a year.

She froze. *Shit.* The last thing she needed was a photo. *Should I use an old one? No, that's a terrible idea. Maybe I should...*

Abandoning the wine glass and laptop on the end table, she marched into her bathroom. Pulling out every makeup bag and hair product she owned, she began dolling herself up, as if getting ready for a date. Lip gloss brightened the pink in her lips. Brushing her long golden locks, she started flipping her hair to one side. Thanks to online tutorials, she was an expert at eyeshadow and decided to smoke-out her eyes so her blue eyes would pop. Her gray top made her skin tone pop just right against the white bathroom walls. With all of this coordinating, surely, she could take a decent picture.

That's it. Now the pose, need lots of eye play. Gotta bring the A game.

Pulling on a sleeve, she exposed a little of her shoulder and looked over her it in classic glamour shot allure. Happy with how she looked, she propped her phone, set the timer, and posed. *Click!* She had it.

She sent a Facebook message to DeeDee, her advocate in this venture and Sinder expert.

[Goldie: How's this for my profile shot? Is it ok?]

[DeeDee: Smokin'! But you need more photos. Full body shots. Show off those girls!]

[Goldie: Are you kidding me?]

[DeeDee: I thought you aimed to get fucked on V-day?]

Goldie's eyebrows lifted high. *She got me. That's the very least I wanted out of this. A bearded man with just the right dick to please me. All night long.*

[Goldie: What's your recommendation?]

[DeeDee: >:}~ A tight, little black dress, braless, and push out more cleavage, girl. Look like you're begging for that dick.]

[Goldie: Does the boss know you talk to our customers with that mouth?]

[DeeDee: Oh, he knows what else this mouth can do, afterhours and under his desk.]

[Goldie: OMG. You're a whore, DeeDee!!!!]

[DeeDee: And proud of it!]

Goldie dove into her closet. These days, she didn't have many dresses, but she never tossed the little black dress. With a slip, she weaseled the dress up and over, using the bathroom mirror as reference. Licking her cherry-flavored glossy lips, she juggled her thirty-two C-cup breasts together, the deep canyon of flesh made her appear more hour glassed. She pinched her nipples to keep them awake and alert.

Another round of timed photos and she sent them off to DeeDee for inspection.

[DeeDee: That's what I'm talking about! Now, post them all!]

Changing back into comfortable grey pajamas, she settled back on the couch. With a few gulps of her wine, she uploaded three photos: her glamour shot, a front body and side body shot. If they didn't want what she offered, then *fuck them.* Her glass empty, she refilled it, preparing for the questions she now needed to answer.

First question, what age range is she hunting for? *Let's keep them within ten years.*

Second question, gender preference? She hovered on *bisexual* for a moment before clicking *male. Sorry girls, I'm in the mood for a nice hard cock. Maybe next time.*

The questions were endless it seemed. From what her ideal date would be, to picking activities for outdoor and indoor. A standard marketing data collecting routine.

Did she like romantic comedies? *No. Though my life feels like one at this rate.*

Do I like to go dancing? *Uh, my experience is bumping and grinding at a crowded club. Does that count?*

Would you rather have steak, fish, or salad? *Depends. Who's buying? Ha!*

She refilled her glass, the heat of wine warming her cheeks. The time had come, to click FINISH. With this, the profile would be live, and she would be waiting for responses to roll in. No sooner had she refreshed the screen, she had thirty requests. *Well, at least I know the tan and makeup do work.* Blinking she sipped her wine and lifted and eyebrow. So many looked hot but lacked beards. She began swiping left for every bare faced man that hit her screen. Many came across the screen with long, short, and medium beards. She didn't care, she wanted them all.

Her imagination ran wild, drunk on wine as she poured the last of the bottle. The liquid courage now had her imagining one of these men between her legs, whether it was their beards or dicks didn't matter. Her pussy throbbed with want. Closing her eyes, she could imagine the tattooed biker man from first beard's profile towering over her. Peeking at his images once more, she could see the bare chest with a happy trail leading down to his pants.

The v-shaped bulge said it all, *he's packing.*

She swiped right. *Yes, please!*

I few swipes to the left brought her to the next eye candy, a serious, furrowed-brow man locking eyes with her. Another swirl and sip of her wine and her mind wondered back to the bottom of the gutter. *I need sex.* She could see him towering over her with that glare, pulling her hair and smacking her ass. Finishing her wine, she swiped right, hunting for at least one more.

After powering through, sliding left again and again, she paused on one. He didn't have sex appeal photos like the ones before, but he was handsome. Lifting an eyebrow, she wondered what hid under that loose t-shirt. The tattoos on his arms hinted to more art across his canvas. He had long wavy hair and a longer beard than the others, as if he were a casual mountain man.

Those hazel eyes sent a shudder through her. *Gawd he's sexy.*

Goldie's hand slid into her pajama pants, pushing her panties to the side. She flipped through his remaining photo, the muscles pulling on his clothes, muscular thighs, and shins. Closing her eyes, her finger dove between her pink folds, her swollen clit slick with her arousal. She imagined undressing him, imagining what those tattoos might look like, how far they painted his body, and how they rolled over his chiseled body.

Laying the phone to the side, her other hand glided under her pajama shirt and groped a bare breast. Twisting a nipple, her fingers dove back inside her pussy. *Oh, what I wouldn't give to have him play with me. All of me. To feel the heat of his mouth on my breasts, to feel that beard between my thighs.* Her fingers returned to circle her clit, her body arching as she squeezed her breast tighter. She peaked, moaning as she collapsed forward, opening her eyes at last.

She swiped right. *Good grief, maybe I need to add NSF to my profile.*

Her phone continued to buzz from Sinder notifications. It appeared beard one and beard two have already responded. Now to set up the dates.

The Guber Driver

Goldie slid into the back of her Guber and tilted her head. Her driver was a cute tattooed hunk. He even had a clean-cut short beard that made his chiseled jaw and pompadour haircut complement his overall look.

He turned to her, lifting an eyebrow as he eyed his cell phone for second. "Goldie, I presume?" His voice was smooth and suave as he addressed her.

Where was his profile on Sinder? "Yes, that's me." She buckled in, searching his hazel eyes. "And you're my Guber, yes?"

He sucked his bottom lip and nodded, turning to focus on driving as he put the vehicle into drive. She stared at him, something about him seemed strangely familiar, as if she'd seen him before. *Not from work or I would've recognized the voice.*

"Are you sure this is where you're going?" He broke the silence.

"That's the address he gave me." Glancing at her phone, she brought it up again. "*Red's Bar.*"

"Have you been there before?" He gave her a quick look through the rearview mirror.

Why the hell would he care? "N-no." Her face flushed, and she glared out the window.

"So, *he* picked it, huh?" Humming to himself, he continued prying further. "Was there some place you'd rather go?"

Is this his way of stealing another man's date? She smiled, shaking her head before meeting his gaze. "Shouldn't you watch the road instead, Mister..." She glanced down at the phone. "Charles."

"Come on. You can't tell me your idea for an outing with your boyfriend was a bar." He flipped the blinker and waited in the turn lane. "Just entertain me for a moment."

Oh, good grief. Why can't I just not reply? "I don't mind bar food," Goldie deflected.

Scoffing, the car turned, and he retorted. "But anyone can do bar food. Hell. Even chain restaurants with better wine selection have bar food."

Goldie opened her mouth to fight him on the matter, but she couldn't. *Dammit, he's got a point.*

"That dress and the way you carry yourself... I bet you're a red wine fan."

Normally, I'd be pissed. But coming from someone gorgeous and the way he said it, it's a bit of a turn on. She smirked. "You got me. And it's not a boyfriend. Just a first date."

"Oh?" He pulled next to a curb and parked. "Well, good luck on your date."

See you nosy-hot-Guber-driver!

Goldie stepped out of her Guber, standing in front of *Red's Bar* and froze. She had seen the good reviews online, but this evening, the parking lot was packed with motorcycles. Her phone buzzed with a message from her first beard, and she ignored it. Biting her lip, she had dressed in a tight little red slip-on dress, complete with matching red lingerie. She expected a hot date, not a party with a local biker gang.

The car window rolled down. "Hey. You ok?"

"Y-yes." She narrowed her eyes at him, feeling the weight of defeat. *Why does the Guber driver look familiar?*

"Are you sure this is the right address?" He questioned the locale and situation.

Putting on a brave smile, she spun on her heel. "Yea, looks like the right place. I just didn't expect a biker gang here too. Blind dates, ha." Her face flushed. *Shit-shit-shit. Why did I let that fact slip? He will think I'm a complete idiot.*

He furrowed his brow, giving her a skeptical smirk. "I can take you back home. Or elsewhere?"

Elsewhere? What is he planning? No. I will stick with the plan. My first beard is waiting for me.

She considered it for a good minute, then said, "No, I'll stay."

"Ok." He shrugged. "But, let me give you my number."

"What?" She leaned into the car window, lifting an eyebrow. "Why?"

He locked eyes with her. "No offense... uh...?" He lingered, searching for her name.

"Goldie."

"Look, Goldie. A pretty girl like you, walking into a bar full of bikers doesn't sit well with me." He scribbled his number on a sticky note. "Just keep this handy, if you ever need me. Tonight, or any other night."

"Do you do this for all the pretty girls?" She laughed, reading his name. "Chuckles? Really?"

"Nickname of mine." He winked. "And no. Only those I drop off at biker bars with no signs of their date waiting at the door."

She stuck her tongue out at him, and he laughed.

"Just, watch yourself in there."

"Yes, sir. See you around, Chuckles." Rolling her eyes, she pulled herself from the car.

"Same to you, Goldie."

With that Chuckles left her standing in the parking lot.

First Beard

T he neon sign, reading *Red's Bar* overhead, buzzed. The rowdy crowd could be heard laughing and hollering within. Adjusting her purse strap, she couldn't help but regret leaving the pepper spray behind to make room for the condoms. *I only needed one. Not the whole fucking box. Shit, I look desperate.*

Her phone pinged, and she pulled it from her pocket.

[First Beard: You here?]

[Goldie: Yes. Just arrived.]

[First Beard: Come on in! Wat r u waiting 4?]

Scoffing, there it was. That annoying lazy text writing she loathed.

Gripping onto her purse strap for support, she marched through the worn wooden door. Inside, she was met with a cacophony of clacking pool balls, Molly Hatchett piercing over the crackling speakers, and shouts coming from the rowdy bikers. Blinking to adjust to the dim lighting and smoky ambience, she paled. They all wore the same biker gang vest, a local chapter of the *Outlaws* spread out before her and she groaned.

Like a deer walking into a den of hungry wolves, the atmosphere came to a screeching halt. The lyrics filled her ears, *we're flirtin' with disaster, ya'll know what I mean.* Smiles rippled across the gang's face, their hungry eyes picking her apart in a way that made her feel dirty and naked. *I didn't sign up for a gang bang.*

The biggest in the group with the older, tattered vest pushed through the core of the group. "Damn girl! You're hot!" A long-bearded man with salt and peppered hair pulled into a tight ponytail approached, loud and monstrous. "Goldie, right?"

Oh gawd, don't tell me this is him. "Y-yea." Panic filled her. *Asshole, you look nothing like your picture! Unkempt beard, much older, and a slight gut? Did you trade in your six pack for another version? What the fuck!* "And you're..." She glanced at her phone. "Tex? Is that short for something?"

A toothy grin shifted under the burly beard. "Besides being from Texas." He laid the accent on thick for this, puffing out his chest which did nothing to hide the gut. "You know what they say about Texas, don't ya?"

Oh no, this is not what I signed up for. This isn't what your Sinder profile had on it, Mr. Texas. Don't get me wrong, you are so much bigger in real life. But in all the wrong places.

"Everything's bigger in Texas. Including me." He groped his crouch, and Goldie swallowed, adverting her gaze. "Hope you came to party, girl. You look just like your pictures. I'm impressed. I can't wait to see if you're a natural blonde under that dress."

"Uh, excuse me. It was a long ride. Where's the bathroom?" *What fresh hell have I gotten into?*

"Right over there, baby doll." The group cleaved, forming a path to the door.

"Thank you." Goldie rushed into the restroom. Much to her surprise, it was halfway decent.

The bar had all the workings of a dive, but the ladies' room was on par with any night club she'd visited. She leaned on the counter, staring at her reflection in disbelief. Scrambling for her phone, she didn't know how to get herself out. The sticky note had come out, she shook her head and shoved it back in her purse. Her thumbs worked fast.

[Goldie: This is a shit show!!!!!!]

[DeeDee: What? You're not talking about First Beard????]

[Goldie: Yes, First Beard!]

A roar of laughter came through the door, and she cringed. She walked into a stall and flushed the toilet. At least, she had to make sure he knew she was using the bathroom. The anxiety of walking out there among the biker gang made every nerve tighten in her joints.

[Goldie: He's older, fatter, and he's a leader of a biker gang]

[DeeDee: WHAT?!]

[Goldie: I don't know what to do! HELP!]

She turned on the sink to buy her time. *DeeDee! Get me out of this!*

[DeeDee: Call the Guber back!]

[Goldie: I am not calling Chuckles!]

[DeeDee: Who the hell is Chuckles???]

The door swung open and Goldie shoved her phone into the purse. A toothy grin spread on Tex's face as he waltzed into the restroom. Eyes wide, Goldie gave him a baffled expression and tilted her head. He closed the door, the men outside whistling, cheering him on.

The door shut, and he locked it behind him, then leaned against it. She was trapped.

He licked his upper teeth, his hungry eyes roving over her, from head to toe, then back again. "I imagine you reached out to me on Sinder, wanting a little more Texas in you."

And it's clear you only responded for the chance for sex. "You just get right down to the point. I was hoping for a real date," she said, afraid to move closer to him.

"Oh, but baby doll, you have me hard already." Like an unsolicited dick pic, he unzipped, and the biggest cock Goldie had ever seen stood at attention.

And now my curiosity is overwriting my logic. "I'm about to go through the big D." Goldie muttered, her eyes unable to break her stare on the huge cock, her loins aching with want. *It's been weeks. No, since what? December? And Valentine's day tomorrow. This may have been a dud, but how can I say no to a chance to ride a dick built like a train car? Fuck it, let's do this. He's got a Dadbod. There's nothing wrong with that.* "So, we're just hooking up for the sex today, huh?"

"Thought that was the plan." He winked and gave her a smirk.

Goldie had to give him some credit. He didn't dare move a muscle from the door, there had been some sort of moral code mixed in with the blatant passes to just fuck. Raising an eyebrow, she didn't bring lube. Surely a dick the size of a giant dildo would need lube, or she'd have to be wet as hell to make this work. She glanced into her open purse. Damn. *These condoms won't fit that monster cock.*

"You got condoms for that weapon?"

"Fuck ya, I do." Out of his back pocket he produced a Magnum XL. And without further ado, rolled it on.

He closed the gap between them, butterflies in Goldie's stomach as the large dick became ever more intimidating. The heat of his hands pulled her dress up over her hip, fingers hooking her lacy underwear and tugging them down. Red lace fell down her shins, over her ankles and over heeled toes.

Tex gripped her, picking her up and propping her on the counter. "You know what blondes and noodle have in common?" His beard tickled at her neck, lips at her ear.

"No?" Goldie wasn't sure if he was trying to be clever or tell a cheesy bar joke. *Oh my God, he sucks at talking on all levels. Just when my libido was starting to heat up.*

"They both wiggle when you eat'em."

Before she could absorb what exactly he said, he had knelt and pressed his lips to her clit. He suckled, his beard tickling her pussy and inner thigh. She leaned back, propping herself on the counter as she spread her leg s wider. The back of her head pressed against the mirror and she closed her eyes, indulging in the pleasure buzzing through her body.

The heat of his tongue teased the opening of her vagina before twirling around her clit once more. She moaned, goosebumps making her body shudder. There was nothing she loved more than the sensation of a bearded man eating her out. He had a long beard, and it wasn't the preferred length for her pleasure, but it beat a bare faced man. Hands-down. Again, his tongue teased her opening, and fingers dove inside. She arched, knees hugging his shoulders, jittering with the electricity of her arousal.

With one hard pull on her clit, he made her shriek. The fingers rode hard and deep, her wetness flowing from her as she began to orgasm. His lips released and she reached down to grip his hair, to demand more of his oral pleasuring.

He smacked her hand from his hair. "Don't touch the tail, sweetie."

Shut up! You're killing my libido again!

It was a sobering cold shower on the moment. She blinked, panting as he stood to fix his hair in the mirror over her shoulder. *Note to self. Don't let this man speak or I won't get off a second time.* His cock rubbed against her swollen clit, and her heart leapt into her throat. *Shit he's big. Will it fit? I can't back down now, can I?*

"Shame we ain't got any lube-"

Goldie pressed her fingers against his lips. "No more talking, just fucking." *I can't take another comment of belligerent biker dialogue.*

The tip of his ginormous cock pressed against her opening. She stiffened and they glared at each other, gauging the reaction as he pressed further, slow and calculating. DeeDee had made fun of her huge dildo once, but it couldn't have prepared her for this. The tip pressed further in, the hard cock like a police baton. Her loins ached in a new way with no room for tensing and squeezing.

She wiggled, calming herself, relaxing on par to being amid a gynecology exam. "Dammit your big," she breathed as he slid a little further in, making her fight the need to tense.

"I'll go slow, baby doll." His hands slid across atop her thighs. "Mmm, you're so tight."

Who wouldn't be! You're fucking half-horse with a dick this size!

As he rode deeper inside, he at last hit a spot that made her feel like he was knocking on her belly button. He wasn't even all the way in but was very aware this was the end of the line for the Texas Express Train. A hand glided between thin, his thumb rubbing her clit. The waves of pleasure were only met with the brick wall of the agonizing inability to squeeze. It was like over stretching a hamstring or bicep.

He began a slow rocking, his dick sliding slowly in and out, gaining more range with each pass. Goldie was in turmoil, pleasure and discomfort mangling through her. She wanted more, and on the other hand, wanted it to end. Tex started to moan, and she secretly sung the praises to whatever guardian looked over her. She relaxed and at last, enjoyed the slow pace as he grinded against her gently.

Bigger dick isn't the best fit, but at least I'm starting to enjoy this!

Tex gripped the side of the counter, shoving in hard one last time as he came. Goldie yelped, convinced her belly button had popped or at least knocked on her cervical door. It was painful and relief filled her as he left her body. She sat there, head leaning on the mirror wondering, what the hell made her think this was a great idea?

Shit. Talk about ruining my climax yet again!

"You need a ride home?" He pulled the condom off and flung it into the trash can.

She sighed. "No, I'll call a Guber."

"You ok, baby doll?" One sink over, he began washing his face and beard as she slid off the counter, wiggling her underwear back on.

"You've ruined me, Tex," she confessed. "Bigger isn't better."

He snorted, drying his face. "But you were so good, sweetheart."

She gave him an unamused glare, and he laughed.

"You could have said something, darling." He unlocked the door and paused. "I didn't make you feel pressured?" His voice had abandoned the rough-n-tough biker tone and softened.

"No, no..." Goldie sighed, pushing into the bathroom stall. "I was too curious. And honestly, I was searching for sex. No offense, Tex, but I didn't realize that some part of me wanted a real date after all."

He snorted. "But trust me, girlie. No man wants a girl not enjoying herself. Next time speak up. And if he takes offense, he's an asshole and you call old Tex to come take care of them."

"Uh, I wasn't expecting a favor from a biker gang out of this." She laughed from her porcelain throne.

Guber Home

Reluctant, Goldie made her way back through the bar. This first date had so much promise, but in the end, Texas was too big for even her appetite.

Sighing, she hit the app. The Guber would be here in a matter of minutes. *How lucky could I get?*

Tex winked at her as she pushed through the doors. The sun had started to set, and a familiar car pulled to the curb, exactly where she had been dropped off. Looking to her phone, the message flipped to, *your driver has arrived.* Then she saw it. *Driver name: Charles. Chuckles didn't leave. Was he waiting for me? Are you kidding me?*

Furrowing her brow, she marched to the car as he rolled the window down. Leaning in, she narrowed her eyes at him. In turn, he raised his own and lowered the music.

After a minute of gauging silence, he tilted his head. "Need a ride?"

No shit, I pinged on Guber and you pulled up. Of course, I need a ride! "Did you even leave?" she blurted. "Chuckles."

He gave a toothy grin, scratching at his beard. "I took a lunch break nearby."

Bullshit! "Thanks for the vote of confidence." Her face reddened, embarrassed and frustrated. *He knew I wouldn't call him. But I don't mind being chauffeured by someone this handsome.*

"Look, if it makes you feel better, you stayed longer than I thought." The confession did nothing for relieving her heated cheeks. "You want to sit up front?" He patted the seat

She snorted, then smirked. "No. I'll sit in the back," she said, wondering if his hand would snake up her thigh if she had taken the offer. *No, Goldie. You still have one more date and possibly a third if beard three ever replies. I wish Sinder showed if someone read the damn message.*

She slid into the car, pulled out her phone and opened the app.

"Home or... somewhere else?" He patiently stared at her through the mirror.

"Like your place?" Goldie lifted an eyebrow, reading DeeDee's text.

[DeeDee: What the hell happened? DO YOU NEED HELP! Answer your text, woman!]

He leaned over the seat, demanding her eyes, but she ignored him.

[Goldie: He had a dick the size of a nightstick! Too fucking big! And now the Guber driver is hitting on me!!]

"Are you fucking with me?" His voice came out low, and she met his gaze.

"You are serious." Goldie's heart raced. "We just met."

"I'm not the one with a box of condoms meeting bikers in dive bars." He pointed at the seat beside her. Laughing, he continued his observations, "And it's quite intimidating to see a box with my name and number stuck to it."

Mortified, she grabbed the sticky note and shoved it into her purse. The chuckling rolling from him agonizing. *Now I know where he got the nickname from.*

"Seriously. I'll take you anywhere you want." He turned away, cancelling the Guber ride. "This one's on me for being a dick. Home, right?"

Biting her lip, Goldie looked to her phone.

[DeeDee: Was first beard hot? Is Guber guy hot? What is happening?!]

[Goldie: First beard was Dadbod. But had a dick fit for a horse!]

[DeeDee: Ok... not a complete lost. Wait, was that Chuckles?]

Looking back up, her breath caught in her throat, locking gazes with his hazel stare. "Take your time. We're not on the clock now. Car's in park. I'll wait."

[Goldie: Chuckles is the Guber driver.]

[DeeDee: And??????]

"Hey, Chuckles?" He twisted back around, and she snapped a photo of him.

"Ok...?" Tilting his head. "You think I plan on kidnapping you or something?" Her silence pleaded the fifth and he snorted. "At least let me pose for the shot."

"Fine." She raised her phone once more. "Ready?"

He wiggled further into view, his broad chest and shoulders visible. "Ready."

She lifted her thumb and as she pressed, he shifted his pose. Lifting his shirt, the ripples of his abs sent a hot wave of arousal over her. His pierced tongue had protruded forward, and he had lifted his eyebrow. Goldie stared at the image. *Would it be wrong to use this as masturbating material later? My gawd he's hot and...* She hit send. The image now in of DeeDee's possession for final judgment.

"Did it turn out ok?" He settled back into his driver seat, pulling on his seat belt.

[DeeDee: Why aren't you fucking Guber Driver Dude!!!]

"Oh, it did." She sucked on her inner cheek. "Your girlfriend must be lucky."

He made a clicking sound with his mouth. *Was that him clacking his piercing on his teeth?*

The car started moving forward and *Red's Bar* disappeared on the horizon. It grew dark outside, the streetlamps fading in and out of the car window.

At last, Goldie asked, "What was that reaction for? When I asked about a girlfriend?" *Now it's my turn to ask personal questions.*

"No girlfriend. She left me for another guy because I didn't spend all my money on her." The car slowed and came to a complete stop, the traffic thick and unmoving. "Ugh, I forgot there's a big concert tonight. I should have gone the other way." He put the car into park.

"You can't just put the car in park while in traffic?" Goldie protested.

"Look, the last time this happened, I didn't move for thirty minutes. Now's a good time to check emails and watch shows on your phone." He pulled out his phone, suddenly disinterested, as if mentioning a girlfriend had spoiled the mood.

I ruined what could have been a good time. Goldie looked to her phone, a message from Second Beard flashing in her notifications, confirming the address and time for their date tomorrow. *Goal achieved. I've got a date for Valentine's Day.*

Flipping through, she pulled up the non-responsive Third Beard's profile. *He looks so damn familiar.* Looking at Chuckles, he was still playing on his phone. The car had stopped under a dark area and traffic hadn't budged an inch.

Let's send another message.

[Goldie: Hi, C.J. I was wondering if you received my first message.]

Uh, I sound desperate. She pulled up the picture of Chuckles, biting her lip as she wiggled in her seat. Tex had felt good in the end but she just didn't feel... satisfied. Her pussy wet, her arousal waving through her. Another stolen glance and Chuckles furrowed his brow as he paid attention to his phone, not her. She gauged the darkness between them. *If I'm quiet, maybe I can...*

Holding her phone in one hand, the other snaked up her inner thigh. Another stolen glance and she was satisfied Chuckles wouldn't even know what fun she would incur in his back seat. Pushing the lacy red underwear out of the way, she began circling her clit, slow and steady.

[Third Beard: Are you available tomorrow night?]

She paused her activities, responding as she slid her thumb across the keyboard.

[Goldie: I have another arrangement at two.]

[Third Beard: Let me convince you to spend Valentine's Day with me.]

Aren't we a bold one? She smirked, returning to playing with herself as she replied.

[Goldie: How about a round of sexting? Give me a preview of how we might end the night?]

DeeDee would be proud of me for this one, ha!

[Third Beard: Ok. I'll play along. You've already got me hard. Tell me, how wet does my picture make you?]

Cheeky!

[Goldie: I grab your hand and slide it up my thigh, letting you feel how slick I am.]

[Third Beard: Leaning in, I whisper in your ear, "I want to watch you come" as I start to circle your clit.]

[Goldie: I moan, your beard tickling my neck. My hands slide down your torso, pulling at your pants. Please show me your cock, baby.]

Chuckles shifted in the driver seat, and Goldie froze. She had forgotten she was still in his car. He pulled it out of park and moved up a car length and parked again. Never once looking her way, returning to his phone. Whatever he was doing, he didn't want to stop playing as his thumbs slide over the screen.

[Third Beard: I help you unbutton my jeans, and I moan as the heat of your fingers wrap around my hard cock.]

[Goldie: I begin rubbing your hardon, opening my legs wider.]

[Third Beard: My fingers slide into your pussy, stroking in and out. You're so wet my cock throbs in your hands.]

She slid her own fingers between her pink folds. Enjoying the imagery he painted, her head tilted back eyes closed. She thrusted in and out of herself, growing more wet with each rotation. Through heavy-lidded eyes, she slid her message, her wish to him

[Goldie: Faster. Please stroke faster.]

[Three Beard: I want to taste you on my lips.]

Goldie lurched forward, her orgasm taking her breath away. She bit her tongue, silencing the moan she would have released if it weren't for–her gaze met hazel eyes in the mirror, and her heart stopped. Panting, the orgasm still sent shiver across her body as she pulled her dress back over her thighs.

"Feel better? Not every day my passenger gets their rocks off sexting in my back seat." Chuckles spoke with intrigue in his voice, a mischievous smirk on his face. "And here I thought I was sexually frustrated."

"You're a creep for watching." Goldie looked away, despair swallowing her up.

"What was I supposed to do?" Frustration filled his voice. "Reach back there and play out what you were sending?" He twisted, raising a brow. "I don't know about you, but it's been a few months since I hooked up with anyone. And you're making this an exceedingly difficult ride."

Goldie paled. "I'm sorry. It's been since December for me and..." At last she wavered and looked back to him. He narrowed his eyes at her, the clicking of his tongue piercing making her shift in her seat. *What would that feel like rolling over...* "I am beyond frustrated. Hot and bothered and not getting what I want," she blurted, much to her own surprise.

"I see that." His eyes studied her, *all* of her. He bit his bottom lip, weighing his next words.

Goldie's heart raced. *Am I about to fuck my Guber driver? Am I really that horny to open myself to any invitation? At least Chuckles seems to care...*

A car horn filled the air, ruining the moment. Traffic had started moving again and for the remainder of the ride, they remained silent. The streetlights only fueled her curiosity.

She looked down at her phone.

[Goldie: Thanks for the good time. Maybe I will call you tomorrow.]

Nothing. Third beard had disappeared as fast as he had made her come.

Never Gonna Give You Up

[Second Beard: Are you here yet?]

Goldie scoffed. *How impatient. I'm only fifteen minutes away. We agreed to meet at two, not one-thirty, buddy.*

The Guber app had given her a few riders, but she had refused them all. She needed to see Chuckles, apologize, or make amends. All night she had tossed and turned. His picture haunting her, and she cursed under her breath. *Why the hell didn't I hook up with Chuckles! The man wanted to. Hell, I wanted to!*

She dug into her purse, then paused. The box of condoms was there, and the sticky note still stuck attached. She cancelled driver after driver. *Dammit, Chuckles. You're going to make me do it.* She punched in his phone number and saved it. Inhaling deep, she began typing the message. She wanted this in writing, not as a call where her panic would force her to hang up on him. *I've done that before. Never heard from that guy again. Let's not completely blow this.*

[Goldie: Hey Chuckles, you working tonight?–Goldie]

She waited, tugging on her slip-on black dress. She had decided to wear the teaser dress with the bra and underwear. She had settled with the idea DeeDee's instructions had led her down the way of one-night stands. Granted, she had failed to make it clear whether or not she was aiming for sex or a date. Who knew what tonight would hold for her? Tex had been upfront and to the point. Maybe Second Beard would want something more. *Or I'm daydreaming.*

The message to Chuckles shifted from *delivered* to *read*. Nothing happened, no signs of him writing. She couldn't stand it. Biting her lip, she thought for a moment. *I will not be ignored!*

[Goldie: Look, yesterday I was a hot mess. I'm sorry. Desperate for a date on Valentine's day. I know, stupid right? C'mon, I had a blind date with a biker and still didn't back down, so you already know I can't make good judgment calls.] She paused and smiled to herself. [What I do know is you're the best damn Guber driver, and I trust you to save me if this blind date goes South tonight.]

Closing her eyes, she sighed in relief. It was done, she let the truth out. *I sound like a fucking moron.*

Her phone buzzed.

[Chuckles: Did you just friend zone me?]

Her jaw fell slack. *Why can't I do anything like a normal human being?!* Sinking to her knees, she wanted to cry. *Great job, now you've definitely slammed and locked that door tight and threw out the–*

A honk from a car made her lose balance, and she fell back onto the sidewalk. The window on a familiar white car rolled down. She couldn't contain her excitement. Her phone pinged; *driver has arrived.* Scrambling to her feet, she snatched up her purse and slide into the front passenger seat.

"Did you seriously just friend zone me for watching? I'm a man, what did you think I would do?" He scowled at her.

"No!" She pulled on the seatbelt. "Look, I just, I already made plans with this guy before I met you and I feel...obligated."

"Valentine's Day," he blurted. "Just one other guy, huh?"

"I doubt this will work out," she confessed, her gut uneasy by the Second Beard's impatient vibe. "And the third guy..."

"Third guy?" The car was travelling towards their destination. "Did you just message every guy on Sinder after downing a bottle of wine?"

Her eyes widened and looked away.

"You didn't!" he cackled.

"I'm so glad you're amused by this." *Asshole.*

"And did you just deny every Guber driver waiting for me?" She spun her head back as he made the next turn. "If so, I can't say that some part of mine finds that kind of cute and attractive."

"I just don't want you to think I'm... easy." Blushing she turned to the window again, enjoying the safety of staring at his reflection through the glass.

"Oh, that box of condoms totally didn't help that impression." Sighing, he glanced down at the GPS. "Looks like we're here. Be safe. You have my number, so..."

"Right." They stared into each other's eyes for a moment. "I'm leaving now."

"I know." He gave her a baffled look. "At least this is some high-end luxury apartments. Hope you have a better time."

Clearing her throat, she opened the door. "T-thanks."

Second Beard

After being buzzed in, the idea of ditching the blind date had vanished. Whoever she was about to hook-up with had money, and good taste. She wondered the halls, isolated in the silence of marble flooring and six panel doors with golden numbers and keycode pads.

She glanced at her phone.

[Goldie: I'm here.]

[Second Beard: 140]

Snorting, she hoped the vague response was the room number. At least, Tex had more manners, meeting her at the door. Searching for his Sinder profile, he wasn't bad looking and had an impressive profile. *John. What a boring name.*

At last, she found the room and knocked. It took a few minutes, and he opened the door.

Goldie's breath caught. He was gorgeous, dark haired with blue eyes, and... *where the hell is his beard? Did he shave it off! What a complete sham! Calm down, no fair to him if I just end the date on that note. I can salvage this.* She imagined him taller when she first seen his images, but again, that was through a haze of wine.

He motioned for her to come in, smiling, hunger in his eyes. A shudder rocked her shoulders as she passed the threshold. Inside, she discovered minimalistic postmodern décor and furniture. Her eyes scanned the kitchen and tall dining room table, and her gut twisted. *Where are the candles? The flowers or even... dinner? Maybe we're going out to eat?*

She recovered her smile and spun to face John as he closed the door. His shirt laid open and unbutton. As he took long strides across the black tiles, he began to unbuckle his belt. Goldie's body took several strides backwards until she locked knees on the couch and sat down.

"Uh, whoa there." She searched for words. *Words would be good right about now!* "John? John, I thought maybe..."

"Feel it, it's already hard," he said, low and breathy as he towered over her.

"Wait, what?" Goldie shook her eyes. *This man is beyond impatient.*

"Here." He gripped her wrist and shoved it on his crotch. "It wants you."

Blinking, she squeezed and rubbed and... *where the hell is it?*

"Yea, squeeze me a little harder. Just like that, baby," he cooed, tilting his hip towards her, eyes closed.

Jerking her hand away, she ducked to the side of him, fleeing the couch. *NOPE! I'm not going to even try. Not after Tex. I just want a normal sized dick, and this guy has failed.* She started for the door, but he grabbed her arm. Glaring down at his hand, she at last looked up into angry face.

She frowned. "Look, I didn't..."

He unzipped his pants and revealed his... *What is that? An elevator button? A mole? A... NOPE! Definitely not getting any satisfaction with bad impression on top of it. I mean, you can't be a douchebag and have a small dick. That's not attractive.* She tried to leave again, but he squeezed her arm tighter. "Where do you think you're going?" he asked. "You promised me a good time." A wicked grin came across his bare face, and he let go. "Come on, baby. I thought you wanted to hook up with me, with this." He motioned to himself, and she paled. "You can't leave now?"

Come on. Think, think. This asshole won't let me go unless he gets something out of me and... "I was gonna get my friend." Her mind spun, cooking up a half assed plan.

"Oh? She wants to join us?"

Of course, you think I meant another female. Fine, I can work with that. "You know, I'll just call her and tell her to head over. Where's the bathroom? Just want to freshen up, you know?"

"Sure, sure, baby doll." He motioned to a room on the exterior side. "What's your friend's name, sweetheart?"

He followed her to the bathroom, and she practically slammed the door in his face, locking it. "Uh, her name?" Goldie looked around the bathroom. The small window by the tub looked like a tight squeeze. "She prefers nicknames in these situations." She turned on the sink faucet, hoping it would drown out the sound of her climbing into the tub and opening the window. *Thank God, he lives on the bottom floor!*

"Oh? What's that?" The knob wiggled and stopped.

CREEPER! Goldie unlocked the window latch and pushed up, opening with ease. "Uh, Tex. Her name's Tex!" *Oh! Where's my purse and phone! Tex did say if I needed him...*

"Why Tex?" He sounded unsure.

"Everything's bigger in Texas," she answered, texting the biker, then shoving her purse strap over her head and shoulder. With his address, the apartment number, and creeper – He'd know enough to throat punch John on her behalf.

"How so?" he asked flatly.

"Double D's, John. DOUBLE," she blurted, pushing the screen off and throwing her heels out the open window. "DOUBLE D's! You ever seen that?" *Double the dick of a normal man!*

"N-no. So, she's a busty girl like Dolly Parton, huh?"

Goldie made a disgusted face. "Sure. If that's what you like?" She teetered on the tub, starting to pull herself through the window.

The sound of motorcycles rumbling was a blessing. She squirmed with more urgency. The sound of a cell phone came through the bathroom door. The wiggling doorknob stopped. He muffled something, and she imagined it meant someone was buzzing to come into the building. *Tex is gonna be all sorts bigger than you expected, buddy.*

Her hips made it pass the windowsill, and she slid out with alarming speed. The ripping of fabric made her breath catch. On her left side, the seam popped open, thread and fabric fraying all the way up to under her arm, stopping at the cross-stitch.

She heard shouting in the room, and she scrambled for her phone.

[Tex: You ok? Where are you?]

[Goldie: Bolted out the bathroom window]

[Tex: Good girl. We'll teach this creeper a lesson. Did he hurt you?]

[Goldie: No. But it wasn't like I wanted to end the date so soon. Scared me.]

Another squeal echoed through the bathroom window, and she cringed.

[Tex: Get yourself home, girl. We got you.]

She stood and realized she only had one shoe. *Fuck it. I can buy shoes.*

The Missing Third Beard

Holding her dress together, she pinged for a Guber driver. Like she expected, Charles snatched her up. She rounded the corner of the apartments, and her phone pinged. Third Beard C.J. had responded. She kept walking toward the front of the building, where Chuckles had dropped her off. Opening the message, she decided she would turn him down. Sinder had just brought her one shit show after another. *No more. Horribly advice at this rate.*

[Third Beard: Is your date going ok?]

Freezing, she glared at the message and scrolled up. *I never said it was a date.*

[Goldie: How did you know that's what it was?]

[Third Beard: You told me.]

Scoffing, she marched with renewed vigor, crossing the front grassy area of the apartments.

[Goldie: I did not.]

[Third Beard: That bad? Is that why you needed a ride so soon again?]

Her heart skipped a beat. *What the fuck?*

[Third Beard: Look up, I brought you flowers.]

Baffled, her head jerked up.

"But I don't think these roses can fix your dress." Chuckles furrowed his brow, taking in her haphazard state. "What the hell happened and why..."

"You!" She glared at her phone and back up again. "The sexting yesterday! That too!"

He shrugged, puffing out his cheeks. "To be fair, I hadn't checked my Sinder profile until you dropped the girlfriend comment, and I recognized you immediately. Thought it was a chance to make a move, but it backfired."

"But your profile picture." She stomped up to him, failing to keep her dress closed. "You look nothing like that!"

"The tattoos don't change." He scratched his beard. "I didn't care for the long hair and beard. Plus, no one wants to ride in a Guber if the driver looks like he just climbed down from the mountains."

Her lips parted, her thought snagging a moment before she conceded, "Yea, you have a point there."

"Let me ask this again." He cleared his throat. "Are you available tonight?"

Goldie looked to the dozen roses. "Yea, for you I am."

"Then get in the car before a hard breeze rips the rest of your dress off." He opened the front passenger door. "W-where's your shoes?"

She gave him a silencing stare, and he didn't dare press the question further. Once she settled in, he shut the door, tossing the bouquet in the back seat and cancelled her Guber. He checked his mirrors and pulled away from the nightmare second blind date. When it all faded into the bleak night, Goldie relaxed. She covered her face with her hands, some part of her glad she had escaped a terrible situation.

A chill rattled through her as the split seam opened wider. The car's air conditioning icy against her skin, but she didn't want to bother holding the damn thing closed any more. Steady breaths, she recalled yesterday in her mind. *When he grunted, I thought he was moving the car but it's because he was getting hard, wanted more, and...*

Through her hands she spoke, "What do I call you?"

"Call me?" The car took a turn and started down a curvy road.

"C.J.? Charles? Chuckles?"

"I go by all three." He laughed. "Chuckles is fine. But if that's too formal, C.J. works."

"Where are we going?" She pulled her hands from her face, looking at the passing streets.

"I figured you'd be hungry, so I'm treating you out." He smirked, and the car took another turn.

"Um, I hate to tell you this, C.J." Goldie squinted at him. "My dress ripped, and I'm half-naked."

"Oh, I know." He gave a toothy grin, a tattooed arm reaching over. His hand hot as it slid over her stomach and down her thigh before gliding up to grip her inner thigh. *A little further up and he'll...* "It's a dinner for two. I'm cooking."

"Cooking?" A heat washed over her as his hand continued squeezing and exploring, weaseling under her black lacy underwear. *A little further, please don't stop.* "You cook?"

"Yea, and few other things." His finger caressed her clit, and her breath caught. "Should I stop?"

"No." She cupped his hand, urging him to keep going. "Just don't wreck the car."

He scoffed, a smirk across his face. "You have no idea how badly I wanted to reach back and do this yesterday." His fingers dove into her pussy and she hummed. "How much I wanted to give you the very thing your sexts had desired."

"If I had–" Another gasp interjected as he shifted his angle. Her pussy tightened on his fingers as he stroked in and out.

"What was that?" He teased, the car slowing as they pulled into a closed restaurant parking lot. "If I had what?"

"Told me." She moaned, opening her legs wider as she fumbled for the lever to lay her seat back. "If you had said something about Sinder... Mmm."

The seat fell back and allowed him a moment to pull away from her, putting the car in park and cut the engine. His seatbelt flew off, and before she knew it, he leaned over her. The heat of his hands sent her heart racing. One flowed across her ribs, sliding under the lacy bra and squeezed her breast. The other rode over her hip and snaked under the front of her panties. His finger circled her clit and she arched.

"Tell me what you want."

His voice barely beat the fog of pleasure rolling through her. The fingers dipped into her, she tightened and her retreated, returning slick as he rolled over her swollen clit. Goldie moaned and he groped her breast tight in reply.

"I want you..." Her hands pushed his down, and he let her guide his fingers back inside her wet heat. "...to make me come again."

Shoving her dress open further, he shoved her bra off her breast and lowered his lips to her nipple. The tip of his tongue circled the firm nub, slow and teasing as his fingers began rubbing and stroking. She propped one leg onto the dashboard, giving him access to thrust deeper as she shivered with pleasure. Her breath quickened, blood rushing with heat and passion.

The knock of his tongue piercing came like an erotic electric shock.

She whimpered, and she lurched forward, only for him to push her back into the seat, still suckling her breasts. Her orgasm exploded, only egging him to stroke faster. Squealing, her body arched, and a gush of wet heat released. With a pop, he pulled away from her and left her alone in the car to catch her breath.

Just Right

Goldie had pulled the seat up right, wondering where C.J. had vanished to when her car door opened. With practiced motion, he had eased her out, kicking the car door shut and carried her into the old diner. Hugging onto his neck as he shoved through the doorway. Goldie looked all around, the remains of a 24-hour diner half tarped in renovations surrounded them. He didn't stop in the rows of booths and tables, passing through an opening in the bar top. They were now traversing a super clean, upgraded kitchen area. The restaurant may not have been ready to serve customers, but it was ready to cook anything you could throw at it.

"Where are you taking me?" She couldn't stop her heart from fluttering against her chest like a caged bird. "Why here?"

"I'm taking you to my bed." He had a serious look on his face, making his beard and jaw breathtaking in the dim lighting.

"Bed?" *Did he mistake the diner for his house?*

Pushing through the manager's door, as promised a bed filled one corner. He sat her down as gentle as he had lifted her out of the car. Turning away, Goldie watched the muscles in his back stretch and twist as he pulled off his shirt and began unbuckling his belt.

We're about to fuck, and something tells me everything is going to be just right. Spurred by his motions, she wiggled her panties off and unlatched her bra. Frustration filled her as the hooks caught on the frayed edge of the ripped dress.

Muttering profanities under breath, she twisted, trying to reach behind her to untangle it. Strong hands came to the rescue, ripping the cross-stitch and with it, freeing her of the dress and bra. Her lips parted to thank him but found his pressing hard, hot, and hungry. Deepening her kiss, she wanted to find the object that had fascinated her about him in that picture from the car. Her tongue slid across the horizon of flesh, searching. The tip of her tongue flicked the piercing, and he moaned into her mouth.

The bed creaked as she let herself layback into nest of bedding, the comforter balled up behind her, making her back arch. His naked body hot between her thighs, his cock hard as he pressed it against her pussy, daring to enter her. She panicked. Pushing him back, he let her and gave her a wide-eyed expression.

"Condoms!"

He laughed. "I wasn't getting to that part yet. Can't a guy have fun first?"

She glared at him, unamused. "Condoms or nothing."

He stood to his feet and sashayed across the poorly lit room. The light bounced off his muscled body, the tattoos distorting the shadows and curves, making his bare skin more pronounced as it trailed down to between his thighs. He rolled the condom onto his erection, nowhere near the size of Texas, but damn, it made her ache to have him. As he closed the gap between them, she balled the sheets in her fist, spreading herself to receive him.

C.J. knelt before her, his arms wrapping around her thighs, tugging her to the edge of the bed. His tongue licked across her pussy and when his tongue piercing connected with her clit, she came alive. The beard tickled and raked her skin. Chills rippled across her, the sensation provocative and goading her lust to have more of him. Her thighs fought to flee the overwhelming euphoria as he circled and flicked the tender swollen jewel. Goldie's fingers tangled in his hair, wanting more, scared of the orgasm building at alarming speed. The hardened muscles in his arms only added to the arousal consuming her body and soul.

Goldie peaked. The cry visceral as she bowed. It was short lived as his lips locked wither her, muffling it. His cock slid in, hard as she throbbed and tightened. Her orgasm still rolled through her as he began grinding against her. The heat of his body weighed over her, her breast pressing against his torso, his arms wrapping under her. Her thighs tightened around him, rising her knees, letting him deeper into her.

He deepened the kiss before pulling away, panting against her neck. "You feel so good. It's hard to hold back."

"A little more." She let go of the sheets, her fingers clawing at his back. "Don't stop."

He grunted, a hand gliding down to her lower back and arching. His back bowed, moaning. She could feel him throb inside her. He pressed his hip against hers, grinding deep against her as he came. Her legs shook and toes curled. At last, she let go, allowing herself to rest in his arms. He slowed until he stopped, still inside her. Pulling away, he looked down at her and pulled a strand of hair from her face. Her lips curved into a smile as her breathing slowed.

"You seem satisfied." He smirked, pushing against her. "How was it?"

Meeting his gaze, she confessed, "Just right. But now, I'm hungry."

He hung his head in defeat. "I'm out of eggs, but I did make some porridge. You game?"

"As long as its not too hot, and not too cold."

The End

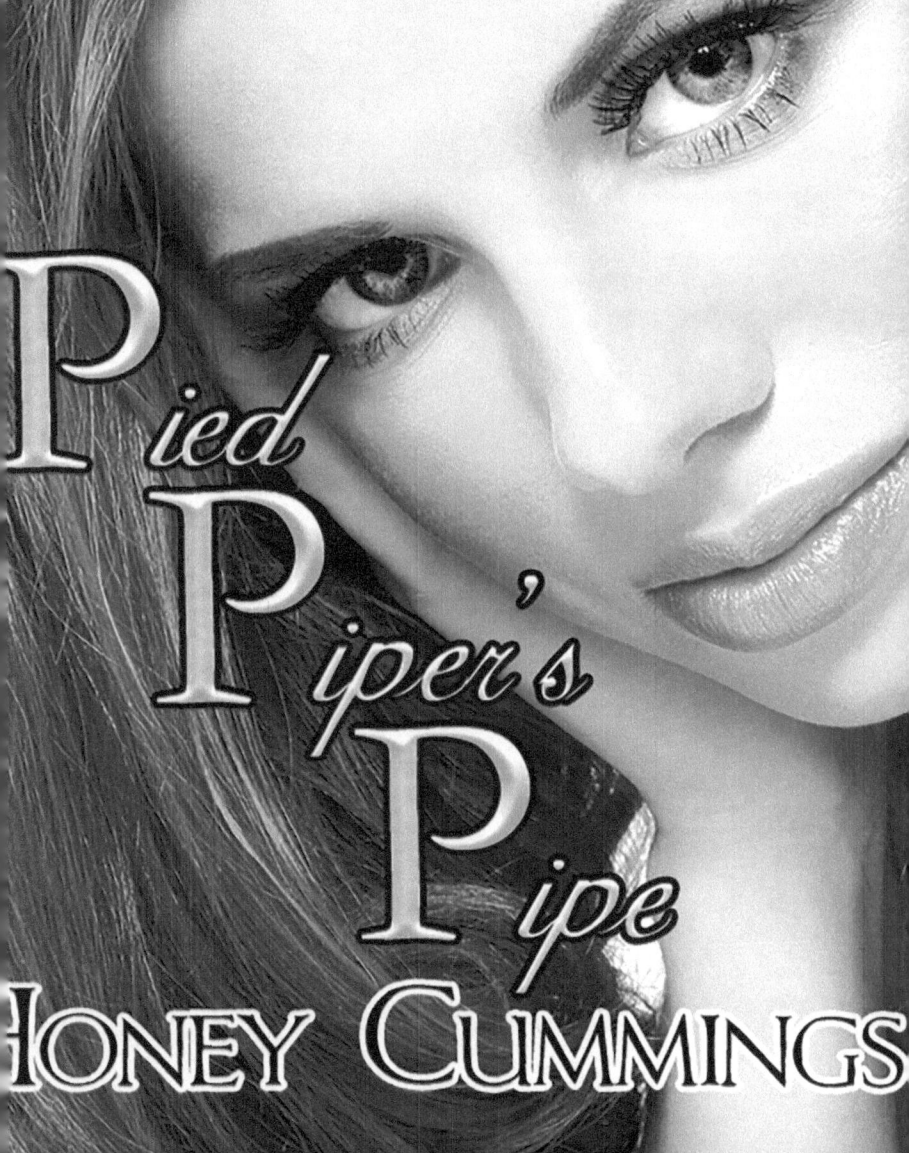

THE URBAN EROTICA FAIRY TALE COLLECTION

Pied Piper's Pipe

Honey Cummings

Table of Contents

THE PIPER

Peter von Schmidt entered *Red's Bar*, relishing the air conditioning as sweat trickled down his temple from early summer heatwaves. Looking at his cell phone, the bar had barely been open an hour. With spring ending, it wouldn't be long before bikers came in droves, on their way into the bigger city for bike week. The worse of it was how they left a wake of unpaid tabs and broken pool sticks at every joint in a fifty-mile radius. This early, the bar was a ghost town, but it wouldn't be long before a cluster of bikers poured in, making a debacle of the weekly karaoke night.

They never bothered him. No one wanted to fuck with a guy who passed as a taller Stone Cold Steve Austin on a bad day. In fact, he had the real deal by about three inches standing at a height of six foot five inches. He often lifted weights, but that was to help him stay fit at the steel factory and the heavy loading of the machines and palettes. Scratching his goatee, he took a seat at the bartop, waiting for the time to pass.

His day had quickly gone downhill. He needed to keep a low profile.

"Hey Peter! You're here rather early." Red came out of the back office, her hips swinging in her jean skirt and red locks bouncing all around her shoulders. "In fact, a few hours early. Are you here for lunch?"

"Let me see the menu," he grumbled, rubbing the top of his bald head. "I have nothing better to do."

She reached over the cash register and pulled one free. "So, you going to tell me why you're at my bar so early today? I imagine it wasn't to watch me prep the ice trough for tonight."

He grabbed the menu. "I got laid off," he said, and her smile faltered. "Slow season is hitting, and they cut the crew in half today. Unfortunately, this year was my turn to get laid off."

"Ouch. I'm shocked no one else came with you." He stole a glance at her cleavage as she leaned over the counter. *If I didn't know better, she did that on purpose to brighten my day.* "Anything I can do to make you feel better?"

He sighed. "I'll live," he said, glancing over the menu. "Just get me a cheeseburger, add bacon."

"Ok, sweetheart." She punched his order into the touch screen. "Are you looking for a seasonal job? Or planning a long vacation?"

"I haven't made up my mind yet." Peter leaned back, enjoying the way Red's body dipped, in and out of her belly shirt. "Was thinking about leaving town for a while."

"Oh?" Her blue eyes peeked over her shoulder, gazing at him. "Heading south for warm beach weather? That's where I'd go if I were you. Some fun in the sun."

"Bah, too hot here as it is." Drumming his fingers on the bartop, he twisted his lips. "Was thinking north, way up north. Maybe Canada."

"Canada?" Twisting around, she arched into the counter, her breasts peaking above of her shirt and he realized she wasn't wearing a bra. "How about I give you a job here? Maybe change your mind about skipping town? Or delay it some."

Is she really flashing those at me? She's must be doing that on purpose and I ain't gonna look away. She's almost too big breasted to be playing that game.

"Oh?" He mimicked her sound, his eyes flowing up and lingering on her painted red lips. "What did you have in mind? Seems like someone doesn't want me to leave town just yet."

"Look, we both know those damn bikers are back and well, they almost put me out of business last year between unpaid tabs and repairs." She bit the tip of her finger, waiting for him to lock eyes before batting her lashes. "You think you can play my bouncer for a week? Until most of them leave town."

"How do you plan to pay me to stay then?" He arched an eyebrow, smirking at the sparkle in her eye. "What makes you think they'll pay their tabs this time?"

"You." She poked him in the chest, making his heart flutter as she bent down, revealing lacy red panties underneath her skirt. "There will be food and drinks on the house for you. That I can promise."

"C'mon Red." He looked away, cursing his luck. *I can't afford a week without pay. She's outta her mind.* "I need cash for fuel. I'm headed north to find a summer job desperate for a strong-armed man to harvest, lift, or even sling asphalt before the mild weather ends."

"I could use some arms for heavy lifting," she said as she filled a large glass with cold beer, then setting it in front of him. "Please, Peter. Stay and I'll pay you with a favor."

Through the bubbly haze of yellow ale, her cleavage shimmered like gold. *What's the worse that happens? I get to fuck Red before I head out of town. Looks like the Pied Piper's back in business.*

"Fine," he drawled. "If not with cash, then with whatever I want?"

She perked up, her breast bouncing as she grinned. "Whatever you want."

Red's Tavern

Belly full, Peter took his time walking the entire parameter. As a customer, he hadn't really noticed there was more to the place other besides pool tables, stage, tables, and bar. The kitchen had all the basics and a walk-in refrigerator and freezer to match. He hadn't expected the dive bar to afford something that nice. Red spared no expense with timers, pressure cookers, and the works so her part-timer cook Chuckles could manage even a busy night solo. Granted, the poor kid was saving up for his own restaurant and even Gubering folks between part-time jobs. Out the back door he found the usual set of dumpsters, pile of milkcrates, and dirt parking lot where her old Wagoneer complete with wood paneling sat.

"Hey!" He shouted through the kitchen. "Should I park back here?"

"I would, makes it easier to leave and no worries that some drunk ass dented your car." Chuckles carried out a garbage bag. "If you get in over your head, let me know."

Peter snorted. "I got a good foot on you, and this ain't my first gig as a bouncer."

Chuckles laughed, slamming the dumpster lid shut. "With biceps as big as my head, I imagine no one fucks with you."

He followed Chuckles back inside. "Where the *hell* is Red?"

"Probably in her room." He flipped the fryer off. "Dammit, did she cook a hamburger on this?"

"Her room?" He walked to the push door.

"Through the office." Then, he shouted, "RED! Next time, clean the damn grill!"

Ignoring the flustered cook, he was back behind the bartop. The usual karaoke crowd was piling in at last, the host setting up and testing the equipment on the stage. He nodded at a few of his singing colleagues before pivoting into the next door. Inside the walls were lined with mismatched filing cabinets, an old computer, and a VCR humming as it recorded a four-panel, black-and-white security feed. *So that's how she knew I walked in.* Continuing to scan the room, he stopped at a far wall where a door lay cracked open.

Red released a frustrated whimper. Alarmed by the sound, he rushed across the office. Peter pushed through and froze. She was on her back, laying across an unkempt bed, her legs spread wide open, her hand diving under her lacy red panties. His eyes remained there as she continued to rub her pussy. At last he willed his eyes up, heart racing as he followed the divot over her belly button, up to where her other hand groped her bare breast, fingers twisting her nipple. She let out another hum, tilting her hips as she bit her bottom lip.

At last, they locked gazes, neither one willing to slow their fun.

"I'm sorry, I didn't..." *Dammit.* He couldn't seem to move his body, the sight of her arousal .... *I shouldn't be here. But...* "You look like you're having some trouble." *I've always wanted a chance to see more and boy, did I hit jackpot.*

She propped herself up, a smile blooming on her lips. "I can't lie, having you here, like this, sets my libido ablaze."

His face flushed, dropping his gaze. "Does that mean you have the hots for me, Red?"

"Yeah." She sucked the side of her cheek, her legs still provocatively spread wide open. "I've always wondered what it would take to fuck Peter von Schmidt."

He laughed, rubbing his bald head before glaring back at her. "You flatter me."

"So..." She arched an eyebrow high, scooting her crouch closer to the edge of the bed. "What will it be?"

"Seriously? You want to fuck now? Here?" Pulling the door shut behind him, he waited for her answer.

"Fuck me, right now." She wiggled out of her red panties, her toothy grin and hungry eyes making his cock throb. "Here, I'll even get rid of the last obstacle. I'm already wet thinking about it today."

He grunted, his hardon pressing against his jeans made him ache. She lifted the jean skirt, giving him a clear view of her shaven pussy. *How can I say no to that?* Yanking his shirt off, he took two long strides across the room as he unbuttoned his jeans. Before he could bend down to her, red painted fingernails were clawing to unzip him, and his hard cock throbbing in her hands. Her lips wrapped around his dick and began to suck. He reached out, bracing against the wall.

Someone's a hungry girl. Good gravy! Glad this was a twin sized bed, or I would have fallen...

He moaned. He was too long, too large to fit all the way into her mouth. The tip pressed hard against the back of her throat and she sucked, tongue wiggling. Looking down to her, blue eyes peeked up making sure he watched as she gobbled up his cock. She began pulling his dick in and out, the tip pressing firm against her lips before sucked hard until he slammed into the back of her throat again and again. He released another moan.

"Keep that up and I'm going to come," he warned, suppressing the orgasm daring to prematurely ruin his fun.

With a pop, she freed his dick from her lips. "Do you have a condom? If not, I have a spare."

He laughed, fingers dipping into a back pocket for his wallet. Flipping it open, he pulled out the wrapper. She plucked it from his fingers, tore it opened, then rolled the condom over his cock.

Another chuckle came out of him as he marveled over how voracious her want for his dick seemed.

If only every time was this—wild and lustful, I would never stop masturbating.

Again, Red laid back and groped her breast. Legs opened wide as her finger dipped between the pink folds of her pussy, demonstrating how much the idea of having him inside her made her wet. Peter inhaled deep and held it. The problem wasn't her, but the bed was too damn low to the ground. With a finger, he motioned for her to flip it around and get on all fours to make this more comfortable for them both.

"You're too tall." She pouted.

"I have to be on my feet tonight, let's not wear out my knees just yet." His hand slid up her thighs, lifting her skirt above her ass. "Mmm-mmm!"

She wiggled her ass. "Like what you see?"

"Definitely." He rubbed his length against the opening of her pussy and swollen clit. "You think you can handle something this long?"

"I've dreamed about it long enough." She reached under, holding his dick against her as she rocked against him.

Humming from her heat, he couldn't stand it anymore. Pressing the tip against her opening, he slid inside her slow. She rocked back, her ass against his hip. With a knee, he made her spread her legs and the rest of his dick slipped in, their bodies snug against one another. She tightened around his cock and he throbbed. Gripping her hips, he pulled out, watching his length come out wet and throbbing until the cap pulled free.

He loved waiting until she leaned back, breaking inside her, and riding all the way in and repeating it until at last, her agony was too much. He moaned as she grinded against him, enjoying how she felt, rubbing his shaft in every sweet spot. *She's such a good fit.* Tired of riding the edge of his orgasm, he throbbed inside her, and she moaned. *Good, she's nice and ready.*

Fingers gripping her sides, he quickened each thrust of his hip until he pounded her harder—*faster*. She screamed, arching as she clawed at her covers. The bed knocked into the wall; *bang-bang-bang*. A deep inhale silenced her shrieks and her body shuddered. Her pussy wrapped tight around his cock and with the last hard shove, he peaked as well.

Throbbing as he came, he slowed his rocking, letting the pleasure of her orgasm coalesce with his own, until both of them hummed.

Several bangs thundered through the wall.

SHIT. Peter paled, his orgasm receding. *That's the kitchen!*

"Fucking Chuckles." Her head sunk into defeat.

Peter pulled out, chucking his condom into a nearby trashcan. "Dammit. I didn't think the walls were *that* thin."

She rolled over, flinging an arm over her face. "It's not the first time."

Peter's heart skipped a beat. *Why the hell does that make me jealous already?*

"Granted, it's been a *long* while," she said as she gauged Peter's reaction. "Thank you, I needed a good release."

"You're welcome... I think." He twisted, grabbing his shirt from the floor. "It's been a while since my last hooked up."

"Wasn't that when that Randi-chick came to town?" She pushed her breasts back into her shirt.

Peter's face flushed again as he tucked himself away. "Y-yeah. She caught me off guard, but it wasn't anything serious."

"Oh?" Red slid on her panties.

He smirked. "When was your last time? Since we're swapping stories."

Her face paled. "I didn't get his name."

Peter blinked, her face turning bright red now as she looked him in the eye.

"I went to some crazy masquerade orgy in the 'burbs." Standing, she straightened her skirt out. "No names, all masks, and so... like a true Red Riding Hood; I fucked the Big Bad Wolf."

"An orgy? In this small town?" He opened the door, motioning her through. *Good gravy.* "Did this town always sex craved?"

THE PIPES

As they left the office, Chuckles was tending to the customers' drink orders. He gave a side glance at Peter before laughing and shaking his head. Whether the other eyes knew what the two of them had done back there was a mystery. He walked around, greeting the other karaoke singers, including Justin, the host.

The stage was set, fog machine rolling into a sea of colorful lights.

The bar was silent as the jukebox was muted, the reigns of entertainment handed over for the weekly event. As always, the cheesy introduction and hype was geared for a far larger crowd than the twelve patrons who barely filled the bartop and two tables.

"Welcome to another Thursday night of Justin-Time-Karaoke!" There was a collective moan in the bar, but it didn't faze the host. "Be sure to grab up the folders and see our collection. If there's a song you want that's not listed, just come see me! First up, let's have Peter up on stage! Singing, It's A Great Day to Be Alive by Travis Tritt."

Oof! I forgot I open with this song and today it's hitting me hard. I got laid and laid off.

The crowd built into a slow, awkward clap as he climbed on stage, grabbing the microphone from Justin. He disregarded the old prompter screen, having sung the song for so long it seemed as if it were a part of him. A foot tapped with the beat, his voice rumbling through and the bar fell instantly silent. If he hadn't been so bald, someone could have mistaken him for the real deal on stage. He picked songs based on the tone and gruff of his voice and he loved how he captivated a room.

One of these days, I just might run off and join a southern rock band. Ha!

In the trance of his performance, he hadn't noticed the bikers enter the bar. The only blessing was instead of the usual cacophony of laughter and cursing, they came in enamored by the big boy on stage singing better than the jukebox could have played. As Peter rumbled the last line and the music faded the leather vested crowd whistled and shouted.

"DAMN! The pipes on that man!" The tallest biker whistled again, gesturing to his crew to join him. "You sing some more like that brother, and old Tex will have to start throwing you some greenbacks instead of the jukebox for a change."

"I'll take your money any day." Peter smirked as he cut across the bar. So, this is the crew she's worried about.

"You leavin' already?" The big biker with TEXAS stitched on his vest scratched his beard. "Aw, don't leave so soon. At least give us another song."

"Don't you worry," Peter grumbled, marching pass the group. "My seat is just right here, near the door, just in case anyone decides to get too rowdy tonight."

"The bouncer?" He gave a toothy grin, then turned his attention to Red standing behind the bar. "You got yourself a bouncer this year, huh?"

"Had to. Last year you and your so-called crew nearly put me out of business." She didn't even make eye contact as she mixed a drink and popped open three bottles of beer. "You want your usual bucket of Coors Light or something with more kick to start off the night."

"Fuck yeah I want my beer and give me a Jagger Bomb!" He swung around in a grand gesture. "Get everyone here a Jagger Bomb."

Red stopped, placing her hands on her hips. "Not without a card. No one's getting shit."

"Aww c'mon, Ginger." He purred, pulling out a wallet with its chain clanking with each step. "Don't be so mean about it."

He slapped the card down and when she reached for it, he slid it out of reach. "I'm in no mood for your flirting. Why don't you sign up on Sinder and get yourself a one-night stand, instead of hounding me like a bitch in heat, Tex."

He released a long whistle. "Damn, girl. Someone needs to get laid."

Coming out of the kitchen swinging doors, Chuckles overheard the comment and choked on his drink, ducking back into the kitchen. Red's face flushed, cheeks puffing out. Peter watched her lips, wondering if she would retort or confess that he had just taken her on all fours barely an hour ago. Nothing. She lashed out again, sliding the card and turned to the register.

"You still want to buy the whole bar shots?" Her tone was every bit of a disgruntled mother's tone when one spoke to a child who had thrown a tantrum.

"N-no." He spun to the bar. "Sorry y'all! I ain't that rich. Perhaps another night!"

The bar filled with groans and laughter. His biker pals were disappointed, but the karaoke regulars sniggered knowing full well what to expect if this was going down like last year. Many had paid for the unwanted drinks to make up the difference, or at least lighten the blow to Red's expenses.

"A Jagger bomb and a bucket, right?" She slid the card.

"Yeah, that'll be good to start with." Tex drummed his fingers on the bar, his smile vanished. "I'll give that Sinder thing a try. So, when did it become mandatory to pay up front?"

"New policy." Red pointed above her head to a sign, pay as you drink, or water from the sink.

"You're just ruining my fun. Can't a guy just open a tab?" He groaned, pulling at his beard.

He pointed to another sign, reading: no open tabs. Pay as you go. "Thanks to you, this is the normal night of fun."

When the receipt finally printed, she slid it, along with a pen and his credit card, in front of him. "Damn. What bullshit. I'm a regular."

"You're seasonal," she amended, nodding at the karaoke crew. "They're my regulars. Coming here one month each year doesn't make you a regular."

"All right, all right. Can we get a pool table for an hour or two?" He gave her a smug look.

She mirrored the goofy grin. "$50 for the first two hours."

"Dammit, woman!" He threw up his arms. "Fred, pay for your damn pool table!"

A skinny twig of a biker appeared. He grinned at her, his teeth green a few already missing.

Peter cringed, but Red remained unphased.

The biker dropped a fifty on the counter, and she pulled out a tray with balls, chalk, and a rack. He took them and a group by the pool table roared to life, drowning out the karaoke. Peter snorted, frustrated that he couldn't hear Wendy nor old Sam sing over the clacking of pool balls and barking bikers. Red came around the bartop, her swaying hips making him shudder as she dropped off and picked up beers from all over the place. For one cook and one bartender, she kept drinks filled, food coming, and tabs ready.

At last she came in his direction and he straightened himself. She flicked her hair back over her shoulder and placed an icy mug of water on his tiny table. The heat of her hand on his shoulder made him think of how those red lips wrapped around his cock, his blood rushing at the thought there might be a second round later. Her breath tickled at his ear, whispering just loud enough to make it clear through the music and bikers.

"Are you ok over here?" Her other hand rested on his knee, making his groin ache to feel her gentle touch.

"I'm fine. Just pissed I can't hear over these assholes." Tex was giving them the stink eye as he leaned on his pool stick. "You handled him like a champ, I'm impressed."

She laughed, her hair slipping off her shoulder to rest on his. "You learn to take no shit in my line of work."

"Well, I hope to make it smoother tonight." Her hand slid up his inner thigh, squeezing until he grunted. *Good gravy, she's making me hard again.*

"It's your turn." She breathed.

He paled. "My turn?"

"Your turn," she echoed, rubbing her warm hand across the crotch of his jeans before pulling away. "Justin's calling you to the stage, sweetheart."

FUCK! She meant for karaoke. He took a gulp of ice water, then marched towards the stage.

The only relief is he hadn't gotten completely hard, otherwise he'd have to cook up some excuse. Chuckles came out from the kitchen and started helping her cater to the demanding bikers, both registers dinging. He managed to get to the stage and realized he hadn't put in for a song number two.

"What am I singing?" He cracked his neck, waiting for Justin to select a song.

With a sparkle in his eye, he gave a devilish grin. "Mustang Sally."

"Of course." Peter sighed, leaning into the microphone stand.

Again, the music started, his heel tapping to the beat as he sang the lyrics. In an instant, the bar went silent once more, and he couldn't stop smiling. Screeching the chorus, he locked eyes with Red and she laughed. It started to feel like a secret conversation, and she snapped her fingers, dancing as he howled on. The song ended and he felt cheated out of the fun of stealing glances across the bar at one another. Whistles and claps came from the pool tables and his grin faltered.

"One more song." He leaned over to Justin. "Let's do another Tritt song."

"I know just the one to match the atmosphere." Justin was pulling it up on the system.

The name appeared on the prompter, and he smirked. "This song is for the biggest troublemaker in the joint, Red."

The music started and everyone whistled and howled. Peter winked at Red, pointing at her as he sang. Fast-paced, he roared the lyrics to T-R-O-U-B-L-E with practiced ease and the whole bar was signing along by the end. Feeling satisfied, he left the stage laughing and thanking the karaoke peers for their compliments. He ignored the bikers and their kudos, intending to march towards the table when Tex's landed a heavy hand on his shoulder.

Peter stopped, twisting to look down at him as every muscle tensed in his bulging arm and heaving chest, forcing his shirt to stretch across his pecs.

"Down boy!" Tex threw his hands up in surrender. "Can I buy you a beer?"

"Why?" Peter returned to his table, gulping down the rest of his water.

"Those pipes. Man, you ever think about singing for a band. I know one looking for a singer like you." Tex waved off his turn at the pool table, handing the pool stick to one of the biker chicks who had come in with them. "Seriously, I bet you could go places."

"I only sing for fun." Sitting down, he locked eyes with Red who frowned seeing Tex talking to him. "Look, I'm working as the bouncer here. Perfectly content with that."

"Well, if you get tired of the grouchy Ginger over there, just hit me up." He slid his cell number on a business card to Peter, and he crushed it in his pocket.

Tex turned back to his crew, but before he could speak the cracking of a pool stick brought everything to a screeching halt. Peter jolted to his feet, blood rushing. Two bikers were screaming into each other's faces, shoving into one another like two raging bulls. A girl was crying, covering her face. Most of the crew were already shitfaced, so they all watched the events unfold in a stupor.

"YOU FUCKING PUT YOUR HAND UP MY GIRL'S SKIRT!" roared the one carrying the broken pool stick. "I WILL CAVE YOUR HEAD IN!"

He raised an arm high, the bulk of bikers pulling the offender away. Peter gripped the wrist hard, wrenching it until the pool stick bounced against the floor. Before the other arm could swing, it too found itself dropping the impromptu weapon and twisted behind him.

"LET ME GO!"

"Don't think so. You're done." Peter shoved him around the pool table and outside with insane ease.

I've lifted steel bars with more bite than this guy.

The bikers followed, none of them challenging Peter. Letting go, the man fumbled forward, pale from the ease he had been dealt with and pulled out of the bar. The girl sobbed, her words belligerent other than his name, Fred, as Peter glared with pure rage.

Tex nodded. "Let's call it a night, boys. We got business to discuss about Fred, anyhow." He motioned a goodbye as he straddled a white Harley Davidson Road King. "Sorry for the trouble. I'm glad she finally has some muscle."

4

CLOSING TIME

Marching back through the door, Red was tabbing out the regulars. Peter returned to the pool table, grabbing the broken stick, then gathering the pool balls into the tray. The music had ended, karaoke disrupted and the lights flickering on. *She's closing down early. That's not like her. I've seen barfights here, cops and all, but she's never just shut the place down over a scuffle.*

He waved farewell to the karaoke crew and helped Justin load his equipment. Silence held strong between him and the patrons as they cleared the parking lot. Walking through the front door, he reached for his empty glass to find it gone. Daring to scan the bar for her, he met Red's gaze as she punched in the tips on the last of the tabs.

"Lock that door, would ya?" He did as she asked.

He sat at the bar and watched her. "You ok? Did I do something wrong?"

"No." She slid the receipts into the slot of the register. "Last time they argued like that, they nearly destroyed this place. I'd rather take a loss by closing early than deal with that shit."

The bedroom in the back flashed in his mind and his stomach knotted. "You live here."

"I do. Sold the house to pay for last year's bullshit. Haven't totally gotten back on my feet just yet." Peter hissed, he had no idea, but

113

Red had always kept to herself. "We didn't do too bad. It helped making those dicks pay as they go."

"Well that's an improvement." A motorcycle rumbled pass on the highway and they both froze, glaring at the front door. "Look, I'll stay until we're both confident that they won't return."

Her brow folded and at last, she looked him in the eyes. "I'd like that. Thank you."

His brow lowered, his voice turning stern. "Did they hurt you?"

"No." She snorted. "I was nowhere near the fight."

He shook his head. "I meant last year."

She froze, then finished locking the register. "No, but it scared the shit out of me." Her shoulders shook. "The cops took forever to get here, and I couldn't afford to hire them as security."

Peter leaned back, drumming his fingers. "Well, you got me this time. Those rats will have to answer to Peter von Schmidt, your personal Pied Piper."

She giggled. "Did you just call yourself the Pied Piper?"

Peter raised his eyebrows, then shrugged. "It's a nickname from work. Kind of grew on me."

Smirking, Red leaned on the bar, training his eyes to fall onto her cleavage. "And are your pipes that voice or something longer and stronger?"

His face flushed, and he scratched his goatee. "You know exactly how to make me blush, you know that, Red."

"It's cute." Pulling away she left him sitting there in silence as she went back into the kitchen.

In the back, he could hear the muffled conversation of her helping Chuckles clean up after a night of cooking. Red came out and sat a cold mug filled to the rim with Bud Light and basket of fries in front of him. Before he could even say a thank you, she winked and disappeared back through the kitchen door. The minutes dragged by, the clanging and sounds of the sink soon falling silent. The lights went out, and she came through the doors, drying her hands in an oversized rag. Flipping open the cooler, she grabbed a Corona, then a lime from the garnish box and slinked around the bartop and slid beside him.

"Your dragging around like an old lady." He smirked taking a sip of beer.

"I do feel old on night's like this." She sighed, squeezing the lime into the bottle. "Seemed like a good night to lend him a hand back there and give the kitchen a good scrub down."

"You keep this place pretty tidy." He gave her a side glance. "When I walked the parameter, trying to gather my bearings, I didn't notice any trash or dust on any surface."

"Well, it's easier to maintain when I live here." She guzzled another long swig.

"So, you opened this joint all by your lonesome?" he asked, curious to know more about her backstory.

Setting the bottled down, she laughed, fingering the opening. "Well, I guess my ex-husband deserves some credit for opening this place. As for keeping it running for the last five years, that's all me." Another long pull on the Corona, she exhaled. "Tex is a good guy, but his biker gang almost costed me the bar last year."

"How can you call him a good guy if he almost destroyed the place?" Peter drained the last of his Bud Light and tossed it into the trash.

"Every month, he still sends me money to repay me for the damage."

"No shit." Peter blinked and watched as Red drained her beverage. "It can't be much though."

"No, but he's never been late since he started last year. I can't talk too much shit about him for that." Spinning in her chair, her hands pressed against atop his thighs as she leaned in closer. "Enough about those assholes. How about you let me play with your pipe once again, Mr. Pied Piper."

Peter laughed, averting his gaze as he blushed at the idea.

"C'mon." Her hands slid slow across his thighs, the heat of them searing through his jeans. "You can't say you weren't hoping for a second round."

Caving, he met her gaze and she batted her eyes. "If I didn't know better, this was never about hiring me to be your bouncer or helping a customer who was out of the job."

"You caught me," she breathed, fingers clawing at his button and zipper.

"Were you planning to pay me in cash or..." He grunted, her fingers teasing his growing erection with practiced skill. "Blow jobs won't keep the lights on, Red."

She blew warm air against the tip and he throbbed in her hold. "You're right."

He braced an arm on the countertop and gripped the barstool under him. Last thing I need is to fall straight back. At least she's going slower this time. A shudder rocked him as she began stroking his cock with her hand, the other cupping his balls. Her nipples had grown hard against atop his thighs as she lean into his crotch. Lips tickled at the underbelly, kissing, and teasing their way from the tip and down the length of his pipe.

Red didn't stop at the base. Deepening her kisses, she suckled and licked his balls, making him moan. She paced herself, stroking his shaft as she made love to the tender sack making him grow harder with each lick. A nibble made him tighten as she denied his balls from toying with them. Her thumb slid to the tip of his dick, circling there, slick with precum as she pleasured her own clit.

She moaned, and he leaned forward, white knuckled as he fought the urge to speed the process.

Pulling off his balls, her blue eyes met his own with a wicked grin. And he throbbed with desire. The pleasure and arousal building at his core made his body feel boiling hot. Wet and soft, her tongue licked from the base to the tip. He moaned, and he closed his eyes, enjoying the primitive sensation of touch, pure and provocative.

The tip of her togue teasing the opening of his penis before her lips slid slow and tight down his shaft.

She changed direction. A firm thumb stroked hard on the bottom half of his long cock as her lips slid to the top and back to meet the rising of her hand. She rolled his balls in her other hand, massaging soft and gentle, adding to the experience. He leaned harder on the counter and at last his hand broke loose from the stool. His fingers entwined with deep red locks, moaning as he pressed his dick deep into her throat, desire taking hold.

She moaned as she shifted, his cock riding across her tongue and connecting with the back of her mouth. She abandoned her play with his balls, leaning in and let him press her where it felt best. He rocked his hips, the stool creaking under his weight as it squeaked against the screws keeping it fastened to the wooden floors.

Thank you to whoever screwed these bad boys to the floor!

She released another moan, and she began sucking, her mouth tight on his throbbing erection. He began panting, fighting his rising orgasm close from exploding.

A little longer... this feels so damn good!

Thrusting in and out, he quickened his speed. Her nails dug into him as if hugging him into her. Slick and hungry, she took him in over and over. The tip of her tongue curled up, the hard nub riding the length of his shaft. And he lost it. Humming, he slowed his rocking as he came. She swallowed, twice more as he throbbed and released for the last time.

He freed her hair, trying to catch his breath. She sat up, a sparkle in her eyes as she licked her lips.

Good gravy. I don't think she's done.

RED HOT

P eter's brow arched high as he watched with erotic curiosity. Red removed her panties, then sat back down, hiking her skirt up. She was barefoot and he marveled to where she had ditched the cute sneakers in all the commotion.

She raised a leg and laid across his thigh, opening wide to show him her world.

That's what he meant by that in Crash into Me! Dammit, Dave Matthews Band!

Tugging her shirt over her bare breasts, she began to rub herself. Peter cursed the fact he was spent for a while before he could go another round. He could feel the heat of her stare as he grunted, balls tensing as her fingers rubbed her pussy. There wasn't a detail he didn't want etched into his memory as he took in every curve, every inch of flesh.

Her breasts were firm, her arousal from playing with his cock still driving her want for him. Nipples stood erect, a subtle brown against warm golden skin. He swallowed.

She tans in the nude. Maybe I should rethink my plans to head south if she wants to tag along.

His eyes widened as she groped her own breasts, raw and rough. The flesh of it bulged from between her fingers and again, he cursed the fact he wouldn't be able to get hard just yet. At last he dared to look higher at the glare he knew awaited him. Lips were caught in the grip of her teeth and blue eyes glossy.

She huffed a laugh. "I want you to watch me play with myself."

He swallowed and let his gaze return to where her finger circled her clit. Her pussy swollen and wet, making him stroke himself, hoping to speed up his recovery time.

"Look how wet you make me."

Another grunt escaped him, some hope building as his dick throbbed under his touch.

"Having your cock in my mouth makes me want to touch myself." She shifted, his view of her pink folds making him throb once more. "Do you want to fuck me again?"

He inhaled deep. What a loaded question!

"You want back inside me?" Her fingers slid slow into her pussy, rubbing in and out.

Peter stroked himself in unison, and she began to moan. He was growing stiff once more, his dick dripping in anticipation of what he saw before him.

"Tell me, Peter." Her voice deepened, dripping with lust. "Tell me where you want to fuck me with that big dick of yours."

He sucked the side of his cheek, unable to look away as her fingers came out, wet, and began rubbing her clit once more. "I want..." Chills rattled him, cutting his words short.

In his peripheral, her lips curved into a wide grin. "Anything you want, you can have it all."

Stroking his cock, he wasn't hard enough to take her. He leaned forward, his lips latching onto her breast, and he circled her nipple with his tongue. She abandoned groping its match, pulling him into her chest so she could balance on the stool. His freehand slid up the inside of her thigh. Slick from her want, his fingers found the hot silk of her swollen folds.

Rubbing her opening, she didn't slow her circling of her bean as he suckled on her breast. He could feel her throb from his touch, and he slid two fingers inside her warmth, pushing knuckle deep. Her body tightened around him.

Twisting his wrist, her legs jittered. There's the sweet spot.

She whimpered, and he rubbed slow, letting her inhale deep and fall into the pleasure of it. Her circling of her clit faltered. He switched breasts, nibbling her nipple. Her pussy tightened on his fingers again and he ran with it. Stroking hard and fast, she grew more wet with each push and at last she shrieked.

Her arms flailed and gripped his shoulders, nails biting into his skin. Peter didn't slow. Her orgasm pulsed through her. Legs shook and she folded forward as a gush of fluid brought his stroking to a halt. He still rubbed himself, his erection still not where he needed it to be.

At last, they met eyes once more and laughed.

"I don't think I've ever hated not getting an instant hardon from a blow job in all my life," he confessed, staring at his dick's betrayal. "You let me down, buddy."

She pushed her shirt down, bringing her leg off him and pulling her skirt back in place. "Sorry, I'm rather brass in the moment."

"I can tell." His eyes widened, a chill rolling up his spine. "And I can't lie, it's super-hot."

Her face burned bright red, and she covered her face. "Please don't blab about my fetish."

"What fetish?" He gave her a baffled look.

"I like it when men watch me touch myself."

"I like watching you touch yourself." The words tumbled from his mouth before he could stop himself. "Wait, that didn't come out as sexy as I thought..."

They jolted in their seats as a loud knock thundered from the kitchen, beating on the back door.

Peter furrowed his brow, tilting his head in a questioning manner. "Chuckles?"

She held her arms and shook her head. "No. He has a key. He would've texted me if he'd forgotten it."

Her eyes fell to her phone on the counter, and he looked to the kitchen door. "I didn't hear a motorcycle. Then again, I was a little distracted."

"Only cops and assholes knock on doors like that." She inhaled deep, holding it a moment before releasing it. "And cops knock on the front door."

Peter stood, tucking himself away and closing his pants. "I got this."

He started to walk away but she gripped his arm with both hands. "Peter. Be careful."

Winking, he marched through the kitchen and halted before the back door. All the locks were in place, a deadbolt, the lock on the knob, even a chain and slide bar. Red's front door had the same array. Another series of banging exploded on the door, and he flipped the light switches. The florescent lights overhead flickered to life and he prayed one of those switches lit up the backlot.

Whatever they did last year, it really shook her up good and someone's about to learn how hard a steel worker punches.

One by one, he started to unlatch the locks.

Another burst of banging. "OPEN THE FUCK UP, BITCH!"

The knob twisted, the last lock still in place.

That's the dickwad who I tossed out front for breaking a pool stick! Oh, he's about to get a fucking fist-sandwich!

Peter threw open the door, locking on a black-eyed skinny biker. His vest gone, he looked like a wet noodle as Peter bowed up. He took a few strides forward and the man countered, stumbling back in alarm.

The door slammed shut behind Peter and the man cowered into the dumpster, falling into a stack of milkcrates as he gave a silent stutter.

"Fred, right?" Peter's voice rolled from him like a growl, his brow low.

"L-l-l-look man," His pubescent voice cracked as he pleaded with Peter, the angry giant, for mercy. "I didn't know she was your girl. I just wanted to scare her."

"Like you did last year?" A vein pulsed on Peter's forehead and neck, every muscle in his body drawing taut with the adrenaline.

"About that, no one knows I did that, and..."

Peter punched the dumpster beside Fred's head, denting the metal. He squealed like a little girl, his knees shaking as he pissed himself. Peter was unmoved as blood trickled in a singular line from a busted knuckle, the blood black against the green paint. Nostrils flaring like an angry bull only made Fred cover his head, waiting for the ass-whooping coming to him.

Reaching down, Peter grabbed him by the scruff like a street dog. A firm grip with a ball of shirt and the back of his pants, it took one hi-ho swing to launch Fred up and into the dumpster.

Satisfied with the result, he slammed the lid closed and marched for the back door.

Red waited there, her eyes wide at the speed in which he had addressed the man.

"Your hand." She sidled to let him in before rushing to close and lock the door.

"This." His eyes looked to the busted knuckle and snorted. "I've done worse at work. Just needs ice."

"I'll grab something from the freezer." She rushed pass him.

6

T-R-O-U-B-L-E

Peter pulled out his phone and the crumbled paper with Tex's number.

[Peter: Come get your trash. Peter.]

The reply was fast.

[Tex: Fucking Fred. Where is he?]

[Peter: In the dumpster behind Red's Tavern.]

There was a long pause.

Red exited the walk-in freezer, a bag of frozen peas in hand. She gently placed it over his knuckles.

"Thank you," he muttered, still glaring at his phone.

With that, she spun, mumbling something about a "first aid kit" and "fucking Chuckles."

[Tex: We'll get him, and make sure he won't mess with her ever again.]

[Peter: Good. Next time he'll become a permanent shit stain in the parking lot.]

[Tex: If there's a next time, I'll help put him there.]

He smirked, his knuckle throbbing and aching. "Frozen peas are a smart idea."

"Don't eat them." She came in swinging her hips with the kit in hand. "I bought a few bags years ago just for this use only."

He glanced at the expiration. "Good gravy, these are older than my grandma."

Red laughed, the tension of the moment passing at last. "Thank you."

"I'm the bouncer," he replied, removing the peas so she could bandage his hand.

She sighed. "Not for that," she said. After taping the gauze, she met his gaze. "Thank you for making me laugh."

Rubbing his bald head, she averted his eyes. "Life's too short not to find humor in the small things."

She put the leftover items in the kit and closed it, leaving it behind. With a come-hither finger motion, he abandoned his bag of peas and followed her out of the kitchen. As she rounded the bar, she wiggled out of her skirt, leaving it on the floor. With a playful pirouette, she pulled her shirt up and off.

At last, she was completely nude. Between the passing time and adrenaline rush, Peter's pipe was back in business. Pacing himself, he followed her across the building where she waited at the pool table. He too mimicked her shedding of clothes, kicking off his boots, pulling his shirt off, and freeing his erection as he shuffled off his jeans. Peter closed the gap between them, stroking his cock.

"Do you think the pool table's high enough to prop me into a more comfortable position?" She smirked.

"Oh yeah." His dick throbbed, gauging the height. "I take it we're picking up where we left off?"

"Unless your knuckle hurts too much."

He laughed, rubbing his bald head with his freehand. "I think I'll manage it just fine."

Red pulled herself up on the pool table. Her legs spread open before him and his eyes fell once more to her pussy. Both of her hands slid down, spreading open her folds like the petals of a pink rose. A single finger slid slow and with great purpose inside. There was an agonizing pause before she drew her figure up and began playing with her clit.

He stepped closer, his eyes locking on the prize. She grew more wet with each passing moment. He timed his rubbing with the slow circling, reaching his tip as the finger rolled over the top and stroking down as it fell. Another step forward and at last he could trail his fingers from her knee to her thigh. Greedy, her fingers dove into her pussy and it made him moan with the desire to be inside her.

Changing tactics, he abandoned his cock and slid his fingers up her stomach until he cupped her breasts. He licked one nipple than the other. She hummed, and he continued his climb fully aware of how desperate her fingers spun and dipped into her pussy. Hands slid over the breasts until they framed her jaw. Pressing his lips against hers, he kissed her deeply.

A shudder rolled over him as they moaned into each other's mouths. Tongues tangled, pulling, and pushing as if in a struggle to decipher who tasted better than the other. His cock rubbed against her thigh until the tip pressed into the back of her hand. Sliding an arm behind her, he coaxed her to lay down. She yielded, lowering, and stretching her body before him. Her hands pulled away, reluctant to abandon their play so soon.

Peter straightened, his hands raking down her body until he could lean back and see all of her. His hard cock rubbed against her wet pussy, teasing her one last time. Her hands reached down, and he grabbed her wrists. Pinning them above her head, she grinned in reply. His cock slid inside, hard and fast. She arched, a gasp then shriek escaping her. He moaned, the tight heat making him throb inside her.

Satisfied, he had pressed as far as he could, he let go of her arms. Bracing himself on the pool table, he rocked his hips, pulling and pushing. Her knees rose high, hugging his torso and he could rock deeper into her. He loved how she bit her lip, staring him in the eye, never looking away. When she started to slide away, he grabbed her thighs and pulled her back to the edge of the table, pressing himself against her.

"You like playing with yourself but..." He licked his lips.

"But?" she grinded against him, her pussy matching the motion with waves of tightening.

"Do you like it..." His words lingered.

"Like it."

His hand glided over her hip, his thumb pressing against her swollen clit. Circling, he felt her spasm around his cock. She inhaled deep, arching as he rolled over the tender nub. Her legs shook where they hugged into him, knees digging into his ribs. The heat of her arousal waved from her and he started to rock his hip again. She whimpered, tilting her head back, eyes shut. Hands reached up, clawing at his arms, unable to pull him free.

Pressing firmer, thumb slick from her pussy, each pull drawing more, making each push quicker than the last. She tightened, moaning louder. The arch of her body higher. He had her peaking. Abandoning her clit, he wrapped his arms around her body, pulling her against him. The fever of their passion pressed into one another as her grind against her, deep and fast.

Fingernails scratched down his back and he fought the urge to peak. Not yet, I want more. She's so wet and...

A howl escaped her before she bit into his chest to ride it out. He pressed hard and stopped inside her, enjoying the pulsing of her pussy as she rode out her orgasm. She melted, muscles relaxing as she let herself lean back into his arms, panting.

"Dammit," he muttered.

Swallowing, she caught her breath. "What's wrong?"

"I don't have any condoms," he confessed, pulling away. "We used the only one I had. Where do you keep..."

Before he could walk off, she grabbed his arm. "I've got a naughty proposal."

He lifted an eyebrow at her. "You plan on swallowing again?"

I'm down for another epic blow job.

"That or..." She slid off the table and twisted around, bending over in a provocative pose spreading her ass cheeks open. "Or you can try something a little tighter?"

"But don't we need..."

She reached into the corner pocket and grabbed a bottle of lube. "I have it right here."

"Good gravy!" He rubbed his head, shaking his head in disbelief. "You had this whole night planned, didn't you?"

"Honestly, I was jealous of you hooking up with that out-of-towner, Randi." She sat the bottle beside her, wiggling her ass once more. "Well, Mr. Pied Piper, which is it? Blow job or this?"

Snorting, he snatched the lube up and squirted some on his fingers. "Please tell me this isn't your first time."

"Not the first time," she reassured.

He coated his dick and rubbed her starfish down. Sucking on his cheek, he pushed a finger into her tight ass, and she moaned. He fingered her, stretching her until two fingers slid in comfortably. She reached under herself, playing with her pussy once more. Another moan and she began rocking against his hand, encouraging him to be rougher, deeper, and more importantly, faster.

"You ready for this?" He gripped her hips, the tip of his cock pressing against her ass.

"Give it to me, Peter." She leaned back and the tip slid in, making her moan. "Fuck me until you come, please fuck me."

Swallowing, he pushed inside, slow, and gauging her every reaction. He didn't stop until their bodies pressed snug against one another. She was so tight, his cock throbbing in the heat of this unknown territory. Her fingers dipped into her pussy and she grinded against him, making him grunt.

"You're making me so wet," she whimpered.

His heart raced, her whimpering and pleading adding fuel to his fire. Licking his lips, he pulled out all the way and dove in a little faster. He repeated this, speeding up as they hummed and moaned in a dark language only they could understand. Curious as he began to fuck her gently, a hand slid over her hip and between her soaked thighs. She let him play with her hardened jewel and she dripped with each push.

"Good gravy, woman," he panted, his arousal cresting. His fingers dove inside her pussy as he fucked her ass. Every touch was breathtakingly erotic. "Did you just orgasm a second time?"

"Don't stop," she demanded. "Touch me more! Fuck me harder!"

His other hand slid to a breast, groping the soft ball of flesh before twisting her nipple. She tightened, both on his fingers and cock. It was like spurs to the horse and he took the opening. He thrusted hard into her. His orgasm peaked. With his cock stiff and hard, she wailed with a visceral scream, reverberating through the bar walls.

The pool table creaked as he leaned his weight into the last push, coming hard inside her. He had held on for so long, the aching release felt bittersweet. Peter sucked in air, stifling his own orgasmic scream. She rocked into his hand and dick, coming for a third time, cupping the hand over her breast as she hummed.

They froze, throbbing against each other as they gasped for air. Swallowing, Peter was the first to move, gently pulling his cock from her ass. She bit her lip, grabbing an ass cheek as his cum dribbled from it in a white stream. The site of it arousing and provocative, like his own personal porno.

If I could just have a picture of that view for those lonely nights. Mmm-mmm!

"You like what you see?" His eyes locked with hers, and he blushed. "The way you stare at my body...it make me feel—wanted."

He let his eyes trailed the cum dripping from her pussy. "You're a wild one, Red."

"And you're a good lover." She wiggled her ass, letting more cum dripping out. "So, you still going to Canada?"

"Canada who?" Temptation called him but his cock returned to recovery mode and his busted knuckle aching. The promise of pleasure and sex made him ache, hoping the feeling to last forever.

Red laughed. "Exactly."

Reaching for her, he slid a thumb into her ass and hummed. "I'm not done working here."

"Oh?" There it was, that signature sound she had given him earlier in the day.

With his other hand, he slid two fingers into her pussy and began stroking her fast, firm against the sweet spot he'd discovered earlier. She squealed, gripping the edge of the table as he overwhelmed her. Again, an orgasm peaked, her pussy gushing with yet another climax. He didn't slow until her knees shook and at last, gave way. Catching her up in his arms, he smirked to see he had at last exhausted his wanton, red-headed woman.

"You got a shower in this place, woman?" He laughed, happy to have out lasted her.

"Through my office."

7

Epilogue

"Come on, Beau." Lou took a sip of beer, nudging his buddy on the left. "What happened to you last weekend? You missed a hell of a sex party! Tell him, Taylor."

Taylor choked on his shot. "Not so loud," he shushed him. "It was embarrassing enough you convinced me to wear that high school play mask."

"Wait." Beau gave a confused expression as his phone buzzed. "The troll mask?"

"Never mind that." Lou put the conversation back on track. "Come on, spill it. You got laid, but with who?"

"I don't know if I should say." Beau smirked, clearly texting someone.

"You boys need any refills?" Red stood with hands on hips, dressed in a crop top and daisy dukes.

"I'm buying these guys another shot, and maybe they'll speak up," Lou drawled, draining the last of his beer. "And I guess a bucket, it's gonna be a long night."

"Coming right up." She began to set up a bucket with ice, crushing bottles of Yuengling into it. "So, what have you boys been up to?"

She glanced up and flinched. Beau and Taylor averted their eyes with flushed faces. Lou on the other hand had a look of pure mischief and screamed, *I got laid, how about you?* She laughed, shaking her head as she shoved the bucket of beers to him. Pulling out two shot glasses she glared at the two shy college boys.

"So, what will it be?" she cooed, enjoying the moment. "You gonna tell me or am I guessing?"

"Taylor! Beau!" Lou smacked their shoulders on either side of him. "Answer the lady."

"I fucked my high school crush at an orgy party," Taylor blurted.

Red blinked, and Peter froze behind him with a face that said, *did I just hear that right?*

Feeling the pressure of Peter, Beau confessed, "I fucked my professor."

Both college kids stared at her, everything about their posture and faces filled with dread as if reporting in against their will. Red laughed until tears shone in her eyes. Peter roared behind them, gasping for air as he patted both of them on the back.

"I was asking about what shot you wanted." Red chuckled. "In fact, that was worth a free shot for you both. Name it."

"Give them some Sambuca." Peter reached between them, grabbing a glass of water that was prepped for him. "They may not want to remember tonight after that one."

With that, Peter left, and Red returned to her customers, sliding shots across the counter. "Sounds like we all got lucky then."

Lou popped open his next drink. "I bet you went to that sex party in the 'burbs too."

Her eyebrows arched. "Yeah, like most of the town."

"I'll have to put in a formal complaint." Lou had a sparkle in his eye, a toothy grin on his face. "Since when did you start wearing bras?"

She nodded, licking her teeth. "Since I needed a way to slow down my man over there." The three of them spun, and Peter waved. "He gets rather jealous if anyone stares at them for too long."

She leaned on the counter, her cleavage threatening to escape her red lacy bra.

The Troll, the Wolf, and Beau paled.

THE END

THE URBAN EROTICA FAIRY TALE COLLECTION

Princess

Pea's Bed

HONEY CUMMINGS

Table of Contents

Party Time

Pearl Hollandale tugged at her dress, aiming for the skirt to skim her thighs enough to cover her ass. Checking her lipstick once more in the mirror, she smirked. Her birthday party was ending. She had snuck into her master bedroom to catch her breath. Granted, the possible hookups proved no different from normal. But still...

So many to flirt with, so little time left to do it in!

Leaving her bathroom, her luxury apartment was filled with guests. Her birthday fell in the middle of the week, so she decided to celebrate early and have a huge gathering. Granted, the idea wasn't her entire concept. The bartender—her close friend Michael, had coordinated and hosted the whole night. When someone had too much, he'd cut them off and call them a Guber.

I wish he'd let me pay him for his efforts. It took everything I had to have him let me pay for catering and alcohol. Still, if it weren't for him handling events, I wouldn't relax. His day job as a project manager gave him an edge.

Buzzing around, weaving around groups of guests, she checked on the remaining few, telling them good night and thanking them for their birthday wishes. The catering company had done an amazing job, preparing an assortment of finger foods to fill her entire large island counter.

Plucking a cherry from a bowl, she smiled, wanting the night to drag on as long as possible. Music thumped over the custom stereo system, not drowning out a single conversation. Yet, there were plenty of folks dancing near the living room miniature bar.

Everything is just... perfect. Michael! You know how to please a girl and treat her to a good birthday. I might have to reconsider dating you one day.

Pearl grabbed a stool from the bar, her cheeks aching from smiling as she suckled on the cherry. Her eyes took in all the happy expressions unfolding between friends, old and new.

A cocktail slid across the counter and she snorted. "I didn't ask for this." She met Michael Hardy's gaze, his smirk making him more attractive.

"But you asked me to keep the drinks coming," he countered. "Have I told you how hot you look sucking on a cherry like that?"

She winked. "Maybe a time or two."

Michael leaned against the bar top, his cologne sending goosebumps over Pearl's skin. She eyed him a moment, biting the cherry at last. They'd been friends a long time, but she hadn't considered him intimately, until tonight.

Her eyes fell to his plump lips, lingering on his toothy grin. Tilting her head, she smirked at his broad shoulders. *I've never seen him shirtless, not even once.* He had passed on every gathering that involved the beach, a pool or even a jacuzzi. Another bite of the cherry filled her taste buds as she circled back to his lips, the smile gone.

"If you keep staring at me like that any longer, I might have to kiss you, Pearl." His voice was a low grumble, making her face flush. "I don't just do this for anyone."

Is Michael making a pass at me? I mean…I don't mind, but that must be a first. Not that we haven't spoken about getting together in that way… but…

Michael always dressed to the nines, like a sexy model attending a work meeting with high-end clients. Tom Ellis could be his brother, the dark eyes and dark hair paired with a devilish smile would make any woman swoon. Granted, the clean-cut beard and pulled back ponytail promised a much wilder man, ready to give you a rawer adventure.

Sharp dressed, serious faced until he gets flirty with a girl. It seems I'm his target tonight. Go figure!

For the first time, she couldn't ignore his smile, knowing it was meant for her. And her *alone*.

"You wouldn't dare." She picked up the cocktail, drinking it while arching an eyebrow.

"What makes you say that?" He furrowed his brow, his eyes lingering on her red lips.

He's smitten with me! Exactly when did this happen? But the man is always top button fastened, long sleeves and suit pants the whole time I've known him. He can't be serious? He's more adventurous than he's ever shown me in our five year of friendship. I mean, he passed on that orgy party a while back! Even the Troll got laid that night!

Placing the drink down, she leaned in and whispered into his ear, "I think you're afraid to even go shirtless around me. You'll need to show me some skin before I take you serious."

Spinning away, she left him in a wake of her teasing. She didn't dare look back, finished her drink, then the last half of her cherry. As she prowled her hallway, she spotted Gaston. The man had muscles for an older man, and he had a strong jawline that always made her heart flutter, catching a glimpse here and there. His back muscles made her wonder if he had competed in strong man competitions when he was younger before becoming a docile professor at the local college.

Their eyes met as she spit the cherry pit into her empty glass. "You weren't supposed to see that."

"Oh?" His blue eyes sparkled with mischief. "But what I wanted to see you tie the stem."

She spun it in her finger, a smirk forming. "I imagine you didn't mean by using my fingers."

"Not with your fingers," he echoed, arching his brows.

Pearl couldn't resist the challenge. Opening her mouth wide, she stuck out her tongue and laid the stem across the pink appendage. Gaston's blue eyes watched with great attention, his body stiffening as he took a few steps closer. She retracted the stem, then began tying the stem in her mouth.

Gaston came closer, drinking a sip of his beer as Pearl's confidence faltered. He began snickering.

She continued to flip it with the tip of her tongue, to fold and bend it to a simple knot and failed repeatedly.

"May I?" He was so close, his hand on her shoulder.

Pearl slumped her shoulders, searching his blue eyes.

He wants to kiss me. Should I? Screw it, it's my birthday. If I want to kiss all the hot guys at my party, then so be it!

In defeat, she nodded.

Gaston locked lips, deepening their kiss in an instant. Before she could respond, he had plucked the stem from her own tongue and retreated. Giving him a baffled expression, she smiled. Unlike her struggle and cheeks rumbling around, his own stayed taut. She opened her lips and he opened his own and there laid across his tongue was the knotted stem.

Pearl blinked as he plucked it with his fingers, chuckling at her expression. "My, lovely Pearl, *that* is how you knot a cherry stem." He dropped it in her empty cocktail glass to join the seed.

"Enlighten me, Professor Gaston. What would this skill say about your hidden talents?" Licking her teeth, her stare bounced from head to toe, then repeating the cycle.

Chuckling, he stared at her, those icy eyes cutting through her. "Maybe one day you'll let me into your bedroom, so I can show you. We both know you're more of a..." He leaned in, his lips close to her own. "...hands on learner."

"Let's have a taste then." Pearl locked lips with him, deepening the kiss.

The tip of his tongue pressed a line down her own, making her moan. Alcohol and cherry flavors mangling in an exotic swap of flavors. The idea of his tongue rolling over her pussy, the firm tip of his tongue teasing her clit sent shivers through her. It's was tempting, to ask him to stay after the party, but she had aimed to flirt with everyone, not settle on one for the night.

Gaston pulled away, and Pearl smiled.

Tempting, but not sold on settling.

"I can't lie." Biting her bottom lip, she started to take a few steps away. "You must be the best kisser I know."

"And always will be." He winked.

"Stop it." Pearl's face flushed, and she spun on her heel. "I need another drink. I'm sorry but private study lessons weren't on my wish list this time, Professor. Please, enjoy the party, Gaston. Surely you can find a more willing student."

"I will, and happy birthday, Pearl." He raised his beer and she waved him off.

Venturing into the kitchen, she stole another cherry for herself. One of the caterers were cleaning dishes and consolidating trays to keep the platters visually pleasing. She plucked another cherry, taking in the tattooed sleeves and bearded face.

At last, he glanced up, arching a single eyebrow. "Something wrong?" His voice was smooth and playful.

She shrugged, enjoying her cherry. "I just enjoy watching a man doing the dishes."

"What else does the birthday girl enjoy?" He rinsed a platter, reached for the next, and started scrubbing it. "Nice place you've got here, by the way."

"I enjoy this and that." She changed course, reaching for a chunk of pineapple. "You don't have to do that. I have a maid coming in the morning, you know."

"It's just habit, part of what I do." He finished rinsing the platter, then shut off the faucet. "So, what can I do for you, birthday girl?"

"Your name and number?" She smiled, slipping the pineapple into her mouth, giving a playful expression.

He laughed, shaking his head. "The name's Chuckles."

"Chuckles?"

"Yeah, and I've got a girl, so no phone number today," he confessed.

Pearl sighed, looking back towards the party. "Damn, now who to hit next?"

"Did you try the bartender?" Chuckles walked around, nodding in Michael's direction.

"Sort of..." She creased her brow in thought. "Why? You think he'll play along?"

"He's been watching your every move. Even cringed when you kissed Professor Cherry Lips over there." He laughed at her baffled expression.

Was everyone watching me with Gaston? And why would Michael care?

"Don't believe me? Go find your next mark and make sure to look in his direction." He nodded at Michael again. "He's a nice guy, you know."

"I know..." She frowned. "But what suddenly makes you an expert on him?"

"His sister bartends part-time for Red." Nudging her arm, he repeated the offer. "So, are you giving the bartender a try?"

"Is that a challenge?" Pearl abandoned her empty glass on the counter, her shield gone.

"I'll put fifty bucks on it." He sucked on his cheek with a sparkle in his eyes.

She gave a smug expression. "Fine. I'll match that wager."

This is my field, and I have the advantage. No way am I losing to a part-time bar cook who caters on the side!

The Bet

Pearl scanned the party stragglers, searching for her next kissing target. At last, she settled on Axle, a coworker and a long-time friend-with-benefits. It hadn't been a secret from their group, which made her curious, *Is Michael fully aware of that arrangement?*

Hell, she had texted him about it more times than she can remember.

If money is on the table, then I'm sure to win. There's no way this will make him cringe. He knows we have a casual sexual relationship.

Axle had a sexy smile and a cute, tight ass, though shorter than Michael and Gaston. In all the years she'd known him, he'd never expressed interest in having a committed relationship (her nor any other female) and took every chance to travel at work. Regardless, under his dapper outfit was a thick muscled athlete who never missed a day at the gym. Granted, his gym partner was Michael: Axle always teased and marveled at how Michael managed to workout in long sleeves during the heat of summer.

No. There's no way I'm losing fifty bucks. Not on always-has-a-shirt-on Michael.

With a wide grin, she kept Michael in her peripheral. She caught his stolen glance and it goaded her to pick up pace. To think a caterer named Chuckles caught Michael's stares before she did!

Reaching Axle, she glided her hand over his upper arm, and like a reflex, he pulled her into him. Her body ached over the heat of it against her, remembering the way he grinded against her. The Adonis belt flexing as he tensed at his own peak, adding to the arousal rolling through her. Shaking off the wanton want, she spun so Michael had a perfect view, just behind Axle.

"Kiss me," she demanded, watching as Michael paused and stared in their direction.

"Depends." He smirked, tucking her hair behind an ear. "What's the occasion?"

"I'm trying to decipher who here's the best kisser," she announced.

"Oh?" He glanced around the party, picking out his possible competition. "And who am I competing against?"

"Professor Gaston says he's the best. Chuckles denied me. And I haven't decided on who else." She stole a glance over his shoulders. "Maybe Michael?"

Axle raised a high brow. "Michael too?" he said, mischief written across his face. "I'm in. Granted, you think he'll go for it?"

"He already implied he wanted one." Again, she gave her playful shrug.

"Then, let's have a go..."

Axle cupped her face; the kiss was simple before the forceful rush of his tongue. He was far rawer and more aggressive than even Gaston. Again, thoughts of them in the bedroom crept forward, his body heating in the wake of her arousal. Even when they fucked, Axled rode her hard and fast. A thought crossed her mind, *always in a rush to go... somewhere*

She changed the direction of the kiss and peeked over Axle's shoulder.

Pearl locked eyes with Michael, and she jolted *What a painful expression!*

She pulled away from Axle, seeping in anger. *How did I not notice sooner?*

"So? Who's winning?" Axle was more concerned with his stats than the confusion building on her face. "Or do you need a second kiss?"

He leaned in for a second round, but her fingers stopped his lips. "No. One attempt to impress. Now, to contestant number three."

Well, if he's truly smitten with me, the kiss will expose him.

She brushed pass Axle, and Michael panicked, taking a shot he had poured while watching them makeout. By the time she climbed back into her bar stool, he had turned away to the liquor cabinet and began organizing it.

Pearl cleared her throat; he turned, slow and unsure. His face was red, embarrassed for peeking, for cringing at her kiss with Axle. She liked this moment, seeing the stoic man, in the suit vest and tie, falter for the first time.

"Come here." She signaled for him to *come hither* with a finger. "Closer."

"What's wrong?" Michael leaned in and she grabbed his tie, yanking him forward.

Their lips pressed tight and she marveled how soft and plump his lips were compared to the others. Michael deepened the kiss, much slower than the first two as his tongue slid between their interlocked lips. A hard-metallic ball rolled between her lips, gracing her teeth, and prompting her to open wider, allowing him in, curious now.

He has a tongue piercing! What? Since when!

Michael's tongue stroked along the length of her own before circling and rubbing. Her tongue wanted to chase the piercing, her aim missing its target, unable to keep up with their unfolding cat and mouse game. He turned his head, locking lips in a new direction, exploring her mouth from a new angle.

Again, she moaned, the piercing sending an exhilarating sensation over her flesh. His tongue began to withdraw, tempting her own to give chase and she thought, *What's that curious flavor lingering on her tongue?*

Cherry-flavored vodka! Is he hoping for me to kiss him next?

She licked the length of his tongue, but, before she could proceed further, he pulled away, denying her another chance of finding his piercing. She eyed his lips, marveling how he returned to his stoic expression.

Her body buzzed with want. *What else might he be hiding under his high collar and long sleeves?*

Michael tried to pull away, but she pulled him back, wanting a second sampling, unwilling to release his tie just yet. Again, he took his time playing and exploring. The heat of his hand cupped her jaw and his kissing made her hungry, her skin pebbling in goosebumps.

This time she pulled away, searching his eyes in astonishment. *He's smitten with me! Am I dreaming?*

He arched an eyebrow. "Are you going to release my tie?"

"Oh!" She let go, blinking for a moment. "Wow, I... I didn't expect that."

"The kiss?" He smirked and poured them each a shot of cherry-flavored vodka.

"Never mind." Heat rose in her cheeks and she wondered, *is my face had red?* "What's the shot for?" she asked.

"Would I be too bold to say this is my winning shot?" he teased, sliding one to her.

"A shot to the winner of the kissing contest!" Her voice caught everyone's attention still lingering at the party. "To Michael!"

The room whistled and shouted their congratulations as they took shots or drinks of their own. She caught Chuckles' smirk as he motioned with rubbing fingers, *where's my money?* Snorting, she met the Gaston's scowl who turned and left down the hall out of view. He had been too cocky, his ego taking a massive hit. Axle lipped a, *wow,* and took a swig of his lemon Whiteclaw.

Turning back to Michael, she frowned. He had gone back to messing with the liquor cabinet. "You won," she insisted.

He eyed her over his shoulder. "You didn't think I could."

"Oh, come on, Mikey," Pearl fussed, panicking. "I misjudged your ability to compete. That's all."

"Oh?" This time, he met her gaze in the cabinet mirror and smiled. "I can assure you, your impression of me isn't entirely wrong. *But* it's complicated…"

"Is that so?" She stood on her feet, squinting at him. "And will you ever dare to show me what you're hiding behind your resigned exterior, Mystery Man?"

Shrugging, he kept silent, refusing to meet her eyes again.

Flustered, she marched off towards Chuckles. He held out his palm, giggling as he awaited his bet winnings. She motioned for him to wait as she snuck into her bedroom, then returned with a hundred-dollar bill.

This time, Gaston had returned and regained his composure. *He didn't find a hook-up and spiraled back for one. Ha! Such a prideful man.*

"The bet was fifty." Chuckles tilted his head.

"Yeah, but you deserve double." She glanced back at Michael, his eyes darting elsewhere. "You saw something I've failed to see for years. Anyhow, you were right. He cringed even with Axle which he knew about…" She shook her head. "So, you earned the money. Go take your girl out to eat or something."

"Nah, I'll just buy her a new dress or some new shoes." He flipped out his wallet and slid the money in.

"That's rather specific list there, Chuckles."

"It's because she lost her shoes, then ripped her dress when…" He paused, then shook his head. "It's a long story, but I feel bad about that whole night."

She sighed. "Well, it's nearing the time for this party to close up," she said, looking at her watch.

"Where do you want the leftovers?" He thumbed behind himself.

"I want the cherries. So place the bowl in the fridge, I like them cold." Scanning over the other platters, she settled on, "The rest is whoever wants to take it home. Otherwise, shove it in the fridge. There's plenty of room to fit everything."

"You got it, birthday girl."

Clearing her throat, she caught the attention of the partygoers. "First off, thank you all for coming to celebrate my birthday with me. I'm overjoyed to see all my friends in one place, enjoying tasty food and great drinks. Feel free to tip the caterer, and don't forget to thank our volunteer bartender, Michael."

Again, a cacophony of whistles and clapping filled the apartment.

Marching back to the bar, she leaned into Michael's ear, saying, "I'm headed to bed. Can you see them out, then lock up afterwards?"

Nodding, he snorted. "I told you before...I would take care of setup and breakdown. I don't break my promises, Princess."

She pecked him on the cheek, and he gave her a confused expression.

"Text me when you get home safely. Thank you, this was a great idea." She turned and disappeared into the master bedroom.

Pearl touched her lips, lingering on the memory of the kisses. Her mind wandered back to Gaston's playful tongue, Axle's domineering nature, and lastly, Michael's slow, lustful kiss. He was a stark contrast from the first two, something lighter and sultry.

I wouldn't mind seeing what else he might do differently to me... if only I can remove that shirt!

Surprise

Pearl decided sleep wasn't quite on her mind. *Not yet.*

She aimed for the bathroom. Her bedroom door locked to keep intruders at bay as she left Michael to flush out the crowd. She could see Gaston trying his luck, he was bold enough to waltz in and join her in the shower or tub. A smile crested her lips as she slipped into her garden tub. Axel on the other hand, he would strip down and wait for her in bed.

Hence why, neither have a key to my place.

She slid down and dunked her head underwater. Coming up, she blew the air from her lips, slow and steady. The steam and lowlighting was calming and soothing, compared to the commotion of the dying party. The music had stopped, voices fading to silence. There was the occasional clink and clack of cups and dishes.

But one of the three does have a key to my door. Has had it for a while now.

Splashing water on her face, she wiped away the last of her makeup, letting her thoughts roam. Part of her felt the temptation of arousing desires pulling at her joints. If she hurried, she could call or text anyone to enter her bed tonight.

Shaking her head, she had planned, no, made a game of it for her own birthday amusement. *I wasn't aiming to get laid tonight.*

A whim of mischief hit her, and she slid down to her lips into the water. Ripples waved out, obscuring her naked body under the water's surface. Her hands snaked over her body, squeezing breasts and dipping between her thighs to play for a fleeting moment. She wanted to spend her real day having an amazing erotic night. The wild orgy had been fun, but it had made her realize something surprising in the end:

I rather be with one person. The sort of partner that would explore every part of me, to the point where they knew my body than I could ever dream. Sure, having multiple partners, back to back, was an adventure. But it felt... unsatisfying. I just want the right one, the perfect fit.

Pulling out of the tub, she inhaled deep and held it. She toweled off and at last, released it as if it were suppressing her thoughts. The dam broke, the sensations flooding as lustful memories and heartfelt desires clashed. Her body, heart, and soul were at war with one another.

Axel is great fun, but sloppy. I mean, he fucks fast and hard. Don't get me wrong, it's amazing, but do I really want that every time? Same shit, different day. He doesn't really change it up much. In fact, I sometimes wonder if he's treating me like a cheat code on a video game: left breast, right breast, up, down, up, down, and unload.

Her reflection scowled at her. The idea of Axel's redundant sex moves was more accurate than she would ever confess. Squeezing the water from her hair, she wrapped the towel around her tiny frame. She sashayed to the bedroom door and opened it slowly. The lights had been turned off, not a soul was in view. Peering out the door further, the kitchen was empty.

She tip-toed into the dining room where the bar sat. She reached the side and before sidling behind it.

Michael appeared, standing up with two liquor bottles.

Pearl screamed.

"Shit!" He grimaced and placed the bottles on the counter before he dropped them.

"MICHAEL!" She clutched her chest, tightening her fingers on the towel, out of fear of losing it.

"I thought you called it for the night?" His eyes drifted over her, and he gave a smirk. "Did you enjoy a soak in the tub?"

Clearing her throat, Pearl countered, "You're just jealous I didn't invite you to join me."

"I would've joined you if you had said *please*. To be fair, I wasn't the only one here, hoping for an invite." He laughed and pulled the spouts from the liquor bottles and replaced them with their caps and corks.

"Oh yeah?" She slid onto the bar stool as he pulled over a few more to flip out. "And who's having a hard time leaving?"

"Gaston at first," He grabbed the hand towel for a better grip and the bottle spout popped lose after a grunt. "Then some girl with a lot of hip and ass caught his fancy and he followed her out the door."

"Good riddance." Pearl offered the cap from the pile on the counter. "Two more."

"Wait, what?" Michael's face flushed before he blinked and redirected his thoughts. "Oh, bottles. Yes, so... why do you lead him on so much, Gaston that is."

"It's just fun." She shrugged, picking up another cap. "Granted, he's not my type so it's been nothing but flirting, groping, and kissing. He's got a hardon for some professor he works with, even though she's got herself someone."

"Ah, I see." He grabbed the last two bottles. "Well, Axel wanted to hang out till you came out. I shooed him out the door. Usually you'd say something if you two were spending the night together."

"Right and I don't let him stay here. I go to his place for that sort of thing," she confessed.

"Well, Pearl. It seems I don't know you as well as I thought." Another grunt and he popped the next spout free and added it to the container.

Damn, is that a monster bicep flexing under that shirt? Wonder if he grunts like that when he starts to come? Wait, what the hell am I thinking? This is Michael! Am I out of my mind? Would he even act on it if I offered? That kiss though, and the hurt expression when I kissed Axel even though he knows that history. He's friends with both me and Axel. They must talk about it. I mean they're workout buddies and...

"...Did you hear me?" Her eyes snapped back to his, and she handed the cap to his outstretched hand. "I asked why his place and not yours?"

"Oh, that," she darted her eyes away, "I don't know if a prude like yourself could handle that answer."

He popped the last bottle, a toothy grin on his face as it brought her gaze back to him. "Want to hear what I think, Princess Pea?"

And there it is. All night I half-expected him to use that pet name for me. Granted, it's only used when we're alone, or text, or whispered to take a stab at me.

Squinting her eyes at him, she smirked. "Enlighten me, oh, prude bartender."

"He's got toys."

Opening her mouth, she stopped herself and reflected on the answer.

"Well? Princess?" Capping the last bottle, he began putting them away and stealing glances through the mirror once again. "Am I right? Old Axel has quite the toy box of playthings, doesn't he? Hmm? A treasure trove of pleasure you don't have here in your castle, no?"

"You can't tell anyone" She covered her face, defeated.

You asshole, Axel! You told him! You do talk about it!

"Why not get your own?" He marveled.

"It's embarrassing and I don't know what to click on," she hissed. "How do you know he has toys?"

He laughed. "A guy as sexually active as him needs a truckload of dildos to keep up with that many libidos coming through his revolving door." Spinning back to her, he leaned across the table. "And he's told me a story or two, matching with our texts, it wasn't hard to figure out who he was talking about. No names. He's at least that trustworthy."

Regular Sherlock Holmes, aren't we?

Sliding off the bar stool, she huffed, "Why haven't you gone home, then?"

"I thought I'd be gone by now, but this took longer to undo than I thought." He motioned to the bar before wiping off the counter. "I must return the spouts to my sister since I borrowed them from her boss at Red's Tavern."

"Fine." She turned for her bedroom door. "I'm going to bed, so don't forget to lock up."

"I have a key, so..." His voice almost came out like a purr over that fact.

"Don't you dare tell anyone about that," she said, hiding behind her bedroom door, fingers tight on the towel.

I'm out of my mind!

A few minutes passed before she heard her front door shut at last. She could breathe again, part of her wanting Michael to give chase and circle back. A laugh escaped her, covering her face over the fact he pinned her for her toy fetish. She had been too afraid to buy or bring home anything. The idea of the playthings made her pussy wet.

Dammit, I can't fall asleep if I'm feeling this horny. I hate you for even bringing it up, Mikey!

4

Sleepless

Pearl clambered onto her bed, abandoning the towel on the floor. She laid back on her silken sheets, her pillows piled high on her pillowtop mattress. Closing her eyes, she let her hands glide over her breasts and across her abdomen. In her mind, she had herself a reverse harem with all the goods.

Her fingers dipped between her thighs, rubbing the opening of her pussy. *I'm so wet... just thinking about...*

Her mind shifted as her slick finger slid up and circled her clit. The pleasure and rise it brought her only fueled the erotic imagination fueling her unrestrained desires. Gaston's tongue played with her pussy, licking and diving in and out, twirling her into knots like that cherry stem. The same hard precise pressure against her tongue she now imagined sliding across her most sensitive of places, wondering how much more enjoyable it would be to roll over her swollen jewel.

Sliding one hand back up, she gripped her breast. Squeezing and pinching her nipple, she arched as she continued to play. Axel would use his teeth or nipple clamps from time to time. It drove her wild, made her drip till her thighs ran wet with her arousal.

She could feel the building buzz of her body, the rising orgasm nearing its peak. *Almost... there...*

The imagery in her mind shifted, and once more, she could feel and taste Michael's kiss. Every part of that kiss said, *let's take our time and play on the edge of pleasure.* Her breath caught, a haunting cherry flavor catching her by surprise. Arching, she was *so close, a little more... a little...*

"Dammit!" She sat up and glared at her mattress in betrayal.

Scooting off the edge, she searched the covers for a while before the sheets and still came up empty. Pressing down on the top mattress, she could still feel the lump. It made the once soft tower hard and unbearable. All this time they had teased her over it and now she knew something was in her mattress or under it or...

"What the hell is protruding into me?" Snorting, she began searching between mattresses and box spring until at last her hand grazed against something cold.

She froze. *What is that?*

Her hand wiggled back to it, pushing her arm deeper between the two mattresses. Again, her fingers found something cold and metallic. She gripped it and yanked it out. Turning on her nightstand lamp she looked closer. The top was adorned with a jeweled disc and as she unfolded her fingers, it became noticeably clear what the metallic item was meant for.

"Is this... is this a butt plug?" She shook her head, wondering where it came from. "Did someone come in here and fuck on my bed? Without me? No, no... this is new. This was hidden inside my bed. But why? And by who?"

She weaseled back onto the bed and marveled over the jeweled item. Part of her wondered if they were real crystals at the way they sparkled in the lamp light. She grinned. *I will put this item into good use for disrupting my orgasm.*

Hands snaked between her thighs. She dipped the plug into her wet pussy, before sliding further down. The plug slid inside her ass until it crested over the widest part and stopped at the disc. She moaned as her fingers glided back to her clit and began circling. The added pleasure of the plug made her peak faster than expected and she lunged forward as she came.

"If only I had a cock or dildo..." Panting for a moment, she rolled out of bed in frustration. "Dammit, that wasn't completely satisfying enough. Where's my phone?"

Looking to her nightstand it was gone. Startled, she rushed to the bar but saw no signs there. She spun back to the kitchen. Relief washed over her to see it on the counter. The screen read, *1 unread message.* Sighing, she unlocked it to see where Michael had sent her a single text:

[Mikey: I'm gone. Door's locked. Sleep well, Princess Pea.]

[Pearl: Thanks. Having a hard time sleeping.]

She eyed the fridge. The idea of eating some cherries without anyone here to see her mess proved tempting. The phone buzzed, slowing her as she sashayed across her kitchen, still nude as she gripped the fridge door. She couldn't stop smiling. Her night had taken an interesting turn.

The phone buzzed once more, and she snorted at the text.

[Mikey: You're still awake! Why would you still be awake?]

How nosy of you! Or...are you calling me out over that conversation, you ham.

[Pearl: There was a lump in the mattress.]

[Mikey: Princess Pea! I knew it!]

[Pearl: Stop calling me that!]

[Mikey: So did you figure out what the lump was?]

Opening the fridge, she paused, paling. The bowl of cherries sat there with a glass object mixed into them. Pulling the bowl out, she hesitated to pull the glass object out.

Walking to the counter, she studied the artful glass... stick. *Didn't Chuckles cover these with plastic wrap?*

She took in the cherry décor, like a ball sack on a long glass stick with red ribbing spiraling into the cherries. The tip and overall shape phallic and unmistakable. This was another object left for her to discover. Looking back into the fridge, there was a notecard, one from her own office stationary.

The calligraphy within it made her blink twice, the handwriting artful as the object itself. It simply said: *Enjoy the birthday treasures.*

She stiffened, thinking of the butt plug prompted her to pull the glass stick from the bowl. The end of it curved upward and she bit her bottom lip.

This couldn't be... do they make dildos in glass? I've never seen one like...

Her phone buzzed again, bringing her attention to it.

[Axel: Just let me know if you want me to return tonight and give you a hand ☒]

Rolling her eyes, she returned to her messages, but another text interrupted.

[Gaston: I haven't given you your birthday gift yet. The cherry stem was a hint.]

This time, she covered her face. She had imagined what he could do with that tongue in all the right places. Shaking it off, she returned to her text chain with Michael. Him calling her out on the toys earned the prude the new bombardment of sexual treasures she had discovered.

[Pearl: Yeah. A butt plug. And now this in my cherries... *Picture of glass dildo*]

There was a long pause before the indicator signaled him responding. She snorted to herself, giggling. *I wonder what he will say?*

[Mikey: Sexy. Butt plug and a glass dildo. Nice buys, did Axel get those for you?]

I knew it! It is a glass dildo! Holy shit!

Looking back to the notecard, she snapped a photo and sent it to him.

[Pearl: No idea. They left me a note. You think I'll find more fun toys in my apartment?]

[Mikey: I can come over and help look. Please tell me you plan on using them.]

[Pearl: For a prude, you're rather pervy tonight.]

[Mikey: You just assume I'm a prude. Don't forget, I'm friends with Axel, Princess Pea. Birds of a feather flock together... or fuck together? Not sure if that sounds as well as it did in my head. LOL]

[Pearl: LMAO]

Pearl shoved the phone aside, plucking a cherry from the bowl. Scanning her apartment, her curiosity and excitement grew. The glass dildo was far too cold to play with just yet. Looking around the kitchen, she picked apart everything. At last, she did a double take on an item in her utensil cup. Something seemed new, longer than the others.

Picking up another cherry, she marched over to the bin and flipped on the kitchen light. "Wow... that's not what I thought that was..." The leather utensil was a riding crop, making her cheeks red. "I don't think I've ever done any spanking with anyone. Oh man, what if these are from Gaston?"

She laid the crop beside the glass dildo. Taking another photo, she was eager to send the latest report to Michael, enjoying the thought of torturing her friend.

Revenge for denying me to figure out that tongue piercing!

[Pearl: See, I can find them all on my own. *Picture*]

[Mikey: Well, well! And who gets to be on the receiving end of that little toy? You or him?]

[Pearl: No idea. I suppose it depends which *him* these are from.]

[Mikey: Oh? Do you have any guesses on who left them?]

[Pearl: Not yet. Though, Gaston doesn't seem farfetched at this point...]

Walking over to the hallway, she flipped on the lights for the living room and bar. Something caught her eye in the blender. She looked back to her kitchen, scanning the area one more time before moving to the bar top. Moving around the counter, she approached the blender. They hadn't used it tonight, sticking to liquor, beer, and simple cocktails.

[Mikey: Still searching?]

She snorted at his text, ignoring it. Opening the lid to the blender, she dipped her fingers in to retrieve the shiny object. Much to her surprise, it was a magic bullet, the same brand and make of the vibrator Axel had used on her time and time again.

A shudder of anticipation rattled her shoulders, her nipples erect thinking of it. She snapped another photo on the kitchen counter, her collection of toys growing quickly.

[Pearl: Score! *Picture*]

[Mikey: I take it you're familiar with this one?]

[Pearl: Indeed, Mr. Prude. A personal favorite.]

[Mikey: Well, at least you have your own now. Any idea who's left you these little treasures yet, Princess?]

[Pearl: Maybe Axel? I mean, this is the same one he has. And he did text, asking to give me a hand.]

[Mikey: You could always ask.]

[Pearl: I'm not asking. What if I guess the wrong person?]

[Mikey: Smart girl. You should keep looking. I'm sure they've left you a good hint on their identity.]

Gaston is definitely dominate whip type. Though, I don't think Axel owns anything similar in his own collection. In fact, I'm a little conflictive about it being either of them at this stage.

Treasures

Heaving a sigh, Pearl sat at the kitchen counter, snacking on cherries. She reviewed her thoughts, separating the items. Gaston and Axel both had lingered here, perhaps the toys were left from both. Shaking her head, it begged the question of when either of them had a moment to slip into her room during the party unnoticed.

I locked my bedroom door when the guests started to arrive, I'm sure of it. So, who left the butt plug?

Picking up the glass dildo with the cherry design, this came from someone who knew she loved cherries. Her mind circled back to Chuckles, but they had just met. There was no way some dorky catering guy would hide erotic gifts in her apartment with such decisive locations. Besides, she had watched him put them away earlier with plastic wrap, so someone followed behind him to place the dildo and note in the fridge.

It had to be someone who has been over here. So that rules out... Gaston. That man isn't as romantic as he makes himself out to be. He's just a beast of sexual prowess and dominance.

Looking at the magic bullet, she smirked. "And I don't think Axel got me this. He's not one to invest in a friend-with-benefits. Hell, he didn't get his girlfriend a gift for her birthday after a year together."

Pearl hummed to herself, walking through her apartment like a nude phantom. She flipped on the lights, peered into vases, drawers, checked under couch cushions. Everything she had found was close to the kitchen and bedroom. Circling back, she double checked the fridge and freezer. *Nothing.* Opening and closing every drawer and cabinet, she snacked on a few cherries in thought. Her phone buzzed.

[Gaston: You still up?]

[Pearl: You can say that.]

[Gaston: I can circle back, tucker you out.]

Rolling her eyes, she was quick.

[Pearl: I'll take a rain check. Trying to figure out who left some items at my apartment.]

This should reveal if it's him.

[Gaston: Oh no. Did someone forget their wallet?]

Sucking on a cherry, she arched an eyebrow. *Nope.*

[Pearl: Yeah, waiting to hear back now.]

[Gaston: Another time?]

Pearl started to respond but deleted the *maybe.* Changing course, she decided to try the same verbiage and see what response she could muster from Axel. Putting Gaston on silent, she moved on to suspect number two.

[Pearl: Did you leave something at my apartment?]

There was a long pause and she waited with patience. The cherries had stained her lips and fingers red, but she didn't care. They were in peak season and sweet on her tongue. The earthy after tone was something she couldn't resist.

Her phone buzzed.

[Axel: No. I got my wallet and phone. Keys on the nightstand. Why?]

[Pearl: Were you asleep already?]

[Axel: Yeah.]

[Pearl: Good night, Axel. I'll find the owner eventually.]

She grabbed another cherry, sucking on it. Staring at her phone, she scrolled through her contacts, reviewing her party guest list. Very few of her past conquests were in attendance, but no one seemed bold enough to leave the smattering of sex toys. She wiggled; very aware she hadn't removed the bejeweled butt plug during the scavenger hunt.

[Mikey: Found anything else?]

No! Her eyes grew wide. *It couldn't be.*

[Pearl: I'm still searching.]

She paused, covering her mouth.

That kiss. Those stolen looks. Could it be he had something far bigger planned for me tonight? With him?

[Mikey: Need me to come over and help?]

Pearl bit into the next cherry, a grin on her face. Goosebumps rippled over her body.

[Pearl: Where should I look next?]

[Mikey: The bar. There's more to be found, I'm sure of it.]

Of course, you are! Suspect number three!

Leaving the kitchen island, she marched back to the bar area. Her eyes fell on something purple on two of the liquor bottles. She rounded the counter and plucked them from the bottles. The two purple silicone items were new and foreign to her. She twirled them in her fingers as she returned to the kitchen where her pile of treasures sat.

A spark of arousal sent a chill up her spine, *these were left for me.*

[Mikey: Well? Turn up anything, Princess Pea?]

He was the last one to touch the bar. I help him finish and everyone had left. Mikey... the prude... he's the mystery man who left me my treasures. He was here long before I even got home from work, he had plenty of time to hide the butt plug under the mattress and considering his nickname for me...

[Pearl: Enlighten me, oh prude bartender. What on earth would one do with these? *Picture of purple mystery item*]

[Mikey: Well that's for this... *Picture of a nipple on a hard plane, tattooed pec*]

Pearl sat down, choking on a cherry. She hadn't expected a picture. Picking up the purple bulb and it became evident these suctioned to the nipples, easily keeping a tight seal. She licked her lips, staring at her phone.

A naughty thought trickled forward, her heart racing at the idea. *Do I dare meet tit for tat? Would he be willing to return tonight and...*

[Pearl: Like so? *Close up of a covered nipple with the purple sucker*]

[Mikey: Wait for it...]

Wait for what?

She furrowed her brow, then... *gasped*.

The purple started to fade into hot pink as the silicone heated to her body temperature. Pearl covered her face. She didn't know if this added to how ridiculous she felt, but there was no denying, he had left her the grand display of toys.

Gathering them into a pile again, she took a photo and sent it his way.

[Pearl: Cute! Now, was this everything? *Picture*]

[Mikey: I don't see the butt plug.]

[Pearl: You'll have to come over to see that one.]

Let's see how far you're willing to go, Michael. Was this just for kicks, or were you hoping to come into my bedroom with me?

[Mikey: Okay. I went home to shower and change. Grabbing the keys now. Should I just walk in? Or knock?]

[Pearl: You got keys to the castle. Come show this Princess how the Prince does business.]

[Mikey: ☒ You ever been licked by this? *Picture of tongue with two inline piercings*]

[Pearl: I got kissed by that today and it was pretty impressive.]

[Mikey: Send me a shot of you playing with your toys.]

So bold!

Pearl felt the heat rising in her cheeks.

Why am I feeling bashful? Is it because I've never sexted with toys? Or is it just intimidating because I'm doing this with Michael, out of all guys?

[Pearl: Aren't you driving?]

[Mikey: Nope. Gubering so I can play along. *Picture of an uncovered forearm revealing tattoos of black and gray koi fish and lotus pond*]

Tattoos! I mean I've noticed some peeking out on occasion of his sleeves and a few times he rolled up a sleeve, but wow! That's some serious ink. Didn't take him for tattoo and piercing type of guy. What the hell? I've known him five years and never once did he ever say anything. To say you're a private man is an understatement.

[Pearl: Okay, how's this. *Picture of breasts, one purple and one pink nipple sucker*]

[Mikey: You crack me up. A little uneven there. Granted, so am I... *Picture of the other forearm with scars and tattoos fighting for space?*]

Oh no... those scars... is this why...

Tears welled up in her eyes. All the teasing and she never knew. This whole time, always rolling up the single sleeve and keeping his shirt on, without a doubt, returned to this one factor. The pieces were falling together with the passing on beach days and the likes.

Dammit. I feel like an utter bitch.

[Mikey: Stop feeling sorry for me. They couldn't cover these, the rest you can't see anymore.]

[Pearl: I'm such a dumbass.]

[Mikey: Send me nudes then. :p I still have half an hour to play! Stop stalling!]

Pearl laughed, shaking her head. He never once took it personal. Just accepted it as friendly razzing. Scooping up all the toys, she scurried back to her bed with all her new treasures laid out before her. Picking up the glass cherry dildo, she bit her lip.

I think I know how I can make this up to him.

Climbing onto the four-post bed, mattresses stacked high enough to make her feel small as she pulled onto it. Readjusting all her pillows, she propped herself up. The lamp lit the area well, casting hard shadows in all the right places. Positioning the camera, legs straddled, the butt plug sparkled from its resting place and the light gave away how wet she had become.

Snapping a photo, she sent it.

[Pearl: Here's the butt plug *Picture of wet pussy and sparkling butt plug*]

[Mikey: Glad you like it. That one wasn't cheap.]

She paled, the thought snaking back to the surface, *are those real crystals?*

[Pearl: You can't be serious! These are real crystals?]

[Mikey: Only the best for my Princess Pea. Now, show me more.]

So, demanding... and to think, he'll be here soon, and all his secrets will be revealed. I can't get my heart to stop racing. I'm nervous, like the first time all over again and well, I can't lie, this isn't what I had in mind nor who I thought I would fuck this week. Michael knows how to throw a girl a birthday party. Showered me with amazing treasures and riding over to join. That's sexy on a lot of levels.

Playful

Grabbing the lube from the nightstand, she couldn't deny her growing desire and arousal to play with herself. By the time Michael would get here, she might orgasm a few times. She dribbled the lube onto the glass dildo, curious what such a hard and ribbed object might feel like against the soft heat of her pussy. She slid it in, slow at first. The glass cool in comparison, making her tense and adding to the pleasurable sensation of the ribbing. At last, it was in until it looked like a set of glass cherries sitting atop her pussy. She snapped a photo.

[Pearl: I don't think I can eat these cherries *Picture*]

[Mikey: No, but don't worry. I'll clean up the juice they make. Starting to get hard. Send more. *Picture of the tent in his pants*]

[Pearl: So, how big are you compared to this little treasure? *Picture of the glass dildo almost all the way out, wet and sparkling*]

[Mikey: What do you think? *Picture of his dick, hard and erect, taller than his hand and thick even in his own grip*]

Pearl paused, glaring at the photo for a moment. Sure, she had been sent plenty of dick pics, but not built like this. This one was worthy of keeping saved in the hidden folders of her phone for later.

She had been with someone with length, but not with the girth she could see in the photo. Her mind recalled how he gripped the bottle tops and spouts. He was no doubt thicker.

Shit, I think he might be the biggest cock I've been with! Happy birthday me!

[Mikey: Not very often I get to render you speechless >:}~ *Another shot of his cock with precum dribbling from the tip*]

[Pearl: You're putting your treasures to shame with that thing... *Picture of the dildo halfway inside her pussy*]

[Mikey: I want to be there *Picture of him making a sad face*]

[Pearl: Too bad *Picture of her sticking her tongue out*]

[Mikey: Almost there. Had to tuck it away before I scarred the Guber driver. Granted, it's Chuckles so...]

[Pearl: Stop it!!! LOL]

Pulling off the nipple suckers, she pushed her breast together and snapped a shot. She took a moment to admire how erect and swollen her nipples had become. The dusky pink now a rosy red like a cherry, seemed appropriate for the way her night seemed to unfold. With a toothy grin, she sent the photo.

[Pearl: The girls needed to breathe *picture*]

[Mikey: You think my cock would fit between them?]

[Pearl: I was wondering if it would fit in my pussy as it is LOL]

[Mikey: Don't tell me I'll be your biggest????]

[Pearl: Definitely the thickest...]

There was a long pause. Pearl puffed out her cheeks. No signs of him writing and panic began building as her anxiety stung her chest. Covering her face, she dreaded she had sent the words.

Why the hell the wave of honesty? What's wrong with me!

Looking down at her phone, there wasn't any signs of a response. She flopped back into her pile of pillows, groaning. Scrolling back over the exchange of photos and words, she paused on the cock shots. Reaching over for the glass dildo, she began sliding it in and out, imagining a cock filling all the space her new toy couldn't fathom to compete with.

Who knew he was packing something this monstrous in those high thread count khakis. And to think, its mine tonight, but I'm nervous. We've been friends for so long and those scars.

Swiping she lingered on the photo, the ink looking fresher in comparison to the other arm. Blinking she became curious and compared the two arms. These were done at various times, usually are, but the scarred arm is definitely recently healed with as dark as the ink held and it seemed to have a hint of lotion or ointment on it.

Was that why he had to go home? Granted, he showed up in that bartending outfit and worked like that all night. Kind of cute he would rush home to clean up and return. I had a shower, but did he want to see how I would react to the toys? Maybe he thought I would discover them in the morning and didn't want to push his luck.

Scrolling back to the dick pics, she bit her lip. Her body throbbed with want. It made her anxious, but it stirred a level of desire she hadn't felt in some time. Tonight would be more than a one nightstand or friend with benefits hookup. If she knew anything about Michael or from that kiss, he intended to take his time with her.

He's so thick, even when holding his own cock. How hard it must get just before he starts to...

Swallowing, she arched, the dildo rubbing against a new area. Her climax was starting to rise and she would peak soon. The more her body squeezed around the glass dildo the more pleasurable the ribbing became. Her breath caught with her rising excitement. Eyes heavy lidded as they took in the photo of his raging hardon, fueling her to thrust the dildo faster.

She turned her wrist, the rubbing tweaking to a new spot. Another swift inhale, moaning as she arched.

"Well, well..." Michael's voice jolted her.

Dropping the phone, it smacked her in the face. "Ouch!"

"Shit!" He rushed the bed, pulling the phone off her face before she could. "That had to hurt." He glanced at the screen and smirked. "It's thick, hard, and heavy when hitting you in the face like that."

"Stop it," she looked away, but his hand pulled her chin back to him.

Michael's lips pressed against hers, rolling his tongue piercing against her own tongue. Both piercings became very clear. The heat of his hand glided over her abdomen and cupped her own hand while still gripping the glass dildo. He began guiding her movements, deepening the kiss and inviting her into his own mouth. The scent of him excited her, freshly showered and a spritz of his alluring cologne goading her sexual tide to peak.

He twisted the glass dildo and rubbed the angled tip downward. This made a new sensation as her pussy tightened in response as the butt plug became part of the playful stroking. His other hand snaked between them, massaging her breast, his thumb circling her nipple. She arched and he broke the kiss to hear her moan. Her bottom lip trembled, teetering on the edge of an orgasm.

Hot lips wrapped around her nipple and she whimpered. He suckled, hungry to taste her flesh before rolling his piercings over the swollen flesh. Another turn of the wrist and he found a spot she had neglected, his thrusting of the dildo faster, firmer. She arched and tried to muffle the scream by biting her lip. He released her nipple with a pop, the wetness he left behind still adding to her arousal.

"Don't hold back. I want to hear you scream." His breath tickled at her ear as he whispered in that suave tone. "I don't give a fuck if you call out someone else's name, just let me show you who I am behind closed doors tonight."

Pearl's eyes were shut tight, the pleasure peaking as his tongue teased her nipple, lips daring to wrap around it once more. The orgasm exploded and she tried the lunge forward. Michael abandoned his play. The glass dildo was quickly replaced with two thrusting fingers and his lips now ensnared her swollen clit. She folded over him, thighs shaking as she came hard. The gush of fluid confirming he had taken her above what she had aimed to do alone.

"Fuck yes!" she cried. "Don't stop, Mikey... Don't..."

Her hands wrapped around his head, grinding in him as she shrieked in delight. The *bump, bump* sensation of his piercings added fuel to the erotic fire he had set ablaze throughout her entire being. When at last the edge slowed and he pulled away from her, she was left breathless. He turned away, stepping just out of the light of her lamp as he pulled his shirt off. Wiping her juice from his face with his shirt, he dropped it to the floor.

The muscles on this man... Axle... he's stacked and not even going to the gym every time!

Mystery Man Revealed

It took a few blinks before Pearl's eyes settled on the artful tattoos etched into his back. The black and white work of art painted every inch of his skin like a full body suit. His pants slid to the floor, the ink never stopping as it flowed over his ass cheeks and down both legs. There were hints of scarring under them as the light hit him. Even the tattoos couldn't completely take them away, but the artwork did well to distract from it all.

A walking canvas and its... gorgeous.

A white crane stood in a bed of lotus, among a flurry of rushing waters and koi as if they lived and thrived on his skin. She propped herself up, eyes wide as she took in the details and marveled over the landscape painted on his chiseled frame. *Hours,* came to mind as to how long it must have taken to cover so much of his skin.

At last, he turned; a puppy dog look on his face softening his features as if unsure of her reaction.

Why is he so worried?

Across the front of his body, Koi fish seemed to battle for space, waves splashing up and over his ribs and shoulders. Her eyes chased the flow of the water down to where he stroked his huge cock, a condom already rolled on and ready for her. She held her breath. That and his hands were the only things she couldn't see signs of having a trace of ink. Again, much like the backside, the water with its koi and flowers spilled over his hips and down his legs, filling his flesh in an amazing form of living artwork.

Is it wrong I'm more excited to be fucked by such a work of art?

When Pearl broke from her gawking, she met his eyes and he waited to see her response. She broke into a smile, fading the tension in his shoulders. Michael had wanted her to see him in the low lighting first. With a few strides forward, the inked skin looked more magnificent. The gray washed shading artfully applied and the rigid line work, bringing depth to the living creatures swimming across the hard planes of muscles.

Her fingers reached out to touch his abdomen and he grabbed her wrist in panic.

"What's wrong?" Pearl's heart raced.

"If you do that, you'll feel them," he mumbled.

"The scars?" she questioned. "It's okay..."

Swallowing, he pressed her palm against his skin and goosebumps rippled over his skin. Pearl furrowed her brow, the bumps, and snags humbling. He had turned away, looking to nowhere while she traced one line up the center of his torso. She inhaled swift. In her lifetime, she had only seen scars like this once, on her father when they had to crack him open for emergency surgery.

Pearl scrambled to her knees, almost making her a little taller than him as he stood beside her bed. "Look at me," she demanded, cupping his face.

"So now you know my secret." There was pain in those eyes. "I was in a bad car crash when I was younger. They had to crack me open, and by some good fortune, they were able to save me. It's the reason for the crane," he shrugged, darting his eyes away from her. "I've spent years getting this ink done, attempting to cover them, but my arm..." Michael lifted the forearm. "It proved too stubborn I suppose."

Pearl kissed him on the lips, but before he could deepen the kiss, she began trailing kisses down his neck. She chose her path well, aiming to battle his wave of insecurities. In this fleeting moment together, everything he'd shown her made her fall in love with him. Trailing across his collarbone, he lips met the top of the scar that ran down his entire torso. He tensed under her touch, holding his breath. She was gentle as she kissed and licked the scar all the way down until at last, she licked the tip of his cock.

HA! A cherry flavored condom! We planned for everything!

By this point, he had taken a breath, his heart thudding fast and hard to the point where she could feel his pulse race under her every touch. Taking his cock into her mouth, she ached to give him enough space as to not nick him with her teeth. She sucked hard and long, sliding his hardened length in and out. Michael moaned, gripping her hair as he began to rock his hips. He cock pressed against the back of her throat and she encouraged him to stay as she shook her head. Another moaned rolled from him before she pulled back and off to inhale for air.

Before she could continue, he stopped her, flipping her onto her back and pulling her pussy to him. He pushed inside her wet heat, slow and a little at a time. She white knuckled the sheets at her sides, tensing at what was to come. He pressed further and further as they watched one another.

Pearl started moaning as he neared entering her all the way and stopped.

"So tight," he breathed, his cock throbbing inside.

"It feels... amazing." She reached down, fingers exploring the thick base of his dick entering her.

"Oh, let's not let this go to waste." He leaned over and made her gasp. "I charged it."

He wiggled the magic bullet and she paled.

"What's that expression?" He flipped it on, and her pussy tightened. "Oh, nervous, are we?"

"Michael, that's a bit much. You're pushing me over the edge," she warned.

He lowered the vibrating bullet, putting it dangerously close to her clit. "I'm pretty sure that was the goal of all these treasures I left you, Princess Pea."

"Mikey..." She looked at him, and he smirked.

The bullet moved down and met its target. She arched, squealing. Her body was electrified with vivid pleasure. Every part of her tensed, an orgasm peaking fast and hard. Another gush and her pussy pulsed around his hard cock. He began grinding in and out, the bullet on its target and unmoving. Her scream heightened, the pleasure making her eyes roll back as he picked up speed.

At last, she couldn't stand it. His cock was growing stiffer and only intensified the erotic pleasure taking hold of her every fiber. She reached down, pulling his hands and the bullet away. He tossed it aside, moaning as he wrapped his arms under her. Pearl wrapped her arms around him, nails digging into this back, only goading him to fuck her slower. Michael would shove forward with great speed and pull back slow, making her arch into his body. Sweat coated her skin and his own, both lingering on the edge of an orgasm.

"Please..." she panted.

"Please?" His breath was hot across her ear and neck. "Are you begging for me to cum?"

"Please... cum for me." She felt his dick jerk inside her. "Michael, please fuck me faster, please cum for me, baby."

"Oh you're mean," he grumbled, arching enough to latch onto a nipple.

She tightened, moaning as she hugged his head into her breast. "Cum for me. Please...I can't... take it anymore."

He caved to her begging, pushing hard and fast, his huge cock unable to deny the tight heat of her pussy. She had gushed until both their thighs were slick and sheets a puddle. He had enjoyed it and at last moaned into her breast, nipple caught in his teeth as he shoved hard. The pulsing, rock-hard cock sent her moaning as she grinded against him, making his own linger longer than he had expected. He released her breast, moaning with heavy lidded eyes. At last they sat still, his cock still inside her pussy. Their gazes met and they both laughed.

"Why haven't we done this sooner?" he asked.

"You shouldn't have waited five years to remove your shirt, Prince Prude," she retorted.

Looking down between them, he pulled his dick from her and frowned, tossing the condom in a small waste basket. "Oh man..."

Pearl's heart jolted. "What's wrong? Did it break?"

"No, no... condom's fine, but..." He smirked, his fingers trailing across her clit, wet opening, and tapped on the butt plug. "We didn't get to pull the plug."

She laughed, laying back as she threw an arm over her face.

"Maybe after we take a short nap?" He crawled onto the bed, pulled her into him and massaging a breast.

"Didn't Axel tell you?" she teased.

"Honestly, I don't recall him spilling the beans about anal." He nuzzled her neck and shoulder before kissing it.

"He hates anal," she announced.

He pressed his chin on her shoulder. "No joke."

She cupped her hand where his squeezed her breast. "But I love it. Do you really need a nap to recoup?"

"You'll have to wait a bit... it takes some... what am I laying on?" Grunting, Michael reached back to pull something out from under him.

After a moment, he reveals the riding crop.

"By the way, was that for you or me?" Pearl takes it from him, both giggling over it.

"It depends. Who's doing the riding."

THE END

THE URBAN EROTICA
FAIRY TALE COLLECTION

Pinocchio
& the
Blow Up Doll

HONEY CUMMINGS

Dedication

For all my wonderful readers, here's a little Holiday Magic with a fairy tale spin!

Happy Holidays,

XOXO Honey Cummings

Table of Contents

Words from the Author

I want to take this moment to thank all my readers. You've all been wonderfully supportive, and I love reading your reactions and reviews. These fantastical books are intended to be fun. For Fairy Tale Erotica Collection, I wanted them written more on the contemporary side by chasing missed opportunities and magical moments the readers secretly wish had unfolded. There's a hint of mischief that magically ends the story on a higher note. Life's funny like that at times!

As for the Urban Legend Collection, this is for all those shifter, paranormal, and fantasy lovers who dream of being swept away into a love story with someone who isn't quite from the same world. There's something thrilling about the not-so-human fantasy characters falling head over heels in love. Throughout the series, funny moments emerge, because for me, love has its share of awkward confessions. In the end, that's perfectly okay; in fact, it's normal!

This book was part of a giveaway earlier this year, a tradition I hope to bring back on an annual basis. It was a chance for fans to receive free books (though the pandemic has slowed the physical prizes from being sent out in a timely manner), and for one lucky fan to win the Grand Prize: naming a major character after them in this Holiday Special.

Congratulations to the
grand prize winner, Zelda!

Thank you to everyone who participated in my giveaway! May you all stay safe during the holiday season!

1

Full Monty

No matter how hard Noc tried to avoid revealing his full name, it always came down to this moment—him standing there as everyone laughed so hard, they almost couldn't breathe.

Family naming traditions were a bitch.

This time he had managed to go almost a whole year at his now not-so-new job as "Noc." Besides, if Noc worked out for Noctis in Final Fantasy XV, how could he go wrong? That is, until the Secret Santa list had circulated the office this morning. Human Resources had listed his *full* name, and the staff came to life, assuming it was some kind of holiday gag.

Pinocchio Geppetto. Dammit, I go on vacation after today. Why now?

Noc didn't look like a pushover. He worked out on occasion, did parkour as a teen, while his mom had him play soccer for a number of years before that. He had decently sized biceps, a six-pack he tried to maintain, hazel eyes, and thick mid-length black hair. Thanks to his Italian heritage, he never lost his summer tan, a natural deep-toned olive skin that was famous among his relatives.

Dread pressed into him as he confessed to his supervisor, "It's not a gag. That's my *real* name. So, whoever draws Pinocchio, that's me. And I'd like to keep that quiet."

At his last job, he'd almost gotten away with using "Noc" and yet, it rose to the surface. Ultimately, the running gag of "knock on wood" jokes had sent him packing. He resigned and moved to a different city, landing a Lead Account Manager position. To offset a potential harassment suit, the company made him sign an agreement and gave him a hell of a severance. Naturally, he used it just to move elsewhere, to start again fresh. Making friends had been easier when no one knew his grand secret.

Thanks, mom. This is the worst name you can bestow a grown-ass man. Dammit, I'd love to change it legally, but I can't. She'd be heart broken. She takes pride in our Italian roots and the story inspired by our family generations ago. It was never meant in ill-intent...

"Let me get this straight, that's your *legal birth name?*" His supervisor struggled to get the words out as he chuckled. "How'd I miss this?"

Rolling his eyes, Noc ran a hand through his thick, black locks. "Everyone assumes it's a gag."

"Yeah, why wouldn't they? It's a storybook character's name." His supervisor continued to giggle as he marveled at the sheet . "What was your mother thinking?"

Noc met his gaze, stern and stoic. "She takes pride that our family inspired the legend."

His supervisor swallowed, stifling his laughter at the heated gaze. "R-right. That's... I didn't realize it was based on an actual legend."

"Well, it is." Noc at last sighed. *Now would be a perfect time to set boundaries. Don't repeat past mistakes here, Noc.* "Look, I left my last job because I was getting harassed by coworkers over this exact reason."

The supervisor cringed. "R-right. Didn't you say you left there with a hell of a severance over a situation?"

"Yeah. A situation just like this." Noc pointed at the paper. "I expect you to make it clear that I won't be bombarded by a billion puns and jokes about my name, Bob."

"Oh shit." Bob's eyebrows lifted high. "It got bad, then?"

"Trust me, it was rough." Noc glanced at his reflection, his hazel eyes piercing him in this tense moment. *I am so pissed, there's no hiding it this time. Is it ok to be this aggressive with my own supervisor? I mean, I suppose considering why I left my last job, I can't fret over the order of command over this. He needs to understand I am not playing around.*

"Look, Noc. I'll keep this at a dull roar. If anyone starts up, let me know." Bob looked at the paper and laughed again. "I'm sorry. I mean, I'm sure it was cute as a kid but, damn dude. Why not get a name change or something?"

"I've thought about it, but it might send my mother to an early grave." He shook his head. "I mean, she's moved back to Italy to take care of my grandparents, so you can imagine the hell that will cause in the entire family if I dare to do that."

"Oh! Aren't you going to Italy for the holidays?" Bob changed topics, shoving the paper out of view.

"I was, but we didn't want to risk anyone else getting sick. This virus hasn't exactly dissipated. There's always Easter." Noc spun on his heel, heading for the door. "Thanks for understanding."

Noc quickly shut the door behind him, cutting off whatever Bob had wanted to say next. Inhaling deep, he scanned the cubicles with gatherings of giggling people lipping *Pinocchio*. His next mission was to confront Gina in Human Resources.

I went as far as filling out my paperwork under my alias. Only HR sensitive paperwork had my full name.

Gathering his nerves, he marched toward the administrative offices on the other side of the sales floor. Her door was open, so he pushed inside and slammed it closed behind him. Jolting, Gina dropped her pen and stared at him wide-eyed. After a few blinks, a wide grin grew on her face.

"We need to talk," Noc demanded.

Gina's cheeks flushed. "Yes? What's the matter?"

"You put my whole name on the Secret Santa list. I *explicitly* requested you not to. Besides, that isn't the name written on my paperwork," he said, getting straight to the point.

She rose to her feet and leaned over her desk. "But you have an adorable name."

Noc's eyes fell to the exposed cleavage under her unbuttoned shirt. His face heated, swallowing as he fought to bring his eyes back to hers. The rest of her attire seemed, unusual. A short skirt, her bright blue bra could be seen through the thin white blouse, and her lipstick darker. Even the eyeshadow screamed she had plans to go on a date.

I don't remember petite, curvy Gina being the type to dress so provocatively. Should I tell her a button came lose or did she do that on purpose? Is that a blue fairy tattoo on breast? Holy shit, Gina has ink!

Gina marched from behind her desk, forcing Noc to step back until his slammed against the door. She approached, hips swinging in her red stilettos until she could reach behind him.

Locking the door, her brown eyes looked him up and down.

He blinked. *Did she just take stock of me? This isn't a club, I mean, last time a girl checked me out like that we ended up fucking in a bathroom stall.*

Her body language was stranger, more seductive than normal, stirring something inside him. Noc opened his mouth to speak, but snapped his jaw closed. Gina winked, smiling wide as she started to shut the blinds that peered into the sea of cubicles. Noc tilted his head, curious what in the world was happening. His initial understanding seeming to be screaming he was about to hook up with his HR rep. Her skirt so short, he swore he could see her ass cheeks and hints of a... *blue thong to match?*

"Let me make it up to you, Noc," she offered, undoing a button, giving him a peek of her blue, lacy bra.

"Excuse me?" He shook his head in disbelief. *Did I just walk into an office themed porno? Where are the cameras? This can't be happening right now.* "Uh, Gina, I don't think that's the kind of..."

She had closed the gap between them, a finger pressing against his lips. "I didn't realize you had such an adorable name to match your cuteness, Pinocchio."

"Wait, what?" The weight of his situation started to unfold in his mind. *No, it couldn't be. Gina intentionally did this because...* "Let me get this straight, you did this on purpose?"

"Maybe?" She shrugged as she unhooked two more buttons on her white blouse, freeing her breasts completely. "You know, I'm a huge fan of those movies."

"Porn movies?" Noc's confusion tangled with the involuntary bulge in his pants. *Shit, she's got a big set of tits.*

Gina blushed, laughing as she finished unbuttoning her blouse, revealing a taut bra filled with soft flesh. "Heavens no." She motioned at a display high on the wall behind her desk, where she perched herself. "Disney movies."

"Oh." He cleared his throat, seeing the unusual amount of older film characters staring down at them. "Right. Those movies."

Wait, are those all Pinocchio themed characters? There's more Pinocchio's up there than I've even seen or been gifted in my lifetimes. Which means...

"So, what do you want first?" she offered, teasingly pulling her skirt higher, revealing her matching thongs.

Noc closed his eyes, sucking on his inner cheek as his logic and cock battled for decision-making rights. "Gina, I don't think this is a good idea. I mean, I'm flattered but technically we're still on the clock?"

I doubt that's gonna stop her.

"I can give you a blow job." Gina's voice deepened with provocative demand. "Or let you lick my pussy." <Insert an action

from Noc.> "Or we can cut to the chase and let you bend me over the desk and hammer me."

Shit! She's out of her mind! He peeked at her, swallowing. "Gina, I just find my name embarrassing and just wanted it..." With practiced skill, she reached back, and the bra came lose, pink nipples erect as the blue bra landed on the floor with the blouse. "...wanted... wanted... you have magnificent breasts." *Fuck! What am I saying!*

"Oh, you're a boob man, huh?" She excitedly jumped to her feet, making her breasts bounce in a way that tightened Noc's pants further.

She's really going to do this. We're really going to do this. When in Rome?

Wiggling out of her panties, only her black skirt and red stilettos remained. Her blonde, wavy hair bounced around her shoulders as she waltzed toward the exterior window. Bending over, she lifted the skirt to show off her pink folds, her pussy wet and ready for him. Noc's cock pressed tighter against his pants, the tingling arousal starting to drown out all reasoning in his mind. Gina pressed her breasts hard against the window and wiggled her ass as if invoking a bull to charge.

Being on the fifth floor, midday, I wonder if someone can see her from here. On that note, would they see me pounding her this far back with her breasts... fuck it, let's do this.

Noc rushed to unfasten his pants, taking one final look at the locked door and closed blinds. "We gotta be quiet. These walls are thin."

"You're assuming you can fuck me hard enough to make me squeal." She smacked her ass cheek hard, a hand-shaped welp already taking shape.

"This isn't exactly what I had in mind as part of my Christmas bonus..." he muttered, approaching with caution. "You get too loud, and it's over."

"Fuck me, Pinocchio."

He blinked, his cock throbbing at her weighted command. "Well, if I'm honest, this is the first anyone has used my full name."

"Fucking lie to me and fuck me with your hard wood," she moaned as her other hand slid between her thighs from the other way.

Noc's eyes fell to where her fingers rubbed across her wet pussy. They dipped between the swollen folds, thrusting a few times before pulling back wet. He bit his lip, stroking his hard cock. Retreating to her clit, her finger circled slow and she moaned once more. He took a step forward, but again hesitated.

Man, this will complicate things...

"Lie to me."

"Excuse me?" He took a nerve-wracking step forward again, heart racing and arousal growing. "You want me to do what now?"

"Fucking lie to me, Pinocchio," her voice deepened with desire.

"I'd be lying if I thought this was a good idea." He half laughed and caught her reflection in the window. *Shit, she's fucking serious.* "I've been dreaming about you, Gina?"

"You lie." She smirked, wild and sinister. "Again."

"I've always wanted to fuck you?" he offered.

"Fucking liar... tell me *more*, make that dick grow for me, baby." Gina seemed hot and bothered by his clueless attempts.

"I only took this job to fuck you?"

"Liar." She wiggled, her pussy dripping. "Look how long your wood is getting. Fuck me with your lies, Pinocchio! Fuck me with your growing wood!"

Noc came closer, his thick, hardened length rubbing along her opening.

"Oh, it's nice and hard."

His hands caressed her tight ass cheeks, gliding up until he could grip her hips under the raised skirt. "Here's another lie, *I have a condom.*"

Wonder if she thought about that little fact.

The Paperwork

N oc locked eyes with her reflection as his cock rubbed against her swollen folds. Silky and hot, he throbbed with the desire to shove inside her wet heat. The way her back arched so that her breasts were pressed firmly against the glass made him jealous. There was no way someone in the parking lot couldn't see those headlights, but she was really into this moment.

I'd rather rub my cock between them. Or better yet, catch one of those cotton candy pink nipples in my teeth for fun. Granted, this is kind of hot.

"Don't you worry, Noc. I plan on swallowing."

He didn't need any more goading. He shoved hard and fast inside her. She bit her lip to stifle her yelp. Her cheek pressed hard against the glass now as he thrusted into her with hard, long strokes. Noc could feel Gina tighten around his cock. She began panting, hands and arms bracing her on the glass. Her legs shook. Noc leaned forward, the building friction of her tight pussy intoxicating. He landed a palm flat on the glass above her, rocking back slow and slamming forward fast. Each time her yelp grew louder.

Dammit, I'm losing it. This is a little unnerving even for me.

Closing his eyes, he imagined someone he wanted more. He agonized on the edge of peaking. His imagination sought out a blonde, elven vixen. Something surreal, something otherworldly seemed more realistic than this unfolding moment between him and his human resource officer. Noc let his mind take him to a moment of licking a breast, having such a noble being kneel before him. IN his mind, he moaned the name of a game character he had crushed one for all his life.

Zelda.

A moan escaped Gina, her hands covering her mouth as she pulsed and gushed. He had grown harder in the moments of gamer boy fantasies. Her orgasm exploded, and he slowed to watch chills roll over her skin like ripples on a lake. Despite it, she was warm and soft under his grip. The pulsing of her pussy on his rock-hard cock tipped him dangerously close to peaking.

"I'm coming..." he huffed, pulling out.

Spinning on her heels, Gina's lips wrapped around his cock. Noc's other palm thudded on the glass, his legs turning to jelly as she didn't let him lose any ground on his overwhelming ecstasy. The bopping waves thrusted to and fro as she sucked on his shaft. Her tongue wiggled against his underbelly. At last, the tip pressed down the back of her throat and he groaned.

What's the etiquette of grabbing HR by the hair to hold a deep throat? Shit...

A hand fisted against the glass, eyes shut tight as he fought the urge to hold her there for a moment longer. He came, *hard*. She swallowed and suckled and brought on another spurt, then a third. Satisfied, he sighed as she slid off his cock with a pop. She ran her tongue from the base to tip one last time, making him grunt. At last he opened his eyes, backing away to give her space to stand.

"It's a shame I'm not free this weekend." She shrugged and brushed pass him. "I wouldn't mind trying to straddle and ride your wood one more time, Pinocchio." Circling around her desk, she plucked her bra and shirt off the floor as she continued, "I'm sorry to expose you twice today." She winked, pulling her bra back on. "But in all fairness, I'm your Secret Santa. I rigged it, and you were mine"

"Well," Noc tucked himself away, glancing at the marks of Gina's breasts, face, and hands on the window, "that's gotta be the strangest Secret Santa gift I've ever received."

She giggled. "No, silly. That was just me wanting to have my way with someone named after my all-time favorite character. I mean, don't get me wrong, you're super-hot, Noc. A real nice guy, but finding out your real name..." She paused, face blushing. "All reasonable thoughts just ceased. Don't you dare say anything about this. Anyway, your gift is in that sealed box in the chair, but wait until tonight before you open it."

Noc turned to see a rather big box wrapped up and a huge bow tied on it. "Why wait until tonight?"

Gina smiled, arching her eyebrows high as she buttoned her blouse with impeccable speed. "You can say I hope you think of me tonight."

Oh shit. This can't be good.

"Noc, look, I am off for the rest of the holiday week too. Thank you for starting my vacation off with a bang." She picked her panties up, then shoved them into her purse. "I'm spending the whole week with Mr. Townsend."

Noc paled, eyes wide. "Wait, my supervisor? B-bob?"

"Oh? Huh, I didn't realize you worked under him." She paused, typing on her computer. "You know, let me do this much for you, how about a promotion? I would love to see more of you and a managerial role would make that possible."

"Gina, Bob's married." Noc sucked on his cheek. "And her name's Mary."

"Yeah, I know." She hit enter and turned to dig in one of her desk drawers. "But you see, every holiday they spend it with... someone else. It's some kind of swinger's arrangement. In the end, I literally get to have a good time in some fancy resort in Miami for the week.

I hate going home for the holidays to see my family. They're in Ohio and the snow is *ugh*." She pulled out paper towels and a bottle of window cleaner. "Look, I'll clean up in here, so you can leave early and get paid for the whole day."

"Then who is Mary spending the week with? I know they don't have kids but..." Noc's curiosity got the best of him as he pried further into this weird dynamic unfolding within his workplace. *Exactly how many people in this damn building are fucking each other?*

"You know Heather in sales?" The sway of her hips made his eyes follow her to the window. "In fact, it's the third holiday they'll be spending together."

"Heather?" He tilted his head. "The same Heather who can beat any man in this building at an arm-wrestling contest? The Gina Carano could be her twin, Heather? But Mary is so tiny and frail, even next to you."

"Yes, that Heather. The big, beautiful gal with her tall, black boots, torn jeans, white camis, and plaid shirts." Gina paused a moment, then wiped breast print from the window. "Now that I'm thinking about it, I bet she's a Nirvana fan."

"How many in the office know about... this?" Noc's brow folded, his mind racing. *What planet did I wake on this morning?*

Gina snorted. "Like the whole office. I mean, Mary and Bob have already made their rounds and don't be shocked if she doesn't offer you a ride in her office next."

"Wait, what?" Noc covered his mouth, his imagination seeing sweet little Mary coaxing him in and shoving the financial reports off her desk. "No, I couldn't..."

"Oh she's a good time, though careful, she gets rough." Stretching on her tiptoes, she sprayed the window and wiped the area one last time where his palm marks had been.

"Rough?" he marveled. "Exactly... what the hell does that mean?"

"Oh? You really don't know about all this?" Turning back to him, she gave him a skeptical look. "How long have you been here?"

"Eleven months," he replied flatly. *Shouldn't HR know that?*

"Ah, well." She returned to her desk, dropping the cleaner into a drawer, then kicking it closed. "My adorable, oh-so-innocent Pinocchio, should be aware she's really, *really,* into BDSM."

Noc's eyes nearly crossed as he imagined tiny Mary in a black negligée, perfectly fitted for a dominatrix featured on PornHub. com. Glancing at the present wrapped with ribbons and bows, he sighed. Again, his mind cooked up what the mystery item could possibly be with all the new, naughty dirt he had gained about his fellow coworkers. *Shit, my bosses. Every supervisor in this joint has some underground sex ring happening, what the fuck is up with that?*

Shaking the images from his head, he turned back to Gina who seemed to be settling back in to... *work?*

"Um, ok, well thank for..." He picked up the rather weighty gift. "This. Um, yeah, heading home and gonna start my holiday week a tad early."

"Oh?" She smiled, her eyes never leaving the screen as she tapped away on her keyboard. "Well, just remember...think of me when you open it and play with your new *toy.*"

Noc inhaled deep. "R-right," he said as he opened the door and dove into the sales floor.

At least no one has seemed to notice our little hookup, but damn... What the hell is going on in this place? They did, they had to have heard that last shriek. Maybe this is normal for them, which would explain why they aren't phased. Have I just been accepted into some weird, secret sex club?

From her open office door, Mary locked eyes with him and winked. Then he stumbled as he watched Heather lean into Mary's ear whispering or... *did she just openly lick her earlobe?*

It was more than enough to turn him for the door and elevator.

I got my car keys, my wallet, fuck my jacket. I'll brave the cold just to get out from under all this... heat.

3

Secret Santa

Noc couldn't shake the nagging sensation lingering in his trunk. Outside, the temperature plunged as another cold front advanced just as the sun began to set over the bustling cityscape. He had left it there, came home and ordered out in hopes he would just leave it there until he found a dumpster big enough to toss it in. The phone buzzed, his order left at the door and he waited. Thanks to the pandemic, his holiday plans were cancelled including his plan B to hit the local bar. Flights back to see his mother in Italy were impossible now with the airport shutting down and freezing ticket sales.

Guess if I even wanted to brave it out there wearing a mask, it's just not meant to happen.

Grabbing his bagged dinner off the stoop, he returned to the kitchen counter. As he opened the containers, a blast of pad Thai and pork dumplings sent his stomach rumbling. He had missed lunch altogether thanks to the event with Gina. His mind wondered back to what unfolded in her office. Shoveling the food faster, he was back to seeing the damned box.

Well, maybe I should at least see what the fuck was so heavy? I mean, it a good-sized box.

Chucking the empty containers into the trash, he snatched the keys off the counter. He muttered curses under his breath as he braved the night air. Snow began to fall as he removed the box from the truck, then rushed into his townhome.

Setting it on the couch, he waited a moment, mind racing with possibilities it held. *Don't tell me Gina bought a sex swing...something for us to use together. I mean, it's big and heavy. How did that tiny blond even get this thing into the office.*

"Fuck it..."

He pulled at the bow, failing to unloosen it. At last, he scoured his kitchen drawers for a knife and at sliced the ribbons away. The wrapping paper ripped away easy enough, but the bare cardboard box underneath gave nothing away about what may be inside. Scoffing, he slid the knife over the packing tape and forced it open. Opening the flaps wide, he took a step back.

No, I think this is the worst idea ever...

Noc covered his mouth, knotting his brow. Blinking, he took in the folded form. Frayed blonde hair, flesh colored skin, red lips stuck in a permanent "oh" as she stared up in helpless blue eyes. The sex doll was deflated and between her flattened breasts was a note. Noc cringed. The implications of a doll for her man-doll sending a shiver up his spine.

My beloved Pinocchio,

Please think of me when you play with her.

Your friendly neighborhood HR,

Gina <3

"Really. Of all the..." Groaning, he crumbled up the note, closing his eyes against the blinding, red anger. "Because...my name's Pinocchio. It doesn't mean I have a doll fetish, lady." Peeking open one eye, he looked down at the crumbled plastic being. "Well, let's at least blow you up and get a better idea what exactly I'm dealing with. I don't think I've seen one of these in person."

He peeled the doll out of the box, then unfolded it. This wasn't a simply cheesy gag gift vinyl made blow up doll. Gina had found something well over the twenty-dollar limit they had set for the rest of the office. The rubber was soft and fleshy to the touch, not as wrinkly as he'd expect her legs and arms to be as they unraveled.

Damn, this is a high-end doll made to be used in all seriousness.

Glancing over the front, his eyes glided over the nipples, down the torso and lingered on the pink slot meant to be her pussy. Swallowing he flipped her over, perplexed there was a slot for anal too. *No fun opening missed I see.* As he searched upward, relief washed over him as he located the valve in the middle of her back.

"Oh man. I was so worried this would be a nipple or worse, in her ass like a bad joke."

Steeling himself, he drew in a large breath and began to blow air into the doll. He watched with each round as her limbs stiffened and soon her torso began making the process difficult. Fumbling with her, breast still not fully inflated as he tried to find some means to hold the naked inanimate woman, he found himself pursing lips against the small of her back.

So...this is awkward.

A hand gripped a breast and he left it there in defeat. After a few more rounds of air, he started to feel lightheaded. The groping of her breast became firmer, more realistic until he reached the point where the air wouldn't go further in without pushing back into his mouth. Using the tip of his tongue to plug the hole, he managed to push the plug in with his hand, then popped it inward to smooth her back.

Breathing in and out, regaining the oxygen he had given her, he stood up and placed her on the couch. She lay stiffly across the furniture, looking surprised to be propped up so haphazardly. Noc crossed his arms, his brow lowering as he observed the inanimate sexual partner he had been gifted. She seemed as nervous and shocked as he did. Without the deflated, squashed look, she curved a little more naturally than he had expected. The straight locks of hair waterfalled all around her like a princess.

Am I really thinking she's hot...? I need a shower. Maybe on the cold side.

Noc's heart raced, his face heating from his rising emotions.

I mean, it seemed like a cheesy mockup, but after filling her out with some hot air...

He stripped down, tossing his clothes all over the bedroom floor as he beelined for the bathroom. Living alone had its advantages, one he had frequently enjoyed while strutting around the apartment completely naked. Setting his phone up to play music, he tilted his head as a ninety's throwback by Santana came on and he left it. The knobs squeaked and icy water rained down on him.

I still feel dirty after my rendezvous with HR, regretting not doing this first.

Gina's perfume seemed to still linger for a moment until he at last reached for the body soap. His entire day seemed surreal. The idea his real name had been exposed to coworkers once again made the muscles in his back tense. He reached for the shampoo and conditioner, scrubbing his hair in frustration. Unlike the last job, this powder keg took an unexpected turn.

Shit, I shouldn't have slept with Gina. She's my human resource officer! "What the hell was I thinking?"

Shampoo slipped into his eyes, stinging. Murmuring profanities, he rushed to rinse it all off. Despite clearing it from his hair and face, his eyes still stung, and he closed them tight. Turning the shower off, he went scrambling for the towel. His hand gripped the empty towel rack. Grumbling more curses, he blindly moved toward the door. As he reached for the doorknob, a towel met his hand. He gripped it and started drying his hair and face, eyes still stinging.

Did I leave it hanging on the bathroom door? That's weird...

"Is that what you were looking for?" The female voice made him drop the towel and take a step back.

"Who the fuck..." Blinking out the last of the soap, he stared wide-eyed.

Before him stood a completely naked blonde with curvy hips and large breasts. She blushed, batting her eyes at him. Unlike Gina, her blonde hair was long and fell in straight locks like a waterfall around her breasts. Pink nipples stood erect and his eyes chased the contours of her body, the way her shaven pussy tucked between thick thighs making him aroused. He covered his cock with his hands, the muscles in his torso tightening with alarm.

"Who are you?" He snapped his eyes to the blue irises glowing with magic.

"I... well, you haven't given me a name yet." She frowned, cupping his cheek with her hand. "But thank you for blowing me up earlier."

Noc's mind raced, thoughts grinding into one another as if gears locking up. "Blew you... up?"

Disbelief hit him, he walked pass her and marched into his living room. The box still laid in tatters and he examined it, smelling it, and shaking it as if some unforeseen chemical leaked from it. Scanning the room, the sex doll he had blown up moments before was nowhere to be seen. He covered his mouth, turning back to the bedroom door where the naked woman stood and smiled sweetly when their gazes met. She didn't seem to be unnerved being in a stranger's apartment, completely naked along with him, and it sent chills down Noc's spine. Standing before him was a real-life version of the doll.

She looks like the doll. Same height, features, breast size. There's something so unnatural about this. It's gotta be acid, or LSD, or...

"What the hell did Gina lace on that damn doll." He started pacing the room, holding his head. "She's my HR officer. She knows where I live. And now...I'm hallucinating on some unknown drug she clearly laced her *gift*." Spinning on his heels, he rushed the front door to flip all the locks, drawing the chain he never used into place.

What if she's already here? Fuck.

Ignoring the completely naked woman in his home, he checked the rest of the house, while his paranoia wondered if Gina had snuck in during his shower. As he continued to inspect his closet and under his bed, he couldn't help stealing glances of the gorgeous blonde. Again, he could feel himself aroused taking in the peachy tone of her skin, the soft pink of her nipples, and the way her lips unfolded like flower petals.

She looked so much like a real life... *a name, she said she...*

"You're seriously waiting on me to name you?" he murmured, as he closed his closet. *Well, it doesn't seem my hallucination is going to fade any time soon. Might as well entertain this idea.*

"Oh yes, I really should have one, don't you think?" She took a step closer to him, clapping her hands with excitement. "Name me anything you'd like, the sexier the better."

"A sexy name..." He sashayed back to the other side of his room until the bed made a barrier between them. "I mean, you're just a fragment of my imagination or high." He reassured himself. "And I'm pretty sure Gina has something to do with all this..."

She titled her head. "Is that my name? Gina?" she asked, a sense of innocence in her voice.

"NONONONO!" He threw out his hands in panic. "*Hell* no."

"Then what do you want my name to be, Pinocchio?" She sat on his bed; her hands clasped on her plump thighs making his cock throb.

"Noc. Please, call me Noc," he said flatly.

"Noc, the Blue Fairy has blessed you with the perfect match. But please, I need a name."

Of course, why hadn't I considered that old story into the mix. Perhaps the Blue Fairy will answer my longtime wish and join us in a threesome I'll never forget.

"Zelda," he said firmly. "Your name is Zelda."

"I like Zelda." Her hands covered her heart, a look of relief on her face. "Thank you, Noc."

"Uh, you're welcome?" He shook his head. "Look, Zelda. I'm going to bed now."

"Wait, I wanted to..."

Noc threw up a hand to silence her. "It's been a long day and well, I think if I can just sleep this off, whatever this is," he motioned to her and himself a few times, "I might wake up a little less freaked out."

"Oh, I had no idea." She cupped her face. "And feeling so tired, you still took the time to inflate me."

"R-right." He flipped back his comforter. "Um, well, goodnight?" he offered.

She flipped her side of the comforter. "Get some rest, Noc."

"What are you doing?" he asked, his words rushed.

"Going to bed with you." As she crawled into bed, his heart fluttered catching a view of her pussy, prompting him to blush. "I'm cold and want to keep you company."

Noc narrowed his eyes. "F-fine, but I mean it. I'm going to sleep."

She's just a figment of my imagination, why the fuck am I getting all worked up over this?

4

Between the Sheets

The heat of fingers slid up his inner thigh, stirring him awake from a deep, deep slumber. He had fallen asleep faster than expected, even with a strange, naked woman snuggled in the curve of his arm, her soft skin and warm body instantly lulled him away.

Granted, he wasn't completely convinced he was riding on some mystery drug trance. Between the "meeting" with Gina and her *generous* gifts, he imagined he was snuggling with a sex doll in bed like some poor, drunk college student.

As the haze of sleep melted away, his mind shifted into erotic thoughts about *Zelda*. Strangely, this version didn't have elven ears. His cock hardened as fingers began stroking his shaft. A moan escaped him; his eyes still closed. The tingling heat buzzed across his entire being as his pleasure increased.

A hot breath blew across the tip and his dick jumped in the grip.

Her fingers tightened around his shaft; the stroking grew firmer, more confident with every touch. A tongue slowly circled the tip of his cock. He hardened further, tilting his hips wanting more of the wet heat and its velvety texture. The tongue glided down and up his shaft, the hot pants promising against dick teased how close lips lay in the vagueness between the sheets. He gripped the sheets, still fighting sleep as his dreams took an erotic turned.

"Zelda," her name fell from his lips with unfiltered, provocative desire.

Lips slipped over the cap of his cock, and he moaned, angling so he could dip further into the slick mouth. A whimper escaped the mouth, and he became very aware his dream was not so imaginative. Eyes popping open, he saw a form covered in his blanket, someone had slipped between his legs. His knees pressed against a hot, soft body. The pleasure fogged his mind, unwilling to push them away as the bopped up and down his dick. He threw back the covers, the sultry blonde gobbling the entire length of his cock, suckling as she went. Breast swayed with her efforts, nipples teasing his thighs.

He inhaled swift. "Zelda," he said more firmly.

Their gazes locked and she pushed further down on his cock. The tip of his dick hit the back of her throat, and he grunted. She kept him there, suckling and wiggling her tongue against his throbbing hardened length as he teetered on the edge of an orgasm.

"Zelda," he breathed, body tensing as he fought the urge to come.

Slow and agonizing, she pulled back off his hardened length, her eyes on his until her lips broke away. "Yes, Noc?"

"You're still here?" he marveled, his mind failing to comprehend the weight of the reality and glancing at the clock. *It's been over six hours and...*

"Of course, I am." She sat up, her body gorgeous between his legs. He hissed as she arched upward into the right angle to present her breasts to him. "I'm yours, and *only* yours."

"R-right." Noc's heart pounded in his ears. "I thought, well." *What am I trying to say?* "I didn't think you were... *real.*"

"Oh?" Zelda smiled, crawling atop him, her breast soft as they brushed against his torso. "What will it take to make it clear to you that I'm very real, a real-life woman meant only for you. I'm not going anywhere unless you send me away. I'm a real woman on every level, Noc."

"I mean, doesn't it normally start with a wish?" Noc smirked as her thighs pressed on side of his hips. "I don't recall making one, to tur a doll into a real––*live* woman."

"No, you didn't. It's not always prompted by the receiver. Sometimes, the Blue Fairy rewards those who have worked hard or have failed to take time to find companionship with someone special." Zelda leaned in, her lips tickling his ear as she whispered, "In your case, you are given someone special when the perfect opportunity presented itself–– when you were gifted with me today."

Whispering into her ear, he challenged, "Even if it means turning a sex doll into a person? A little inappropriate for the Blue Fairy I would think."

"A doll is a doll." She kissed his neck and he shuddered. "But... would you rather me be a fragile, porcelain princess, Noc? Or someone...less anatomically correct?"

"Are you implying," he paused, inhaling her familiar, intoxicating, flowery scent before he dared to finish the sentence, "...that you were built to fuck me?"

She grinded her wet pussy against his hardened length. "You did blow me up, Noc. Now I can return the favor and blow *you*."

"That I did." He held his breath as the grinding sent shivers through him. "I just didn't think magic worked like this... and exchange of blowing one another."

"Touch me, grope my breast." She jerked his hand from his side, his palm cupping the soft flesh forcibly. "Touch me like you did when breathing life into me, Noc. I want to feel you kissing down my back once more, your breath against my skin like it's the first time all over again."

Noc shifted his hips, his cock sliding between her slick folds. Her pussy tightened as he rode, slow and deep. She tried to sit up, but he wrapped his arms around her, pulling her into him as he rocked back and forth, making her moan. His tongue lashed out, sliding across a nipple and her breath caught. Sucking the flesh between his lips, his appetite for her growing with each thrust. Every long suckle of her nipple rewarded him with the tightening of her pussy around his cock.

"Oh, Noc," she moaned his name, rocking her hips to deepen his penetration. "Noc, don't stop."

He switched breasts, enjoying the soft pillow of flesh. His hands wondered down the small of her back. One hand slid beyond the other until he could grip her ass. Her legs shook with her rising bliss. He sped up his thrusting, his lips releasing her breast so he could look up to see her face. Zelda arched her back, palms pressing down on his chest so she could shift once more to let him fuck her more deeply. He hardened under the heat of her hands.

"Noc, I'm..." her words failed her, his hands sliding over her body to hold her hips in place. "I think I'm..."

"I can tell..." he panted, trying to not lose the pacing and motion. "Come for me, Zelda."

"Y-yes." Her fingers dug into his chest as her pussy tightened on his thrusting cock.

"Give it to me, I want to watch you come for me," he confessed.

Sweat trickled down his temple, he suppressed his own orgasm, his groin aching for release. Zelda gasped. At last, an ecstasy filled cries escaped her, body arching as her orgasm started to edge closer. Her breasts bounced with each entry of his cock. His thighs were wet, her body gushing to receive him over and over again. Her panting and closed eyes left him wanting to see her blue irises. She was so tight, so close to peaking as her muscles tightened throughout her body.

"Look at me," he demanded.

Under heavy lidded eyes, her glowing, blue eyes peered down at him. "Don't stop," she begged.

"I'm so close," he muttered, slowing down. "I want to come with you but..."

"Fill me," she pleaded, grinding against him to regain the lost momentum. "Come with me."

"But..." he swallowed, the wet friction making his cock throb inside her. "...what if... if I cum inside you can't you..."

"I'm a fuck doll, Noc. FUCK ME!" She gripped his wrists, moving him off her hips, then shoving his hands onto her breasts. "Fuck me and fill me. I am yours! I want to come with you!"

Squeezing her breast hard, her pussy tightened as she continued bouncing atop him. He returned to the rapid, deep thrusting. She shrieked, her pussy squeezing his rock-hard cock and he lost his fight. He moaned and she screamed. He released her breasts and pulled her back down into him, pushing hard into her as he filled her with his cum. Her fingers clawed at the sheets, and he kept thrusting to make their orgasms linger until exhaustion claimed him. His heart beating fast and hard.

I've never had a moment this incredible with someone... holy hell...

After a moment, he released her, allowing her to roll off him. They panted, sweaty from the energy spent in the heat of passion. Noc slowly turned to face her, watching as she continued to ride the buzz of ecstasy. One of her hands gripped a breast, the other gliding down her thighs. He watched her as he caught his breath, curious as she began pleasuring herself.

At last, he rolled to his side, propping his head up with an arm to get a better view.

Her eyes were shut tight, arching as she twisted a nipple. Following the length of her arm, he at last stopped where a finger circled over a swollen clit. Her fingers dipped inside her swollen lips often, drawing the wetness across the flesh to fuel her play. And then, she released a muffled moan.

"Are you using my cum to masturbate?" Noc sucked on his cheek, jealous and turned on by the notion.

"You felt so good..." she cooed, not slowing her work. "I just want to keep it going, just a little longer."

Shit, and I'm spent for a while. Dammit, I'm aching to go again.

"Don't stop," she huffed, fingers dipping and thrusting in and out of her pussy.

He furrowed his brow. "Don't stop?"

"Don't stop watching me, Noc." The wanton want in her voice made him shiver in excitement.

Her brow furrowed, struggling to release a second orgasm. He ran a hand across her stomach, and she moaned. Her body twitched. A smirk crossed his face, trailing fingers over her arm, down her hip and over her thigh. He squeezed and rubbed Zelda's inner thigh, daring to knock knuckles with her working hand.

Is it wrong for me to embrace this fantasy, to be with Zelda? To taste and make love to her until I wake up from whatever dream, or high, I'm on...

5

Taste of Honey

W hen her legs began to shake, he knew she was drawing close to peaking once more. His refractory period would be a while, but he wanted to explore her body more. Leaning closer to her, he began suckling on her ear. His hand pulled her thigh against him and his cock. Licking and kissing, he was slow to taste her salty sweet taste.

She tilted her head to give him access. "So close," she breathed, encouraging him.

His hand slid higher, her fingers retreating to circling her clit. Fingers slipped inside her and she whimpered. Burning kisses continued down her collarbone, he worked his way back to suckling her breast. Her pussy tightened around his fingers and he began stroking, enjoying how she began him helping her get off. Her hips shifted, helping her grind against his hand. The shaking in her legs increased, visibly fighting the urge to clamp close in fear of stopping the pleasure he brought her.

"Feels so good," she moaned.

Abandoning her circling she gripped onto his wrought iron headboard. It goaded Noc to change tactics and he pulled away. She panted, breasts rising and falling in the faint light spilling across them from his open bathroom door. Forcing her legs open, he positioned his body between her knees. Bowing before her, his hazel gaze watched as her blue eyes widened with wonder. Running his tongue flatly across her opening sent her in a squeal of delight.

I suppose this means I'll be the first to taste her... and that's a rare treat.

Her clit was swollen, the pink pearl erect, easy to circle and flick with the tip of his tongue. Knees dug into his torso as a shiver rattled her entire body like an electrical shock running through her veins. His fingers slid back into her, stroking faster than before. Arching, she allowed him better access and he couldn't resist to take advantage.

Enjoying the jolts and jerks, he explored her pussy further. Giving her clit a break, his tongue teased her opening. She inhaled, holding her breath. He licked inside her, thrusting his velvety tongue in and out of her. Her moaning betrayed her, and he reached up to rub her clit once more using his thumb. Honey dripped as her body desired to keep him there.

He grew aggressive, making love to her in hunger as his tongue wiggled in her wet heat, unraveling her. The cries of passion escaping her drove something animalistic in him. He wanted to make her come. Wrapping his lips around her clit once more, he sucked and stroked inside her with his fingers.

"YES!" The visceral exclamation didn't make him slow, teeth teasing and fingers rubbing a new side in response. "OH! OH! FUCK YES!"

Zelda's orgasm peaked, her throbbing pussy gushing around his stroking fingers. Noc could care less about the wet sheets, wanting to see her body react to him more. His cock had begun to harden, and he towered over her, pushing his cock inside her. Groaning, he grinded in and out of her as she wailed. Hands released the headboard, clawing at his back as if desperate to keep him there. Moaning, the fire she invoked only made him grind harder, deeper.

I love how she touches my cock when she orgasms. I want to keep her going...

The way his torso waved against her, breasts keeping them tantalizingly close and apart all at once. Her screams faded into moans as she continued to cling to him, her knees rising to improve their connection. His arms flexed under his own weight, unwilling to stop looking at her face.

"I'm coming again..." she confessed.

"Then look at me," he beseeched, grunting as she tightened around his cock.

Noc's breath caught, mesmerized by her bright, blue irises glowing with a magic as he slowed each movement.

"Beautiful..." he searched her face. "Are you really mine and mine only?"

"Forever yours." She pulled him closer, locking lips.

Noc kissed her, hungry and passionate. He moaned as he began to peak, her tongue slipping into his own mouth wrestling for real estate in a fit of desire. To go this far and kiss for the first time. He pushed hard against her, releasing as she tightened. His arms dove under her, pulling her into him as they continued to kiss passionately. They rolled and he found himself under Zelda. Breaking their kiss, she sat up, straddling his waist. He grunted as she tightened on him.

As the orgasm dissipated, Noc could feel how exhausted his entire body had become, how every aching muscle begged for proper rest. He had never gone this hard and long with someone, but somehow, his inability to maintain the stamina pained him.

"Unfortunately, I'm spent," he relented.

"Oh no," she scrambled off him, his cock losing its stiffness. "You're deflating! Sh-should I blow you up?"

Her hands scoured his body, tickling him as she searched for his valve.

"No!" He grabbed her hands and pulled her back beside him. "How about you and I get some rest, and we'll give this a proper second round. Maybe try this out in a hot shower?"

Spooning her, he pulled the covers up. He nuzzled her neck, enjoying her natural, flowery scent.

"You can do this bathing?" she marveled.

He laughed. "Zelda, as long as you're willing, we'll try it in every humanly way possible."

"That sounds wonderful." She held his arms into her.

He started to doze off, but his anxiety kept him awake. His mind raced, and his earlier suspicions resurfaced, his beating heart haunting him.

At last, he forced himself to whisper his greatest fear. "Will you still be here when I wake up?" He swallowed, waiting for the reply.

"Of course," she replied, patting his hair.

"But will you still be..." he choked on the question and at last, pushed out the rest. "...still be you and not a... sex doll."

She sighed. "I will be whichever you prefer me to be."

His heart fluttered at the answer. "Then you stay as you are, no matter what."

"I'd like that very much, Noc." She laughed. "The Blue Fairy will be very pleased."

Another moment of silence lingered and at last, he thought to ask, "Who is the Blue Fairy?"

"Well, some people know her as Gina," replied Zelda. "Once she returns from vacation, she said she'll join us for a threesome."

Noc paled. "Join us?"

Son of a... I guess it's true.

Be careful what you wish for.

THE END

THE URBAN EROTICA
FAIRY TALE COLLECTION

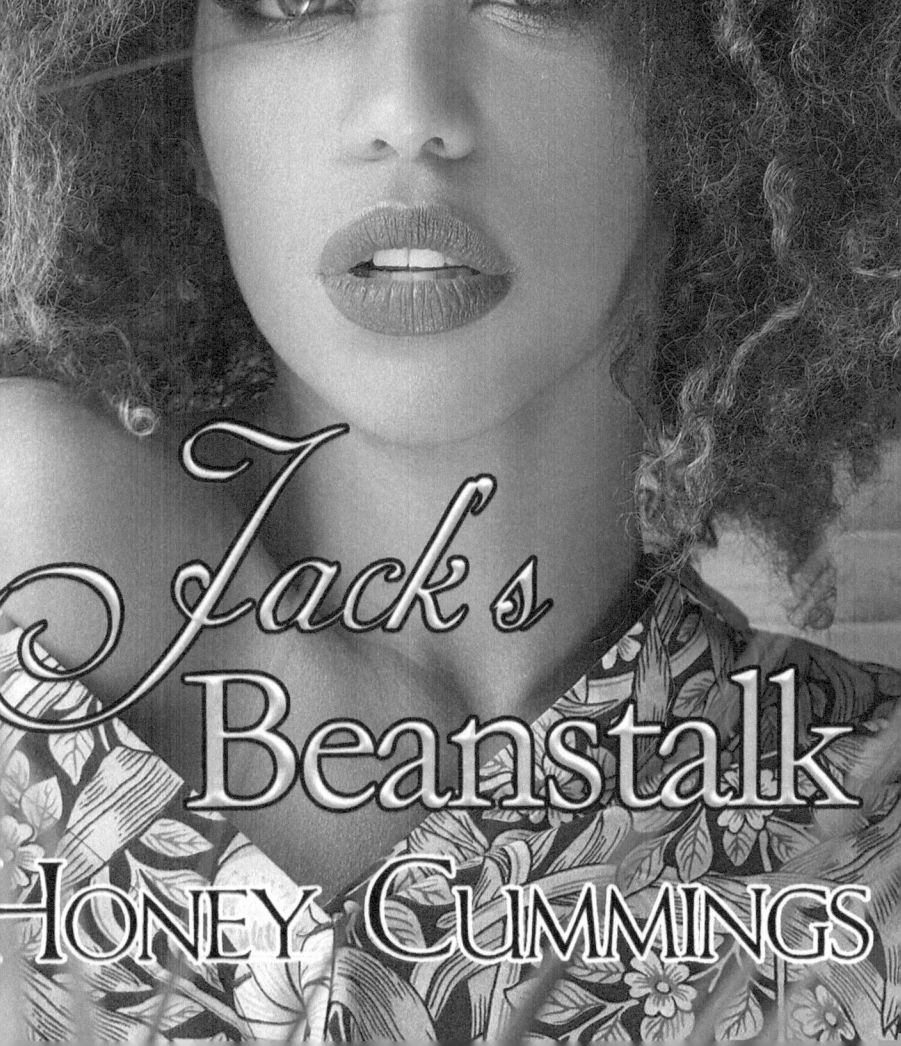

Jack's
Beanstalk

HONEY CUMMINGS

Dedication

To my personal friend Jenn
and her adventures in exotic bromeliads!

XOXO Honey Cummings

Table of Contents

1

Jack Spriggins

"What shall we do, what shall we do?"

K endall Warden adjusted her miniskirt once more before picking up her martini. Michael, an acquaintance from one of her father's firms, was playing bartender tonight. *At least the view is delightful. Even Axel is lurking about,* she laughed to herself before hunting for her best friend Pearl—the mastermind behind this party.

They had met in high school, and in adulthood, had become closer friends. Then, by some twist of fate, they managed to work together as client and contract lawyer. It made for fun nights in Costa Rica and Holland at elite plant shows as she locked down new customers to sell their exotic variants of bromeliads, while they partied and ate meals with the biggest names in the industry, never turning down a chance to have some fun in a darkened corner.

"Dammit," Pearl whined as she looked at a cherry stain on her white blouse. "And I was being so careful too."

Kendall giggled. "Why on earth would anyone in their right mind eat cherries in a white shirt?"

Pearl smirked, grabbing another from the bowl on the kitchen island before shrugging. "We both know I've never been in my right mind."

"Hey, at least you're at home and can change," Kendall offered before taking a sip of her martini. "Not like you have to drive or stumble upstairs."

"Oh, you're right!" Sucking on the cherry for a moment, Pearl said, "I'll change in a minute."

"Don't forget to lock your room or Axel might slip inside."

Pearl watched as Michael served another round of drinks to a few girls. "What can that man *not* do?"

"Hmm?" Kendall followed her stare. "You referring to the elusive Mister Michael?"

"Yeah, I mean, he's a beast as an advisor at the investor's firm, but..." Pearl sighed as if unsure of her own thoughts. "Where did he have the time to learn bartending? Every day I discover some new skillset that he's flawless at every time."

"I think his sister works as a part-time bartender at Red's. As far as I understood, something bad went down in their hometown, and he's been taking care of her ever since she moved in with him. She has a bad hip or something like that from a car accident." Kendall shrugged, adding her assessment. "He seems like a good guy and a smart man. Mmm... so much, man, you think he's stacked under all those clothes?"

"He's single, Kendall." Pearl laughed, spitting a cherry pit into her napkin.

Scoffing, Kendall took a silencing sip of her martini. *Yeah...but he has the hots for you, Pearl. For some time now, he's had that hungry look in his eyes. Even when I last spoke to him on the matter, he would do things his way and in time. Perhaps tonight might be the night, and he'll finally find a way to get your attention. If only you knew what was coming...I have been sworn to secrecy!*

"He's fair game," offered Pearl, raising a brow.

"He threw this party for you, Pearl," Kendall breathed before draining the last of her martini. "Something tells me he's aiming *elsewhere*."

"No way." Pearl rolled her eyes. "I mean, he's best friends with Axel, my friends-with-benefits."

"Like that would stop a guy. That just tells him you're single too and a horny bitch." Laughing, Kendall scanned the room and she scowled, "Oh no... speaking of horny and bitchy."

"What?" Pearl froze, her hand hovering over the cherry bowl. "I don't like it when you make that face."

"Who invited Professor Gaston?" Kendall whined.

Taking a cherry, Pearl whispered, "I did."

"Why?" exclaimed Kendall, her shoulders shuddering.

Sucking on the cherry in thought, she finally admitted, "He's great eye candy and fun to flirt with, though at times, a little too forward for my taste."

"He's always a little too forward." Kendall gave her a skeptical look.

Kendall looked back but dodged making eye contact with Gaston. *Shit, shit, shit! Someone else, look at someone else!* At that moment, Axel waved at her when she met his gaze, and she laughed, waving back. *Saved by the horny dork in the far corner. Thanks, Axel! I can always count on you for an infamous, awkward wave.*

"I can't believe you and Axel are each other's booty call." She glared over at Pearl. "Is he really any good? Or just easy access?"

"What? He has toys," Pearl defended. "He's definitely not relationship material, but I don't think he's actively looking so it's convenient. But I do like that collection he has..."

"Buy some for yourself!" fussed Kendall. "You must be the only woman I know who doesn't own a vibrator or a dildo. Considering you seem the type who likes having a man in control of the toy while he fu—"

"Shhh!" Pearl choked on her cherry. "Dammit, I accidentally swallowed."

"Sure, you *accidentally swallowed*." Kendal smirked, making Pearl flush.

They fell silent as a tall, dark man walked past them, folding out of view as he inspected the array of beers and drinks from the fridge before finally selecting a beer. They had been alone up until this moment, but the stranger's side glance he gave them made it clear of his intrigue of the gossiping girls in the kitchen.

Kendall arched an eyebrow, enjoying how his ass looked in his pants, shooting Pearl a look before lipping, *who is that?*

Pearl shrugged. *I blast-texted every number.* She motioned with her hand as if she sprinkled magic dust over the entire room.

You a horny-bitch, lipped Kendall. *All of them are on your phone? Really?*

Pearl shrugged. "So?"

They started sniggering as the stranger returned his attention to them. He was well over six feet tall, broad shouldered with a striking set of hazel eyes. He might as well been a model from a Ralph Lauren commercial. *Well-dressed and that cologne... I wouldn't mind taking him home or sneaking off for some quick fun.*

Kendall straightened herself, correcting her slouch. She flashed a big smile, *thank you, Lord, for my dark complexion, because I tend to blush more than Pearl in these kind of situations!*

"Good evening, ladies." His deep voice sent a shiver through Kendall. His smile wide, and the dip in his eyes as he appraised her sent an excited flash of heat through her. "So, birthday girl, who's your friend?" He offered his hand, and Kendall obliged as he kissed it. "I don't think we've met."

"My name's Kendall," she answered as heat rose to her face. *He's checking off all the boxes of who my dream man would be. If he escorts me to my car later, I'm in so much trouble.* "And you are?"

"JACK." Clearly, Pearl had been searching for his name as it left her lips, louder than intended.

Chuckling, he nodded. "Jack Spriggins. A pleasure to meet you, Kendall. So, do you work at the firm or are you a client of Pearl's?"

"Childhood friends," she offered.

"Well, I better go change out of this stained shirt," Pearl's voice trailed off as she disappeared through her bedroom door.

Kendall's eye widened, her cheeks puffing out as she glared at the door. *Pearl! Girl, you did me dirty! You almost didn't remember this man's name and now, you're hiding in your bedroom! Punk ass bitch... I see you.*

"Oh, I guess it's just the two of us. So, childhood friends, that's pretty awesome." He took a sip of his beer, his hazel eyes searching her face. "I don't think I've seen you around the firm before."

"Y-yeah." Kendall's nerves tightened. *Damn you, Pearl! I needed a wingman for just a bit longer!* "And I suppose you can also say we collaborate on important business trips. Um, so Jack, what do you do for a living? You work at the firm, then?"

He cringed. "Well, I did, until...I was part of that wave of layoffs last month."

"That sucks." Kendall tilted her head, curious at his transparent reply. "Sorry to hear that. How's the job hunt going?"

"Yeah, not so great. I haven't found anything promising, and it's looking like I might have to roll-up my sleeves and get my hands dirty." He shrugged, guzzling his beer a little harder as his charisma faltered.

"Dirty? How so?" He now had Kendall's attention. *What I wouldn't give for you to get dirty with me by the end of the night...*

"I don't like going too long without a steady income, so I usually grab a labor job in between the corporate ones." He thumbed the label on the beer bottle, their roles flipping as he became the nervous one. "Anyhow, Kendall, it was nice meeting you. Hopefully, we cross paths later." Without warning, he spun away, his face hidden from her as he added, "Bye."

"Wait—" With that, he was gone without another word. *Really? Self-rejecting before I had a say in the matter? Granted, I had planned to reject you when you mentioned you were laid off? Because, a jobless man comes with risks. But still...someone with a plan is another matter. Wonder what Michael thinks of—*

"Well, if it isn't Kendall!" Gaston's voice sent a harrowing shiver up her spine. "I haven't seen you since my Business Proposals course."

Inhaling deep, Kendall faced him and said flatly, "Professor Gaston. Imagine meeting you here. How's your girlfriend doing?" *Please tell me you have one so I can lower my guard. Weren't you chasing the English Literature Professor across the hall from you? Pray tell she folded to your advances.*

"No woman can tie this bull down," he announced.

FUCK. He's been rejected, I see. Can't say I blame her for saying hell no *to him.* Wincing, Kendall searched the room. *Michael's making drinks and has his back turned, Axel has a hand up some girl's skirt, Pearl must be taking a damn shower at this rate, the catering dude has already left to take a call on his cell, and...*

"There you are!" Jack's booming voice caught her by surprise, the heat of his hand soft against the small of her back. "I lost you for a moment there, baby. Didn't realize you were in a conversation with... mister? I'm sorry, have we met?"

Baby? Kendall looked up at her towering savior in awe. *Wait, had he noticed my panic, then circled back to save me? What a gentleman! Regained some points there, Mr. Tall-Dark-And-Handsome.*

"Professor Gaston, and you are?" Kendall tensed at the aggression in Gaston's voice, and Jack pulled her into him.

His two massive hands squeezed firm. The crushing exchange made the threads of his muscles flex in both forearms. Jack flashed a grin, and Gaston cleared his voice as if signaling their shift into the second round.

Kendall snorted before rolling her eyes. *Sometimes, I feel like I should take bets when shit like this goes down.*

"Jack Spriggins, Kendall's boyfriend," he announced with utter confidence.

Kendall's smile strained. She turned her head slow, eyebrows rising high. *What? Did he just... he just called himself...* Blinking, she puffed out her cheeks, her brow furrowing in disbelief. *My boyfriend?*

"Oh?" Gaston released the shake, then took a step back as if there were guidelines on how close he should be to a claimed woman. "Nice to meet you. I thought you came alone..."

Creeper! Did he watch me from the parking lot or something? "He had to work late..." Kendall shrugged and rubbed Jack's back. *Oh my, the muscles on this man's back! Does he workout with Axel and Michael? Either way, at least he was able to force Gaston to back off. I should remember to bring up my "boyfriend" if Gaston tries this again. Even if I still don't have one.*

"I rode in with Axel," Jack offered, his hand sliding to her hip. "But I suppose I'll have to play designated driver tonight if you continue to drink those martinis now, huh, honey?"

"Oh?" Kendall let her hand slip down his back until she could squeeze an ass cheek, making him choke on his beer. "How many martinis do you think I've had? I'm not here to get shitfaced, baby."

"I was hoping to have a little fun later." Jack winked, his eyes searching her face as he returned the gesture and goosed her.

Kendall yelped and covered her mouth. *He did not just pinch my ass!*

Gaston scoffed. "Well, you two lovebirds enjoy your evening. I see someone I need to say hello to."

He's leaving! YES! It worked!

2

Climbing the Beanstalk

"Two in each hand and one in my mouth"

K endall turned her attention back to Jack. *Well, I didn't take him for a smooth operator after his earlier defeat*, she marveled at his intuition.

Her hand glided back toward his back, his muscles hard underneath his shirt. Face hot with lustful thoughts, she admired the moment of authority he had taken with Gaston. Kendall's body buzzed with desire. *Maybe he'd be in the mood for a quick hookup at the very least... dammit, Pearl! You've corrupted me with all your 'let's have a little fun' on a whim.* Inhaling deep, Gaston was finally out of view, and she hadn't seen exactly where Jack had appeared from. *Regardless, I think he secured me immunity from Gaston for the night, if not for a while!*

Kendall hugged Jack, relief washing over her. "Thank you! You saved me!"

"Sorry, if I only knew leaving you alone would bring over the only shark in the room," he glanced over to the hall where Gaston had disappeared down and snorted. "I would've braved talking with you longer."

"No, no. I just…didn't want to entertain his forwardness tonight." She broke away, frowning at her empty martini glass. *Come on, Kendall. You can't start with, 'So you wanna? Wink, wink.'*

"Speaking of forwardness." He lifted an eyebrow, giving her a smug expression. "I wasn't expecting you to rub up on me like that, then squeeze my ass."

Biting her lip, it was her turn to dip her eyes up and down to devour the view. "Well, I can't say I didn't find you attractive too, Mr. Spriggins."

"Is that so, Ms. Kendall," he mimicked. "Do you need an escort to your car? He might try to follow you there too."

Kendall placed the glass down. *I've only had three drinks tonight, but it might just be enough liquid courage. Before I leave, I want a taste of what this man has to offer. Show me your world, Jack. Are you willing to trade a cow for some magic beans tonight? This hot mama's hoping that by the time we make it to the…* "Yes. Walk me to my car." She grabbed the beer from his hand, setting it on the counter, then pulled him behind her.

"Hey, I at least wanted to finish that." He let her tug him down the hall, passing the leering Gaston and out the door. "Are you that worked up over the professor?"

"You can say that" Kendall snorted. "But it's not Gaston that has me flustered." She winked up at Jack as she pressed the elevator button.

"Is that so?" Jack's grin widened, briefly looking away before meeting her gaze again. "Are you leading me into a dark corner somewhere to play?"

Kendall shrugged, feigning shy. "Maybe…"

The elevator opened. No one but them slipped inside as the doors closed. As it began descending ten floors toward level 2 parking, she wasted no time. *I want him now, not later.* Fisting his shirt, she tugged his lips to hers, bending Jack to her will. He followed her lead, opening the gates just as her tongue entered the hot crevasse. She moaned as his heated hands glided to her ass cheeks, squeezing tight, pressing her into his body.

He backed her into the corner of the elevator. The numbers counting down behind them as she sucked on his tongue. Her breasts pressed against the hard planes of his torso. Arousal waved between them, their hands exploring one another in an unapologetic aggressiveness.

She slipped her thigh between his legs, his hardon unmistakable under the now taut pants.

He moaned pressing it against her leg and—

"Please, no sex on the elevator," screeched the unseen security guard through the intercom, cutting the laugh short.

Pulling apart, Jack cleared his throat as she straightened her miniskirt.

"Shit," muttered Kendall.

"Does that happen often?" Jack rubbed the back of his neck, staring toward the elevator camera.

"Dammit, Jay! Why you gotta ruin my fun," flustered Kendall as the elevator dinged and the doors opened.

"Love you too, Kendall!" The security guard laughed as the intercom crackled.

Kendall flipped a middle finger at the camera and stormed out. Jack rushed to catch up to her. She couldn't decide if the heat in her face was from her arousal or embarrassment. *How could I forget the fucking camera! This must be the third time now that they've caught me making out, hot and heavy.*

"You know the security guards?" Jack walked parallel with her, following her through the columns of yellow lights.

"They make themselves known." She laughed. "And it doesn't help that I've him down at least twice in the last year or so. Something about a man in uniform driving a golf cart reminds me of a mall cop doesn't exactly do it for me."

"I see." Jack nodded, hmphing to himself. "So, where's your car?"

"Over here next to..." The lights of her Jetta blinked as Kendall hit her unlock button. "...Gaston. Dammit. I should have known." *I must've been in such a rush, I didn't see that creeper watching me from his car.* "I got an idea, if you're into it."

"Well, I'm really into you at this very moment," retorted Jack.

"Fuck me on his car," she blurted, tugging him by his shirt, pulling it free from his pants.

"Wait..." Jack looked at her car, then at the one she was scooting atop the hood. "The Mercedes? You want me to fuck you atop... Gaston's Mercedes?"

"That's right, my Jolly Green Giant." Her feet left the ground as she pulled him against the car. "Fuck me on his car, right here, right now."

"We just met..." Jack's voice broke into a panic. "What about the car alarm?"

"I bet his alarm settings are set so low you can pound me until we make this bitch rock." She slipped her miniskirt up her thighs until her pink, lacey underwear caught his gaze. "Besides, I came to the party hoping for a quick hook up... and after that rescue, I want to show you my gratitude."

Judging by his facial expression, he's never done something like this before, even though he secretly wants to. This is your chance, Jack! Show me some grit!

Jack covered his mouth, his face visibly thinking as he peered across the parking lot. His cock still strained against his pants, and Kendall wanted to see exactly how much of that bulge was length versus girth. She unfastened the first button of her blouse, then the next, bringing his attention back to her. A matching pink-lace bra poised her amble breast, while her dark nipples peeked between the lacey gaps.

As her shirt laid open, a sound escaped him as if his favorite meal had been set before him.

"I'd like to see you after tonight," he confessed.

"Then when we're done here, give me your number..." She reached for her bra's front latch. *This damn bra's uncomfortable as hell, but the easy access in the heat of the moment is well worth it!*

Her plump breasts lay exposed in the cool air, erecting her nipples. Jack closed the gap, groping the pillow of soft flesh, carefully pinching each nipple. His lips pressed hard against hers. She could feel his hard cock underneath the fabric as he grinded against her pussy. Having his body between her knees made her ache as his hands fell away.

The heat of hands slid up her thighs as she deepened the kiss.

His cock jumped where it pressed into her.

I want you so bad. Give me more...

She lashed out, coaxing his tongue to explore her mouth only to suckle it instead. Arousal waved through them; her breasts pressed hard against his chest as their hearts raced one another. His fingers rubbed against her opening, her panties leaving nothing to the imagination. He rubbed hard and aggressive until she moaned into his mouth. Once more, she pulled him against her, relishing the fire building between them.

Her lacy panties soaked in the rising excitement, her pussy throbbing with want.

Jack broke the kiss as his fingers shoved her panties aside, slipping two fingers inside. She shivered with pleasure, exhilarated by the heat of his breath against her neck. The soft warmth of his lips added to the slow thrusting of his fingers. He burnt his way across her collarbone, travelling in rhythm to his stroking. Kendall's skin pimpled, her imagination painting scenes of how those same lips would feel on her more sensitive places.

"Are you sure about this?" he whispered into her ear in a silky voice, and she inhaled swift. "I've got a condom if you're serious about this."

"Yes..." She moaned as his fingers stroked in and out, gaining speed. "Quick... before Gaston arrives..." She bit her lips, muffling a shriek of ecstasy as he rubbed her in all the right places. "Before I come..."

At last, Jack pulled away, unfastening his pants. She could... *Holy beanstalk!*

She blinked her eyes several times. *Is his long, girthy cock real or some part of my phantom erotic dream.*

He unfurled a Pasante Super King-sized condom over the tallest erection she had ever seen in person. Pulling her from the car, he flipped her around. She yelped as her breast pressed into the Mercedes' cool, metal hood. Fingers tugged her underwear down and rubbed her already dripping, wet pussy. She was on her tippy toes as he pressed the tip of his monstrous cock against her, then slowly sliding it inside, gauging how far he could go.

"Oh..." breathed Kendall, his cock filling her.

She hummed with each pull as it retreated, then slowly reentered, each one gaining more depth than the last. Her legs shook, bringing her chills of pleasure with each rotation. Panting against the hood, she watched his reflection, his intense focus on its waxed surface as he watched himself slide in and out, making her tighten. His head tilted, fighting the overwhelming pleasure rushing through him.

Jack's fingers gripped her hips, his cock throbbing deep inside her. "I'll start slow, but we have to be fast before someone sees us."

This time, he completely slid his length out before pushing back in.

Kendall moaned, her pussy squeezing around him. "Don't be slow. You feel fucking amazing."

He laughed. "As tight as you keep squeezing me, I won't last much longer, baby."

"You said make it quick." She pushed herself into an arch like a cat stretching in the sun, forcing his cock to slide in deeper as she pressed her ass against his waist. "Fuck me, Jack."

He arched an eyebrow. "No one's ever climbed my beanstalk so eagerly before."

"Stop. You're ruining the moment with that cheesy line." She laughed. "Just give me what we both want, big daddy."

"As you wish..."

The heavy panting soon turned into moaning and humming as he continued to push in and out, hard and fast. His huge cock filled her and rubbed into places she never knew existed. The spot she often reached with only her toys were being rubbed by his huge dick. She could feel the rig of his cap and... *I will peak hard at this...* She bit her lip, eye clenched shut as she came. *Yes! YES!* His cock was hard as a rock now, and in a few more strokes, he pushed hard into her with his own moan.

Breathless, they froze, still throbbing from their peaking orgasms. Then a ding from the elevator echoed through parking garage, ending their ecstasy.

"SHIT." Jack pulled out of her, making her gasp before tossing the condom onto the ground between the cars. "Well, uh, I guess..."

"Thank you, Jack," Gaston's voice echoed through the garage, sending Kendall to shove pass Jack and slide into the driver side of her car. "I'll get your number from Pearl!"

"W-wait." Jack rushed to zip up his pants, marveling over the breast-prints reflecting off the Mercedes' black hood. "My number... She doesn't..."

Kendall was backing out of the parking spot when he saw Gaston in the distance, making out with a girl at the elevators. "Well, shit. Guess I better go before he notices me."

Kendall glanced at the awkward wave in her rearview. *SHIT! I should have gotten his number before.* She wiggled in her seat. *Oh, God, I am still riding out the orgasm that man gave me, and I want more. Pearl, you better have his number!*

3

It's Getting Hot in Here

"What have you done with my golden hen?"

The air conditioning had completely stopped... *again.*

She glared toward the overhead vent in her tiny office with disdain. Kendall had fought the owners over budget cuts and forcing the damned, outdated piece of equipment to last for another year. Frowning to herself, she thought, *it wouldn't be so bad if my office wasn't connected to a fucking greenhouse!*

Standing up, she stretched and shuddered as a droplet of sweat snaked down her spine. Unbuttoning her work polo, she sighed, wishing there were more than three measly slots at the top. She marched out of her office and into the greenhouse's stifling, humid heat. Travelling down the length of the main lane was the only way to reach the owner's office where a brand-new air conditioner had been installed two years prior. Stopping at the door, she inhaled deep, securing her commanding aura in place. Cracking her neck, she at last banged on the door like someone from a SWAT team before a raid.

It swung open and her father grinned. "Why, Kendall, what brings you to this side of the greenhouse?"

"Well, Da..." She cleared her throat. *Keep it business. This isn't Dad, this is one of the owners.* "Mr. Warden," she corrected. "The air conditioner is done for."

Despite his reflective reading glasses obscuring his eyes, she knew he'd dodge the issue. *Again.* "I see... I'll tell you what..."

Kendall crossed her arms, waiting for the distraction or excuse he'd cook up this time.

"I'll get with Bo Smith and see what he can do about this."

She snorted. "I'd rather see an air conditioner man hunched over that outside unit, handing you an estimate to replace that archaic thing. It's been here longer than I've walked this earth, and I'm not exaggerating."

He nodded, spinning them around to walk the humid greenhouse again. "I understand," he assured her. "In that case, could you give the new guy the grand tour and make sure he completes all that HR stuff? He starts today."

And there's the distraction. Granted, he'd rather deal with a new air conditioner than train anyone for anything around here. Kendall narrowed her eyes, her voice flat and agitated at best. "And who did you hire to do *what* exactly?"

"J... J... Jay Spudnik?" He winced. "It's a J-name. Anyhow, he'll help us rework the heating and cooling computer systems. Some sort of software engineer that isn't afraid to get his hands dirty. Real nice guy, tall as hell. This way, we figured you and the rest of the staff wouldn't have to rush out here in the middle of the night during a cold snap anymore. Dealing with the heaters or closing and opening the vents in the middle of the night is a pain. I'm too old for that."

And why do I question his intent on this? Goosebumps rolled across her skin. *And my gut is screaming. Something's off about this...*

"I thought you said you were hot?" Her father chuckled, and she rolled her eyes. "Just kidding, Kendall. I'm serious. Old Frances across the building had already railed me on the failing AC system. Bo and I will get you, office girls, squared away. Promise. Just, do me this favor and train the new guy by starting him on those HR videos."

"Fine." At last, she unfolded her arms. "When does he arrive?"

"Now. He's already waiting in Frances' office." He stopped midway through the greenhouse, waving her on.

Rolling her eyes once more, she muttered remarks about her father's levels of procrastination he had mastered. She opened Frances' office and closed her eyes. The blast of heat radiating from the open door was stifling. *The greenhouse feels cooler!*

"Fran, would you like me to prop open the door?" she called out, searching the ground for the door stopper.

"At first I didn't want to." The elderly woman's voice sounded exasperated. "But I can't work like this. Especially if the open door gets my papers soggy. But that blast of cool air says I'll cook in this oven of an office if I don't."

"I can give you a dehumidifier to lower the humidity level, but it's hotter than the greenhouse in here, honey." She spotted the doorstop between the wall and filing cabinet. "Dammit I'll have to get on all fours to reach that." Dropping down, she stretched her fingertips, barely grazing her target.

"I can move it." Jack's voice sent her heart racing. *Oh no, the hot beanstalk man from a few months ago. It can't be.* Her fingers clawed it closer, and she gripped it.

"I g-got it." She stood, keeping her back faced him. *SHIT! This can't be happening!*

He cleared his throat, admitting in a low, confident voice, "Wasn't that the same position you were in the last time I saw you? Pearl wouldn't give me your number, but this almost seems like... fate."

Her heated face surged with a rising tide of anger and embarrassment. "She should have." Spinning with renewed confidence, she slapped the doorstop in his hand. "Prop open the door while I grab the dehumidifier, Jack."

"Ah, so you do remember my name after all, Kendall." The goofy grin and the glint in his eyes said he intended to pick up exactly where they'd left off.

"And to be fair, she said she couldn't find your number," she confessed.

"That's because she doesn't have my number," he called after her.

Kendall's heart pounded hard. *This will be interesting.* Pulling a humidifier from the janitor's closet, she shoved it into Frances' office. Her mind racing, memories of their rushed, steamy session atop Gaston's Mercedes boiled to the surface. She hadn't been satisfied; she had wanted more... *dammit, I even went home and...*

He grabbed the humidifier and lugged it into his arms with a wink. The bulge of his biceps in his short sleeve sent her body ablaze with want.

What the hell am I going to do? Do I pick up where we left off? Not the fucking part, but do I want a relationship with him? I barely know him... Come on, girl. Let's be real. You let this man bend you over a Mercedes. At this point, all formalities are out the window, aren't they?

She waited at the door, listening to how he politely addressed the old woman, and without any direction, had her setup in no time. Jack returned to the doorway, flashing a handsome smile that could make any girl swoon at how tall and thick he'd looked. *I wonder what he looks completely undressed...*

Shit. My mind's will be stuck in the gutter all damn day.

"I didn't realize you were in the plant business," he started, rubbing the back of his neck as she stared up at him.

Oh, how I imagined those lips on my...

"Breasts. I mean, Bromeliads," she clarified. "We travel all over the world for shows and conventions in fact."

He smirked, trying to remain professional as he replied, "Yeah, Mr. Warden had said you have greenhouses all over the place, including Costa Rica, right?" His flirtatious tone had fully faded now. He was talking business this time.

Thank you! BUSINESS. THINK BUSINESS, ME!

"There, and partners in Holland." She motioned for him to follow. "You already met Fran, the accounts manager. Janey, the scheduler and secretary, is on vacation and their assistant is Sammy. She's either at lunch or on PTO. The four of us work on this side of the greenhouse. The owners, Mr. Warden and Mr. Smith, have offices on the other end. As for the bathrooms, there are two here, but we keep the left one locked. Over here is my office. I'm the Sales Manager and further down, are the other sales representatives. Halfway down is the breakroom, the Greenhouse Manger's office, and the server room..." He followed her in silence, looking at everything she pointed to with a stern expression. "...that'll be your office. Though I have no idea what state it's in after they fired Greg."

"Fired?" Jack asked, curiosity riding on his voice. "What did he do?"

"Lied to the owners. Said he was actively reprogramming the fan vents parameters, only to discover he had no power flowing into his office for an entire *three* days."

"Wow." He hissed, gritting his teeth before prying further. "And how did you figure that out?"

Kendall smirked, shrugging. "Maybe someone flipped the breaker, wondering how long it would take for the lazy ass to figure it out. I suspect he was watching YouTube on his cell or sleeping the hours away."

"But how was he clocking in and out?" Jack followed her into her office, the heat of the room startling. "Holy smokes."

"Yeah, hold on." Walking toward the window, she lifted the blinds to reveal a window unit and plugged it in, turning it on. "It will take some time for it to catch up. I should've turned it on before I marched down there..."

"Why don't you keep it plugged in?" Sweat beaded on his forehead as he whistled, fanning himself.

She pointed at the overhead vent and drawled, "Because *this* is supposed to cool the room."

"Oh," he said, reaching up. "It's actually blowing hot air. Want me to close it?"

"Yeah, then come sit." She motioned to her chair and desk. "I'll get you started on the mandatory human resource videos. Then we'll see what state your office is in. Be warned, it may be just as hot. Let's pray the AC man gets here today and replaces that ancient unit."

She leaned over him, both of them hot and sweaty as she clicked on the computer. In the screen's reflection, she saw his eyes lock with her cleavage hovering over his shoulder. A grin curled her lips. *Yeah, it seems we both were unhappy with how that night ended. Fate, you say? Maybe...* She reached down and grabbed his hand, placing it on the mouse. Flashes of how he gripped her breasts and hips made her pussy throb.

They locked eyes.

Jack's body stiffened as he froze. She could tell he was feeling the same reaction. Kendall's body moved before she knew what she'd done.

Her lips pressed hard against his. Strong arms wrapped around her as he deepened the kiss. Their tongues licked at one another until he suckled on hers, making promises as to what else he would suck if given a chance. Her body buzzed with arousal. The chair squeaked as she leaned harder into him, shattering her desire.

She flew back a few long strides, covering her mouth. "I'm sorry, I don't know what came over me..." She lowered her eyes toward the ground, afraid to see the expression on his face. *SHIT.*

Jack laughed, and at last, offered, "Will you at least take my number this time?"

"Y-yes." She grabbed her cell phone and keys from the desk. "Give it to me now. Jack... Spriggins, right?"

He sighed, grinning from ear to ear. "Yeah, 321-555-1234. That's my cell phone. Maybe after work we could… have dinner or grab a drink?"

"Y-yes. If you—"

"We will be covering Sexual Harrass—" The video had finally loaded and started to play.

"Wow," he marveled, rolling closer to pause it. "Is the internet really that slow here?"

"Yeah, but I suspect he didn't run the wires right." She shrugged, making her way toward the door. *I can't be in the same room or this man or I might find myself bending over my desk this time!* "Um, I need to take care of some things. This should keep you busy for at least a good hour or so."

"Usually how this goes." By the smirk on his face, she knew he found her nervous body language adorable. "I'll text you if I need you, then?"

"Y-yeah." She spun on her heels. "Just text me."

She was out the door, breathing easier as it shut behind her. Eyeing the locked bathroom, she glanced down at her keys. *So glad I thought to grab these.* Looking around, no one seemed to be working this afternoon. *Shit, that's right. It's New Year's Eve. Most of them already asked for PTO or already heading home at any moment. Dammit, dad! This is why you ditched the new employee training on me! SO YOU COULD LEAVE EARLY!*

Gripping the keys tight, she marched toward the locked bathroom and slipped inside. She stared at herself in the mirror, flipping on the fluorescent lights. Heated desire filled her thoughts, making her body ache. *I can't walk out of here until I've blown off this steam.* Opening a drawer, there sat a purple vibrator, still hooked to the charger. Her greatest secret revealed. When in need of releasing her work stress and frustration, she'd slip inside the recently renovated bathroom and pleasure herself.

No one ever questioned why she kept it under lock and key. *One of the few perks of being the owner's daughter.*

"Well, little buddy... with Jack working here, you might be seeing a lot more action than what either of us signed up for." She reached into the shirt pocket, searching for her golden pen but found it empty. "Huh, must have left that on my desk."

4

Avoiding the Giant

"There you are again with your fee-fi-fo-fum."

K endall double-checked the locks and froze. Outside, she could hear Jack's voice and... *crap! It's dad!*

"Where's Kendall?" Mr. Warden chuckled to himself. "Well, I guess the air—"

Kendall dropped the vibrator into the drawer and slammed it shut before rushing out of the bathroom. Jack and Mr. Warden jumped, wide-eyed.

She narrowed her eyes at her father, crossing her arms with murderous intent. "What about the air conditioner?" Kendall gave a deep growl.

"I was going to say," started Mr. Warden, dodging her gaze. "They'll be here tomorrow." He turned his attention to Jack and said, "How's your training coming along?"

Jack rubbed his neck, shooting a confused glance at Kendall. "Well, I'm almost done with all the HR formalities. Kendall already gave me the grand tour, and I look forward to seeing what I can do about this shotty internet connection. I've had to refresh a few times, so it's a tad bit agonizing, to be honest."

Mr. Warden's eyes widened, his voice filled with excitement as he said, "You can fix the internet?"

"Maybe." Jack laughed. "Judging by the looks of the IT room, it will need a wire or two replaced."

"Please. I'd like to make an order for my clients without having to double checking whether it disconnect midway or not." Kendall unfolded her arms, her abrasive demeanor fading. "I figured you'd leave with the rest of the staff."

"Well, I came to say bye," confessed Mr. Warden. "And your mother wanted to know if you were still coming over to watch fireworks by the lake?"

Shit! I wanted to go out with...

"Ah, father and daughter," Jack interjected. "I was trying to figure out if you two were related and how but I was too shy to ask and come off as rude."

Mr. Warden chuckled, throwing an arm over Kendall's shoulders. "We do our best to remain professional here at Firebird Nurseries. So proud of my baby girl. She used to be a greenhouse laborer and worked her way up to Sales Manager."

"Proud indeed." Jack smirked at her as she brushed her dad's arms off. "Well, go home, old man, and let me finish training Jack."

"Fine, fine..." Mr. Warden waved her off.

They watched him leave, an awkward silence filling the air.

Jack and her briefly exchanged glares before he said at last, "I guess I should finish that video. But before that... I'll take a look at the wires real fast in IT room, is that ok?"

"Uh, sure. If you think you can fix it, that would be great." The buzz of arousal blossomed through her again, her thoughts reverting back to the drawer and the purple prize awaiting her. "I'm going to... uh..." She pointed and reached for the door. "Just heard

Dad and know how slimy he can be... back to what I was about to do... I guess..."

"R-right." Pivoting, he marched down the hall, while she escaped into the bathroom once more.

Crap! He's gotta be feeling just as aroused as I am. That look in his eyes... I'm melting in my panties! She settled into position atop the pristine closed toilet, pants and panties abandoned on the floor. Dripping lube on the purple vibrator, she held the button and it buzzed in her hand.

Spreading her legs, she let her mind slip back to the Mercedes, the kiss in the office, and... *If only he'd fuck me in my office, but the walls are too thin for the pounding I want.*

First, she slid the vibrating tip over her clit, back and forth across her opening, the sensation enlightening. The tension in her shoulders started to fade as she began to relax and enjoy the release she aimed for. After a few teasing glides, the vibrator ran slick with lube and her own rising wetness as the tip rubbed against her swelling clit from her building orgasm. Her sensitive nipples became erect, pressing through her bra and shirt, adding to the desires racing through her mind.

Oh, how I wanted to feel him lick my pussy...

Her breathing quickened, her heart racing. She slid the purple appendage downward, pressing and threatening to enter her slick folds. *Oh, how girthy he felt knocking at the door, so slow and...* Shifting her position, she wanted to open further in anticipation for penetrating herself over and—

Bling!

She ignored her phone, the text notification ringing out. Closing her eyes again—

Bling! Bling!

Clenching her eyes shut, she pushed the vibrator inside, slow as the buzzing made her pussy tighten against the soft—

Bling! Bli-Bling!

Closing her thighs, cheeks puffed out, she shuffled in her pant pockets for her phone. "I swear, this better be an emergency…"

[Jack: You coming out of the bathroom any time this week?]

Kendall's face heated. *Dammit, I'm taking my time, but I thought he'd be stuck with slow internet…*

[Kendall: I thought you were playing with wires? Don't you have a video to finish?]

[Jack: Internet is out. There's a rat nest in the box. Like *literally* a rat and his collection of candy bar wrappers in there, but I don't know what to do.]

[Kendall: Ask Fran.] She settled back into place.

[Jack: She's gone.]

[Kendall: Yeah, they have a half day today. I imagine it's just us now.]

She settled back into place, the vibrator still buzzing where she held it between her legs, making her body heat as it excited her pussy.

[Jack: I can't stop thinking about you.]

Licking her lips, she opened her thighs and returned to teasing her clit. She slid her thumb over the touchscreen. *I wonder what the chances are that he'd be willing to entertain the idea of this…*

[Kendall: I can't lie. I've been thinking about that night…]

[Jack: Oh yeah? I wasn't done but you left in a hurry. Shame you don't have a lock on your office door. We should fix that.]

[Kendall: That's why the bathroom has one and I've got the only key.]

There was a long pause. Pushing the button to increase the vibrations, she circled her clit more aggressively, stronger until she could feel herself creep closer to an orgasm.

[Jack: Tell me what you're doing. Right now. I'm agonizing not being able to kiss you again.]

[Kendall: Playing with myself while I think of you.]

Another long pause and she grinned. He was being cautious, and it only made her bite her lip in anticipation. *What will you with that knowledge, hmm? Mr. Jack? Will you play with me? Are you jealous I can touch myself and you can't?*

[Jack: I would trail kisses down that gorgeous body and suck on your nipples until you beg me to stop.]

[Kendall: Show me that monster beanstalk again, Jack. I want to climb your one-eyed giant again.]

[Jack: *Dick pic.*]

She inhaled, slowly sliding the vibrator into her pussy. The image was fresh, the terrazzo flooring and her desk in the background. He was hard just thinking about her touching herself. Just like her, he was thinking about fucking her all over again. She thrusted the vibrator in and out, eyes on the hardened cock she had dreamed about having inside her once more.

[Jack: I want to see how wet you get as you think of me.]

Swallowing, she pulled the vibrator out, shutting it off and placing it atop the vanity. Adjusting once more, her fingers spread her folds and after a few attempts, she managed to take a selfie, revealing the state of her swollen, dripping clit.

[Kendall: *Pussy pic.* I can't stop touching myself. I want you.]

His paused reply made her grin. Her finger circled her pink jewel, her legs shaking with the rise of her incoming orgasm. She scrolled back to his cock, a rush of arousal waving through her. In a flash, she was bent over the hood of Gaston's Mercedes once more. Jack's rock-hard dick sliding inside her, jumping and throbbing in response to her own pussy tightening.

[Jack: Send more pics. Show me those lips, those breasts, those fingers dipping in places I want to be in right now.]

She inhaled swift. The words resonated as her pleasure buzzed through her.

[Kendall: *Pic of her biting her lips.* Talk dirty to me.]

[Jack: I want to feel those lips wrapped around my cock, feel that dirty tongue wiggling underneath my dick.]

[Kendall: *A single breast and erect nipple.*]

[Jack: I want to suckle those titties and play with your pussy.]

[Kendall: *Closeup of her fingers dipping into her pussy.*]

[Jack: I want to bend you over and pound you until you beg me to stop.]

[Kendall: You are terrible at this.]

[Jack: Yeah, sexting is not my strong suit.]

Knock-knock-knock!

Kendall straightened, staring at the door in alarm.

[Jack: Fee-fi-fo-fum... may I come in and join?]

She laughed. *Be careful what you wish for.*

[Kendall: As long as the giant promises to gobble me up.]

The door opened and shut fast; the lock flipped with a loud *clack.*

Crap, I forgot to lock it earlier!

"I've been waiting to get you alone after work but..." He smirked at her provocative position, spread-eagle atop the toilet seat as her phone hit the floor. "...it seems you couldn't wait that much longer either."

5

Begging for More

"Be he alive or be he dead, I'll grind his bones to make my bread."

A chill snaked up Kendall's spine. She jerked up, standing in alarm. In a blink of an eye, her sexting session shifted into a secret office rendezvous. *This is a first...* The way her heart raced, pounding loud and fierce, her chest aching.

Jack flicked his eyebrows high, his grin ever growing on his face. Tugging at the buttons on his shirt, she followed his fingers as they filleted his shirt open, revealing the muscles she had felt months before. Kendall couldn't contain her smirk as they raced downward where his pants were already unbuckled, tightening around his hardening cock.

She scoffed. "It seems someone else couldn't wait either," she said as he unzipped, and his dick stood erect, free from his pants.

"Come here." His voice was deep and soft all at once, commanding her as she dared to close the gap.

If this goes as wild as last time... The heat of his torso underneath her hands added to the fiery passion she could no longer deny. *I've never felt chemistry this hot and hungry for anyone before.*

Jack cupped her jaw and pressed his lips firmly against hers. The kiss was slow, teasing, and loving. His lips parted, and she dipped her tongue between as a sacrifice to give her more. Hot hands moved to hold her hostage against him. His hard cock throbbed between them. *He wants me now, but he's taking it slow, unlike last time. Yes, show me this other side... give me the time I denied you...*

"Show me what I missed out that night," she dared him, her voice sultry as he began to kiss her neck.

Jack stayed silent as he worshipped her body with his lips. Removing her polo shirt, he shed his own as she abandoned her bra at last. His hands gripped her hips, guiding her between him and the vanity before sitting her on top. A halo of lights crowned her head as she leaned back to take him all in as his pants fell to the floor. The icy mirror against her back wasn't the reason for her shivers and moans. His hungry, hazel eyes told her where he wanted to go next. So she parted her thighs, giving him full access to everything her body wanted to offer him.

Closing her eyes, she wanted to savor every touch. Hands glided up her thighs, teasingly close as they slid up her torso and cupped her breast. The heat of his breath against her pussy made her tense with anticipation. With a twist of her nipples, the hands retreated the way they had traveled. Squeezing her thighs, he pushed them wider. His silken tongue ran across her opening, hot and wet. She inhaled swift, the sensation exhilarating. He moaned as he licked slow and intentional, the tip of his tongue circling her clit once or twice before repeating the pattern that made her legs twitch.

Kendall arched her back and reached down. She held him into her, returning his moaning with her own. Her legs jittered with the oncoming orgasm that teetered on the edge as he continued eating. His tongue thrusted deep into her, wiggling as her fingers clawed the back of his head. *So hot, so soft... I'm so wet, and he just laps me up with such greed.*

"Don't stop," she breathed, shifting the tilt of her hip to give him a better angle. "So... so close..."

He licked upward, playing and rubbing her swollen jewel as if needing to be taste at every angle. Again, her legs shook. Hands rode over her torso to grope her breasts firm. Kendall's breath caught. Lips wrapped tight around her clit, sucking hard and long, ringing the devil's doorbell.

She abandoned his head, throwing her arm over her mouth to muffle her squeal. *I can't be too loud, just in case...*

A harder suckle, and she raised her knees. Her teeth bit into her arm, back arching. Two fingers slid inside, thrusting, and she peaked instantly for him. He didn't stop. Lips surrounding the swollen pearl of flesh, her pussy tightened on his thrusting fingers, the sound of her wetness filling the room.

Jack's moaning added to her peaking orgasm. Kendall's body tensed, folding forward. With a pop, he released her clit and kissed her. She could taste herself on his tongue as he kept thrusting in and out of her.

Yes! YES! This man has the golden touch!

He rose up before her, his erection hard and veiny. His fingers left her, but the tip of his cock pressed against her throbbing pussy. She wrapped her legs around him, pulling him into her as they touched foreheads, pushing him inside her pulsing pussy. His body waved, grinding into her, the muscles in his torso tensing and relaxing as he banged her slow and rhythmic. *Oh, how I wanted another ride on this monster cock!*

They stared into each others' eyes, seeing each other's pleasure.

"Shit, condom," Kendall panicked, lost in the heat of the moment.

"I already took care of it while I was enjoying my appetizer." His arms wrapped around her, pulling her further away from the vanity ledge.

The counter began to wobble, threatening to break away from the wall. Jack spun them around, carrying Kendall until her back hit the opposite wall. She could see over his shoulder, his bare back and his tight ass in the mirror where she had sat seconds before. The way his muscles waved, tensing and loosening in a way that, was hypnotic to watch in the reflection.

He gripped her knee, raising her leg higher so he could grind deeper into her pussy. She moaned, and he began kissing her neck once more. Her entire body heated, buzzing with another rising orgasm. His cock throbbed, hardening with each thrust as her pussy tightened in response.

At last, Jack panted, "I'm about to come."

She begged, "Please, a little longer."

He pulled out, shrinking before her as he brought her leg over his shoulder. His arm glided across her torso, groping her breast. Once more the silken heat of his tongue ran across her pussy. Her breath caught. Finger dove between her swollen folds as his lips wrapped around her pink pearl. *So sensitive!* It was driving her wild as she clawed at his shoulders. Kendall couldn't decide if she wanted to fight him off or allow him more access. *He's driving me wild!*

Again, the tip of his tongue ran across her opening, from where his fingers stroked against her swollen clit.

"Don't stop," she breathed. "So close..."

Another orgasm began to build. She pushed against his hand, grinding to deepen his fingering. Her pussy tightens around them. His other fingers tightly pinch her nipple. Picking up pace, Jack suckles hard and long on her clit. Her clawing hands rack across his back and shoulders, abandoning their fight to keep him away and encouraging him to continue.

Covering her mouth, she screams into her palm. Her knees shake with her orgasm as it comes, hard and fast.

Flawlessly, Jack abandons his play and pushes his hard cock back inside her. She arches her back, no longer worried about containing her scream as he moans. He quickens his pounding, in and out, in and out, so hard and fast. Jack's arms wrapped around her, pulling her into him as he begins to suckle her breast.

Her entire body vibrates with pleasure unlike anything she's ever experienced before.

"Yes! Oh fuck yes!" she cried out.

"You're so tight when you come..." he panted between each thrust. "Fucking come for me one more time... I'm so close."

"Don't stop, don't stop..." she breathed, clawing him into her.

Lips hot around her nipple, he teases her with his teeth, and she screamed, visceral and wild. Her orgasm peaks further than its predecessors. He gripped her leg hard, his moaning loud as he pressed himself deeper into her, their bodies tense and tight against each other. Their shared throbbing made their pleasurable higher and linger.

Minutes pass, both frozen and afraid to move in their sensitive state.

At last, his gaze meets hers and he grins wide. "You still want to have dinner?" he teased.

"How about you join me at my parents? Fireworks and free food," she offered.

"Only if we're going steady," he countered.

Laughing, she covered her face. "Yes, Jack. I suppose I can't say no after fucking you twice."

"Good, I guess I can return your golden pen."

Kendall made a bewildered face. "Why did you take my pen?"

"Well, I needed an excuse to come see you again and took it while we were kissing." He laughs, explaining, "Don't you know the story, *Jack and the Beanstalk*? He was a thief after all..."

THE END

Pulling Rapunzel's Hair

Honey Cummings

Table of Contents

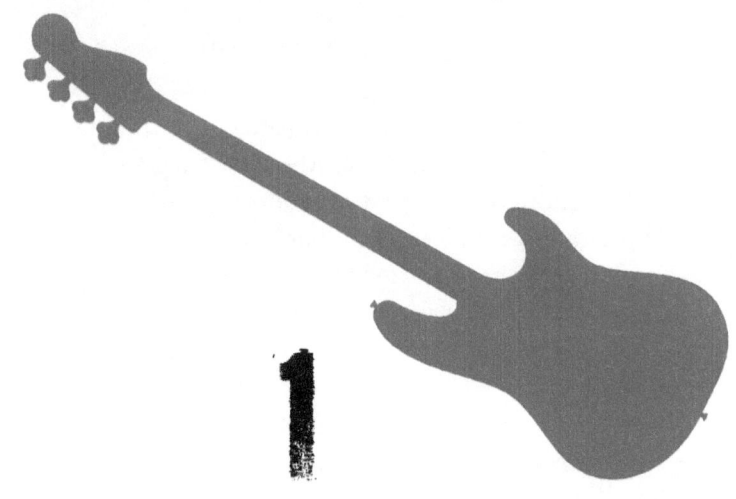

Rapunzel, Rapunzel

Rapunzel Ramone brushed a bleach-blonde-and-purple dread behind her shoulder before leaning back into her bass to continue tuning the instrument. *Red's Tavern* was still quiet, though the locals were coming in more steadily as Friday afternoon shifted into the evening hours. Being a freelance musician, she didn't belong to a particular band and rather enjoyed cherry-picking her nights and music as she saw fit. Tonight, she would be playing with a cover band that would satisfy her itch to play some classic rock for a change.

And maybe I can hook up with an outrider afterward.

Glancing up, some college undergrads with goofy grins settled at a front table, and she rolled her eyes.

Not them. They can barely grow enough chin hair to shave each week. I need a manly man, someone who knows how to treat a girl and spoil her twice over. Enjoy the view, boys, because this is as close as you're getting to me.

They all loved to come and gawk at the curvy, tattoo-covered vixen who plucked on a bass. Tonight, she wore a thin tank top that did nothing to hide her purple bra, Edgar Allan Poe themed hand-sleeves, a plaid schoolgirl skirt with a studded black belt, fishnet thigh-high stockings with a hole over one knee, and black leather boots.

A smirk came to her face as she twisted the tuning peg. *Yup, every man's wet dream, complete with dreads–that's me. Granted, I'm only scantily dressed because the cam lights bake the fuck out of me on this damn stage. Wonder when Red will take Bob's advice and get them changed out or add a minisplit air conditioner to blow down cool air. A tanning bed is more forgiving than these tiny bastards.*

"Rapunzel, right?" The deep rumbling voice sent a chill up her spine as she turned to the lead singer, Jasper Holden. "You're my stand-in bassist tonight?"

"Yeah, Red called me and said you guys were in a pinch." Rapunzel stood, slung her bass behind her, and exchanged a firm handshake. *Shit, my hand feels tiny in his. He could be a stunt double for Bradley Cooper. Damn.*

The lead singer had an amazing voice; she had seen them play once before, and Rapunzel couldn't wait to hear if he continued to impress or if she was just too drunk to care that night. He stood at about 5'10", a few inches taller than her even with her boots on. He wore an old Metallica shirt three times too big with the arms and sides cut open and scruffy jeans to complete the old rock-n-roll bad boy ensemble.

That shirt swamps him; he looks like a kid wearing his big bro's shirt. Ha!

Jasper ogled her from head to toe before arching a brow. "They didn't tell me they were getting me a gorgeous punk-rock-princess in place of old Bob."

"Old Bob?" Rapunzel gave a sheepish grin. "As in Bob Pinkerton?"

"Yeah, you know Bob?" he marveled.

"He's taught me everything I know. Is he okay?" It was hard to tell if her heart was racing from Jasper or the idea that something could have happened to her precious mentor. "He's not in the hospital, is he?"

"Oh no, no, nothing like that." Jasper's face flushed, and he rubbed the back of his neck. "He's in Florida on vacation, and well, honestly, we completely forgot we needed a bassist for the next two weeks."

"Rather dangerous," she snorted, enjoying the red in his cheeks as his hazel eyes darted away in shame. "Two weeks, huh? Hope this is the only gig."

"Well, that's my next question for you." He inhaled deeply and puffed his cheeks out a moment as the bar grew noisy and guests claimed the last few tables. "We've got a few more shows until he gets back, and we were wondering if you're available…"

Rapunzel put her hands on her hips and pressed, "But you haven't even heard me play."

"Look, anyone taught by Bob must be pretty good." His eyes shot to the neck of her bass. The five o'clock shadow on his chin made his jawline more prominent and her heart raced. "And I can tell you know how to tune and play. A hobbyist doesn't drop the cash for a pink and gold Ibanez like that because they can. You only do that when you can play, show it off, and earn the money back fast and hard."

She bit her lip in thought and with a wide grin offered, "Okay, Jasper. If you like my playing tonight, and," Jasper met her gaze on the pause and she continued, "I have a good time tonight, I'll consider it."

He narrowed his eyes at her, sucking on his cheek before agreeing. "Okay. I can do that. Definitely will make sure you have a good time tonight no matter what."

"Promise?" She winked and slung her bass back into her hands, plucking a riff from *Seven Nation Army*. "I'm hard to please."

"I might surprise you, your Majesty." Winking back at her, he spun to the mic and switched it on. "Are you ready to get this show poppin' tonight?"

The bar roared and whistled with their drinks raised high, lights brightened on the stage, and the audience faded into darkness. Rapunzel glanced back to see the drummer ripping through his set to get more out of the patrons. The lead guitarist jumped in, and she was hot on their heels, earning a '*damn girl*' expression from Jasper. His grin widened and again her heart fluttered as his deep voice rolled across the room over the speakers.

At least Red's has great acoustics—Rapunzel's thoughts halted as Jasper began singing "Pour Some Sugar on Me" by Def Leppard. *Holy shit, the man can sing! Being on stage, I can hear it sans-mic and… oh, I think I'm going to wet my panties.*

Shooting a look across the bar, Red locked eyes with her and lipped, *He can sing!*

The guitar and drums thumped through the speakers; the volume of the music vibrated through her lungs, getting her blood pumping and adrenaline climbing. She stomped across the stage, bouncing to the beat of the song as the bar began to clap. The lead guitar ripped through the solo, adding a bit of creative flair to it and bringing a smile to her face. Jasper's part followed and he spun to her, leaning in as he began the next chorus.

"*You got the peaches, I got the cream…*"

Rapunzel's face reddened as those bright hazel eyes caught her gaze. His smirk widened, and she spun to lean into him. The bar whistled as Rapunzel wiggled her ass and dipped down before they broke apart.

A chill of arousal tingled up her spine. *That was too thick to be the microphone wire. Holy shit! Someone is quick to reply to that little hip shake.*

The song ended and he called the next set back to them, "Kickstart My Heart."

Shit, going hard and heavy with old school metal! I'm digging this... Motley Crüe, here I come!

Again, the bar began popping, singing along, but Jasper's voice rose above the cacophony of nostalgic drunks. The music brought more and more patrons into the club as the last strips of daylight stopped flashing through the opening door. A whole gang of bikers stood at the pool tables, too distracted to play a full round.

This man is worthy of being a siren with the way he catches everyone's attention! Even Tex is enjoying himself.

Rapunzel and Jasper could feel the reaction of the audience enjoying their shenanigans. The game of tit-for-tat from playful body rubs and ever-braver gropes between them seemed to fill the air with a sexual charge.

"...a lady with a body from outer space."

Van Halen's "Runnin' with the Devil" slowed the room down and gave everyone a moment to catch a breath. Rapunzel's heart thudded in her chest, fingers and arms aching from the tension of playing hard. Sweat trickled down the divot of her back. Looking at Jasper, as sweat dripped from his chin and locks of hair plastered to his forehead, made Rapunzel's heart skip a beat.

I wonder if he sweats that much while—what the hell am I thinking? What a horny harlot I am tonight! But really, do I dare sleep with the lead singer? How cliché... She watched as he sang to the audience and paced on stage. *Well, it's not a habit, and he's singing and working the stage as good as any pro...*

Rapunzel blushed as Jasper continued serenading her in his rock-metal ballad. The last time she had lost herself to this kind of music had to be when she went to see *KISS* live. Each stolen glance was clueing her in on key lyrics.

"Got nobody waiting at home…"

Laughing, Rapunzel was picking up on exactly what Jasper was doing, or in this case, messaging to her. *This crazy man is picking songs to let me know he wants to hook up, isn't he? All this eye-fucking and rubbing on each other. Clever man. Can't deny it's sort of hot!* The song shifted, and he took a swig of his water by the drummer before returning to the stage.

"How we doing tonight?"

The crowd roared, a few folks dropping cash in the tip jar on the stage's edge. "Keep bringing those tips, and we'll keep bringing the jams. One more song and we're gonna take a break to cool down." Jasper turned back to the band and whispered, "Princess of the Dawn." He licked his teeth and winked at Rapunzel.

Goosebumps rolled across Rapunzel's skin. *I haven't played this song since practicing with Bob. Not just anyone knows this fantasy-fueled memento of old school metal.*

The band played it slower, and she skillfully adjusted. *He's challenging my skills.* She locked eyes and his leg bounced in the slower tone as the riff started, the build exciting and agonizing. *I love this song…* Jasper sang the first line, deep and haunting unlike any version she'd heard before. He had made the song his, and now his rough, thunderous voice made her weak in the knees.

"…her kiss is bittersweet…"

Rapunzel leaned into him once more, his cock hard under the shirt and jeans, pressing against her ass cheeks. Her breath caught, fingers threatening to fumble on the neck of her bass guitar. An arm snaked between her and the bass, pulling her into the hard planes hidden under his clothes. Jasper took the heat up another level, grinding gently against her, promising what he'd rather be doing at this moment before turning away as the song ended. Rapunzel watched him leave with hungry eyes as she dropped her stare. Jasper's shirt was too long for anyone to see what she had firmly felt.

Exactly how big and worked up did you get on stage grinding on me?

The drummer and lead guitarist ended the last notes, and the race between Rapunzel unstrapping her bass and Jasper sliding the microphone into the stand began. Her hair caught the neck of her bass, and she muttered every curse trying to untangle it. The bar erupted into a roar of voices, laughter and the clinking of glasses commenced the intermission.

Jasper had disappeared.

Shit. I was hoping for some intermission fun, but...

2

Let Down Your Hair To Me

Flustered and heart racing, she squinted at the crowd. Through the surge of people placing tips and song suggestions in the glass jar or rushing the bar for drinks, she couldn't see where Jasper had disappeared. The lead guitarist blocked her way off stage, insisting he shake her hand. Shaking her head—she hadn't heard the words he said to her—she gave a haphazard smile.

"I'm sorry." She pointed to her ears. "Say that again—I didn't hear you."

"I said," he inhaled deeply and projected his words to her, "that was great playing!"

She laughed, shaking his hand firmer. "I appreciate that. Granted, I have to say, you guys work well together, and that makes it easier to fall in line."

"I'd dare to say that you're better than Bob!" His eyebrows rose high, his voice deep and throaty like Sam Elliot; he could pass for his younger brother. "The name's Chad. Please tell me you'll be joining us for the next few shows until the old coot comes back from his vacation."

"Ah, you know, Jasper was trying to convince me of that too…" Her voice trailed off as she looked through the crowd for the lead singer. "Speaking of which, where did he go?"

Chad, being so tall, peered over her and shrugged. "Not sure. Getting a drink, out back for fresh air, or might be taking a piss."

Of course. What else is there to do in a bar between sets? Rapunzel snorted. "Th-thanks. Well, we'll see how the whole band feels about my skills by the end of the night, if I can keep up with a rowdy group of boys like you all."

He scoffed, chortling. "You give me too much credit. We don't get shit-faced like in our green years. Not into the groupies, no energy to keep up with them."

Smirking, Rapunzel teased, "Then you should tell that to old Bob."

"Bob has a sex drive like no other," guffawed Chad. "One day he might find a gal that can keep up. I still can't believe he hosted an orgy at his place a while back."

"I'm pretty sure he's at a nude resort or beach at this very moment!" Laughing, Rapunzel patted Chad's arm and slipped past him off the stage.

Again, she spun around looking for Jasper only to find her view blocked by a wall of college undergrads. *These gawkers from the front table, ugh!* She frowned, recognizing them as the crew who had whistled and heckled her during the first set. Taking a step to cut through an opening, she found it closed quickly. *Shit! Not this again…*

"Hey good lookin'," cooed the backward cap undergrad. "We were wondering what you were doing after the show."

"Um, look boys, I appreciate the playful banter, but I'm working—"

They all took a closer step to her, and she became very aware that she was cornered. She was stuck in a dark nook, too far to shout to the stage; the only escape was the men's restroom behind her.

Time to initiate the "mom voice" to see if I can push these jackals off. I am not in the mood for this bullshit tonight.

Clearing her throat, she shifted to a stiffer pose and raised her voice. "Look, I'm working. I'm not here to pick up a date."

"So, after you're off work, you're coming to hang out with us, right?" offered the pock-faced friend.

"No," Rapunzel's voice carried a stern chill to it. "I'm not going anywhere with you three."

Another step forward forced her to bump her back against the men's door, making it open slightly. *Dammit, every man I trust in this place is out of shouting range and pisses out in the parking lot like a dog.* Her hand gripped the door's edge, keeping it from closing. *If this gets bad, I am not against locking myself in the shitter and shrieking like a banshee.*

"Oh c'mon," he whined, making a pouty face. "Look, we'll buy you drinks, and we got a whole liquor cabinet at the house, baby doll."

"Don't call me that," she replied flatly.

"Guys, this is going too f—" They shoved the third friend who shot her a pitiful expression.

Rapunzel cocked her head. "Look, you're making me uncomfortable. Back up and get out of my way."

"Say please," the pock-faced undergrad licked his lips, eyes dipping provocatively before whispering to her, "Or we can save the begging for when I'm behind you—"

"HEY!" Chad's booming voice made everyone jolt, and the third grad walked away from the stage.

Oh shit, their friend saved me!

"WHAT THE FUCK YOU TWO DOING WITH MY BASS PLAYER?"

Thank you, Chad, for—

A hand gripped her wrist, pulling here into the men's bathroom. The door shut hard behind her. The force of the thud took. A hand reached behind her and flipped the lock. The man had her pinned between him and the door, her arms above her head as he leaned in over her to listen. Looking up, she saw Jasper staring down at her, his brow furrowed with worry. Blinking a few times, Rapunzel's heart skipped a beat.

I feel like I just stole a moment with my high school crush. Am I really into him this much?

"You okay?" he murmured down to her.

"Now I am." She shrugged. *I want to ask him to back away, but some part of me is enjoying how close we are... wait...* "Have you been in here the whole time?"

He pulled away, freeing her. "Y-yeah." His face flushed red before he spun his back to her. "I uh..."

Rapunzel gave a sheepish expression, able to see his face in the mirror. *He's embarrassed... did he... no... it couldn't be?* "Did you come in here to..."

His eyes met hers in the mirror, widening as he bit his lip.

"...unload?" Now she was beaming at the idea, recalling how hard he felt rubbing against her on the stage. "You know, clear the pipes so-to-speak?"

Jasper cringed, closing an eye before confessing, "I can't exactly control that I'm very attracted to you, and well, the body knows what it wants before I do."

"I can't lie..." Rapunzel walked to the vanity and pulled herself onto it, legs swinging. "It was turning me on too. Not that I make a habit of sleeping with band members either."

"Look, I don't want you to think I'm that douchebag who has to go around sleeping with the female band members or fucking groupies in the back alley." He seemed on the defense, marching into the single stall and flushing the toilet, making her snicker. "So, yeah, I'm not that type either so… I didn't mean to go too far on stage…"

She scoffed. "I didn't say you were."

Jasper leaned on the stall door, his lips twisted as he looked her over. "Enough about my cock—what was happening out there?"

"College dirtbags." Again, she shrugged but looked away with a sense of insecurity. "I was handling it."

He snorted, walking closer, his finger gentle under her chin to lift her eyes to his. "It's okay to scream if you want. That's more than enough to spook anyone who aims to do you harm."

"The only screaming I want to do," Rapunzel's voice came out in a sultry tone as she gripped Jasper's shirt, tugging his ear to her lips, "is when I get you all alone to myself."

His hand rode up her legs, snaking under her skirt, as he cooed, "In that case, we're all alone right now." Hot lips began to blaze a trail down her neck and shoulder. "I might have ruined my chances for some fun…" Jasper squeezed her thigh before rubbing her underwear and teasing her pussy through the thin fabric. "…but I don't see why I can't make you feel better."

Rapunzel moaned, "You're a tease."

"Maybe." His finger pushed the fabric to the side, sliding between the folds and making her gasp. "Have I mentioned I'm really good with my fingers?" Slick with her wetness, they slid back up to her swollen clit and she inhaled swiftly. "Aren't we worked up?"

"I told you, I—" She struggled to get the words out as her knees squeezed tight on his hips where he stood. "Dammit that feels… so good." Her body arched and Jasper began kissing at her neck as she whimpered. "So close…" she huffed.

"You going to cum for me? Hmm?" His voice rumbled low as his finger slid down again and dipped inside her, stroking slow as her pussy squeezed tight around him. "Cum for me, baby."

"Oh, oh so close… don't stop," she panted, gripping the edge of the counter.

Jasper pulled his finger over the span and once more began circling her pink jewel. Rapunzel's legs shook with the rising pleasure. Her hands white-knuckled, she clung to her perch. Her breath caught, and he slowed the motion, making her moan.

"You know you want to cum." The heat of his breath washed over her neck, adding to her arousal. "I want to make you cum. Are you going to let me make you cum?"

Rapunzel's heart fluttered, the dirty talk adding to the erotic moment, something she hadn't experienced before. "Y-yes…" It was hard to talk as she tried to relax, to allow herself and her body to indulge in his touch. "I want to cum for you."

He nuzzled her neck and sucked on it. She tilted her hips, and he dipped his fingers inside a few more times, stroking her. Moaning, she rocked against the motion of his hand. The fingers retreated and a more aggressive onslaught with two fingers made her yelp.

"So close…" she whimpered, eyes shut tight as she teetered on the edge, the sensation agonizing. "I want to cum for you…"

Jasper nibbled at her neck and began to moan like he too would cum. "Come for me, baby."

"Y-yes… just… a little…"

The orgasm hit her hard, and she kicked and bucked.

A swift inhale and jolt of her body made him change course. Fingers stroked hard and fast, making her squeal in ecstasy. As his stroking slowed, she came back to earth and looked him in the eyes.

"I've never cum like that before." Heartbeat racing, she panted from the mountainous release he had brought her with his fingers.

Chuckling, he pulled away to start washing his hands. "Well, that's only the appetizer. We keep running around on stage like that, and you might need to give me a hand next break someplace more private."

"I think I can return the favor." She slid off and took a moment to find her legs again. "Give me a moment before we sneak out."

I can't believe I've got baby deer legs from him playing with me like that. Wonder how well he can work that massive single digit he's hiding in his pants...

3

A King's Son

Jasper peeked out of the bathroom door first, waving her out as she darted for the bar. All she could think is how desperately she needed a drink. *I can't believe we just did that. I've never had a man finger me until I came like that, and when he moaned on my neck...* A shudder shook her as her skin dimpled. *So, fucking hot.* Red was quick to open a bottle of Yuengling and slide it to her.

"You okay?" Red raised an eyebrow. "You look a little ... flushed."

"Just overheating some..." Taking down half the bottle, her lips popped, and she inhaled as if coming up to the surface for air. "Hey, next break, can uh, can I use your office to talk business with Jasper?"

"Business or pleasure?" Red leaned on the bar, watching as Rapunzel's face reddened. "Darling, if that energy on stage is just the tip of the iceberg, I say kudos and feel free to unload next break... literally." With a wink, Red rushed to help another customer.

Best wing man ever.

Downing the last half of her liquid courage, she headed for the stage as the band started to settle back into position. Chad gave her a nod and pointed with his chin. The table where the college dirtbags had sat was now occupied by some giggling housewives having a girls' night out.

Phew, I guess the bouncer Peter sent those assholes packing! They were cackling loudly, whistling at Jasper, and gobbling him up with their hungry eyes. Another look, and Rapunzel shuddered. *Isn't this just replacing one form of harassment with another? And who will save Jasper if Grandma's harlot crew corner him by the bathroom?*

Jasper stiffened his posture, giving her a large span to walk by, as if he'd decided to give her bigger boundaries. *No, don't do that! I'm totally into you. Forget about Granny and the old farts! I will not let them squash what I have going on—what happened in that bathroom was amazing!*

The energy Jasper had started with drained from him with each cat call as if he was afraid to release any form of sexual attraction in the gapping jowls of the harpies in the front row. When he stumbled on a lyric, Rapunzel shot him a bewildered look. That's when she saw it, the same look she had on her face in the first set at one point and decided it was time to act.

I can't watch this farce go on any longer. Who knew some retirees could make Mr. So-bold-I-just-jerked-myself-and-her-off-in-a-public-bathroom cower on stage! He saved me, so time to save him!

She sidestepped in front of Jasper to block his line of sight to the table of feral cougars, leaning back into him like they had done during the first set. His entire body, tense and hard as a wall, took a moment to react to the way she slid up and down him. The onlookers whistled as Rapunzel wiggled her ass into him, the familiar rise in his pants egging her on as he pulled her into him. *That's it. He's starting to relax and focus on me now.* Together they dipped down, earning another wave of cheers as he sang the lyrics with newfound vigor, and she shouted into the mic with him.

"Shook me all night long!"

And now the whole bar was shouting along with them.

Chad leaned into the solo, and Rapunzel marched up to him, her dreads swaying to the beat as she plucked to mirror him. Jasper leaned into the mic stand, getting his groove back. He shot a look her way, grinning wide. Rapunzel laughed, shaking her head as she focused on the riffs and returned to her spot on stage.

There we go. Got him back on track!

The song ended and he spun to the little table by the drummer, guzzled down a bottle of water, and poured the last bit over his head. The cam lights overhead rained heat down on them, and there were more songs to choose from. He dipped into the jar of slips, looking over a few before nodding his head at one in particular and dropping the unchosen back into the fray.

He flashed the paper to the crew, then to Rapunzel: "Unskinny Bop" by Poison. Reaching out, Rapunzel gripped his wrist and pulled him close enough to whisper in private.

"Hey, I don't know this one," she whispered in earnest.

"You've got a good ear. The bass in this one is basic. I mean, you know one Poison song, you've played them all." He leaned into her ear. "The lyrics may remind you of our fun in the bathroom."

Pushing him back, she laughed, face red. "Fine, but if I play like shit, it's your fault."

"A price I will gladly pay!" The music began and he locked eyes with her, singing the provocative lyrics with a playful smirk on his face.

Rapunzel took a few stumbles until she finally caught a signal in the drums to aid her. Chad shook his head approvingly, impressed how the fumbling was hidden from untrained ears. Jasper was back to teasing and grinding her from behind.

How the hell no one see this giant cock in his pants under that baggy shirt is beyond me!

The whole bar was jamming, and after a few more songs, they were glad to hit the next break. Sweat dripped from Jasper's chin, and she set her bass down, leaning it on the back wall. They were all breathless and glad to escape the stage's heat lamps.

Glancing at the audience, she flinched. The flock of harpies were coming for the stage exit, or rather, coming for Jasper. Rapunzel, startled, half-ran to catch up with her precious lead singer. Gripping his wrist, she pulled on him and found herself jerked backward, unable to budge or lead him anywhere. He gave her a baffled expression as he stood like an anchor.

"Where are you taking me?" he mused with a sparkle in his eyes.

She glanced over his shoulder at the old cougars stalking ever closer. "I'm trying to save you…" Clearing her throat and giving him a serious, low-brow expression. "Let's go talk about my pay in the office. You owe me for this last-minute request."

"The office … about the request?" Catching the licking lips of one of the grannies, he let her pull him through the crowd. "Yes!" He was shoving her forward now, talking loudly. "Let's go discuss payment." He smirked, chortling. "I owe you more than one night's worth of payments, don't I?"

"Damn straight you do." She pulled him through the office door, slamming it shut.

Now she found herself locking the door and pinning him there. *Wow, talk about a complete gender role flip from the last break session.* Granted, she was so small it seemed goofy and awkward. On the other side, they could hear the older women bickering amongst themselves.

"Dammit, Ethel," screeched the Harpy. "You spooked him!"

"I just wanted to give him a nickel for his pickle," hissed the cougar.

Patting Jasper's chest, Rapunzel smirked. "You totally owe me."

"I'll gladly owe you whatever you want if you keep pulling me out of danger like that." He leaned down, kissing her deeply as their tongues met before breaking away to add, "I kind of like being the damsel in distress."

"Stop." She turned away from him, but he pulled her back and wrapped his arms around her as his hands started wandering. "About that payment…"

I guess we'll be using the office for pleasure after all.

4

He Could Have No Peace

Jasper's hand slid under her shirt, shoving her bra up so he could squeeze her breast. Rapunzel moaned, leaning into him where he teasingly grinded against her. He nuzzled and kissed her neck and shoulder, humming into her as his cock grew harder. His other hand glided downward, dipped beneath her skirt, and trailed downward until his finger graced her swollen clit. She inhaled as he began circling her jewel.

"I love the way you moan," his voice rumbled low into her ear.

Another gasp escaped her lips as Jasper pinched her nipple. His cock throbbed under his jeans against her. *He's so big, it sends shivers through me.* The heat of his body added to the arousal building at her core; the desire whispering in her mind: *Yes, touch me more, talk dirty to me with that sexy voice, and tease me with that...*

Fingers slid across her pussy, teasing that they might enter her at any moment. She spun around, her hands pulling him into her, clawing at his back to ensnare him. Rapunzel's body ran hot with passion. *I've never been so hungry for a man to fuck me.* Her fingers relaxed, gliding over the hard planes of Jasper's back and up across his shoulders until they tangled in his wet locks. Cold droplets shook loose and fell down on her skin. Dimples waved over her like ripples on a serene lake.

Teeth nibbled her ear, and she whimpered, "Talk dirty to me."

"Oh?" He snorted, the heat of it making her shudder in pleasure. "You're going to have to beg me for it."

"Please." She tilted her hip, and he coyly pulled away, still leaning in to nibble on her ear. "I want…"

Fingers teased the opening of her pussy, wet with anticipation. "You want me to dive into the deep end already, hmm?"

"Y-yes." With two fingers, he slid slow and agonizingly into her heat, and she arched into him.

"Have you been a good girl, Rapunzel?" A hard twist of her nipple and she gasped; her thighs squeezed against his hips as he pushed her onto the desk. "Hmm? Have you been a good girl? I'm waiting…"

"Oh…" Jasper started stroking in and out, slow as her pussy tightened around his digits. "I've been… b-been…"

"You've been what?" He mused before licking across her shoulder and up her neck. He whispered, "Tell me, have you been naughty or nice, Rapunzel?"

She tried to rock her hips to deepen his stroking, but he wouldn't lose the agonizing speed and depth, making her crave for more, for *rougher.* "I've been good!" she blurted at last.

Snickering, Jasper began picking up speed as his silken words blessed her ears. "What do you want for being such a good, good girl, hmm?"

"To be…" Another gasp took the words from her as his hand slid to her other breast to pinch the erect nipple. "I want… fuck…" She moaned as his wrist twisted and began rubbing her pussy in a new direction, her legs shaking with the slow rise of an orgasm. "I want… t-t-to be…"

"To be?" he cooed, pulling away from her as he began to open his pants. "Come on, I'm giving you a moment to catch your breath and tell me what you want so badly."

Rapunzel's heart pounded through her like a thousand horses racing with no end in sight. *I just melt when this man touches me and whispers in my ear… holy smokes, where has he been all my life!*

Swallowing, she willed herself to speak her desires. "I want to be naughty. I mean…" She spread her legs wider, her own fingers dipping between her folds. "I want you inside me."

Without Jasper so close, hidden away in her neck and dreads, his face turned red. As his zipper slid to rock-bottom, his cock stood at attention, the tip swollen and dripping from his own agonizing excitement. Biting her lips, Rapunzel slid off the desk and knelt before him, still playing with herself.

I owe him from last session, don't I?

A moan escaped him as her silken tongue ran hot across the underbelly of his cock. Through heavily lidded eyes, Jasper peered down at Rapunzel, meeting her gaze. Her plump lips cupped the tip of his cock where her tongue began circling. A shudder rattled through him, the erotic pleasure peaking as he watched her fingering herself as she pulled his length into her mouth.

"I'm doing everything I can to be a good boy." He now bit his bottom lip, his gaze never breaking.

She rocked back, her lips popping as they released his cock. "Oh? And what would we do if we were being a bad boy?"

He paused, searching her face a moment as she ran her tongue up and down his hardened length. "Grab you by the hair and fuck that dirty little mouth until I cum," he confessed, face flashing red. "But I don't think—"

"Do it," she dared him with a provocative tone as her tongue circled once more before pleading, "Teach me a lesson. Make me sing, bad boy."

He looked away, sucking on his cheek. A smirk crept on his face as his eyes came back to her in time for her to suck his dick back into her mouth. Her tongue wiggled and slid underneath, the suction pulling him deeper until the tip pressed firm against the back of her throat. Groaning, he reached down and gripped her ponytail, pulling Rapunzel's hair until she almost came off his cock. She smiled, tongue wagging up at him, before he slammed her forward and deeper onto him.

Her breasts jiggled as he repeated the motion a few times, occasionally allowing her to catch her breath. The heat of her panting rolled over his dick and added to how he teetered on the edge of cumming. Pressing back between her lips, she resisted slightly, eyes on his and smirking with rebellion. That look of indulgence, knowing that at any given moment she could take his pleasure away, excited him.

She moaned, her hands diving between her thighs as he fucked her mouth. Panting, he watched as her legs shook. She screamed but was muffled by his cock as her orgasm peaked. Pressing deep into her throat, he inhaled swiftly and moaned as he released. Tilting his head back, he grinded into her throat until his cock at last finished.

Hands pulled him back between plump lips; Rapunzel wasn't done with this blowjob just yet. *They're always super sensitive after they cum, so if I...*

He let go of her hair to steady himself on the desk. Hungry, she suckled, pulling, and pushing herself in and out on his dick. Jasper covered his mouth with the other hand, eyes rolling back with the wave of pleasure it brought. A grunt escaped him as he forcibly came again, leaving him aching.

She stood, giving him some hearty slaps on the shoulder before chuckling. "That's my thank you for what you did in the bathroom earlier."

"Oh?" His brows rose as he stood, riding out the wave of his own orgasm. "I don't think anyone has forced me to keep going after... well..." He lost his words as she licked her lips and shimmied off her panties. "What are you doing?"

"They're soaked." She chucked them in the trash can. "It's uncomfortable to wear wet panties, don't you agree?"

"I, uh," Clearing his throat, he stood straight and tucked himself away. "I suppose I can't argue with that. But are you sure you want to be on stage sans-panties like that?"

Spinning back, Rapunzel cupped his face and smiled. "You're assuming I haven't done that before. Cute." Patting his cheek, she giggled and opened the office door, adding with a wink, "I'll think over the payment, but I might need a little more. Let's bang out the details after this last set."

Definitely need to bang it out after the show. Standing tall, she strode out confidently, fluttering on the adrenaline of their secret moment. Another beer washed down his salty flavor, and they were back under the heat of the cam lights.

5

The Ladder into the Tower

The old hags at the front table had left. The bar was thinning out as people led by designated drivers stumbled toward the door. Now, the front door was propped open to let the cool night air in, and a flicker of headlights signaled another Guber driver or ride had come for its passenger. Jasper met her gaze, face flushing, before turning back to what remained of their audience.

"Last set for the night, folks. Be sure to tip the waitress and lovely owner, Red, there in the back. Closing time will be upon us shortly." Jasper held up a whiskey on the rocks, and a few regulars whistled and held up their drinks in turn. "So last call for alcohol for those thirsty or still needing some liquid courage!"

He took it down, shoulders shuddering as he placed it next to a fresh bottle of water on the stage table. Diving into the fishbowl of requests, he rifled through them. Chad started plucking the *Jeopardy* theme and Rapunzel joined in. At last, he glanced at the paper and flashed it at the rest of the crew, "Thunderstruck."

As they began the famous opening, the audience joined in, humming along with the band. They banged on the tables and stomped their feet to add to the thunderous beat of *THUN-DER;* everyone shouted the words in all their excitement. The entire bar was all smiles as Jasper pitched his voice high enough to capture the song in all its glory.

"No help from you!" he sang, pointing at her, and everyone whistled.

The lyrics flew, adding to the expressions and tit-for-tat that unfolded. *Damn, dude. You need to get more blowjobs if this is how it unfolds on stage!*

He wobbled his knees, shaking them, and she turned away trying to keep her laughter from hitting the mic. Jasper pulled her back in time to announce the chorus more. At first, she shook her head in denial before nodding in agreement, and he let out a hissing, *"Yeah."*

Everyone sang loud and clear. The next song continued at the same level, closing the night with a strong set of old school rock and classics no one could resist joining. The energy popping through the place was like a grand finale of a firework display. They were down to the last two songs before the amazing night would be at its end.

Who knew tonight would be so incredible, so sexy...?

This time Jasper made the first move, a knee sliding between her thighs from behind. He lifted slightly, and she grinded her pussy against it and stiffened, leaning back into him. She bit her lip and lowered her brow at him but only got a knowing wink before he pulled away. Again, he surprised her that with each time he came near her, he could make her pulse flutter.

I want him to bend me over and fuck me on stage at this rate.

The songs began to wind down, but Jasper's moves grew bolder, and they seemed to be slow dancing with one another on stage. The creeping hard-on hidden under the oversized shirt added to how her loins throbbed with want. Singing over her shoulder, the heat of his body and breath called forth those erotic moments in the bathroom and office.

Touch me and fuck me, baby. I'm all yours!

Jasper's hand slid over her hip, hidden from prying eyes behind her bass. His fingers trailed down the fabric of the skirt. Her body twitched against him, and she became very aware how muscled his body was, like a wall behind her. Squeezing her eyes tight, she tried to focus on the riff as he rubbed over her clit.

Did he read my mind?!

His cock firm against her ass, she wiggled and returned the motion, partially to bring relief from his fingers making it damn near impossible to play. As he groped her pussy, she struck the wrong chord. Jasper was gone as if it spooked him, and he was back at the mic stand trying not to laugh. Chad and the drummer were chuckling.

How dare he do that to me!

"Goose her again!" slurred someone from the bar top.

Jasper choked on the lyrics and the song fell apart. "Sorry boys, I don't know about you, but I want to make it back home in one piece."

A roar of laughter erupted, and the lights overhead began to flash before staying on. The whole place groaned. *Red's calling it. The signal has fired off to pay up and get the hell out.*

"Ah, looks like closing time. We'll be here next week and hope to see you then, folks!" A few whistle bursts and the crowd turned for the bar to tab out in one mass group. Jasper clunked the mic in place and leaned in to whisper to Rapunzel, "And I hope you follow me off this stage."

His hand grabbed her ass and a chill snaked up her spine. *At this rate, I will follow you and that monster cock anywhere, Mister Magic Fingers!*

Before she could say much, he was throwing cash at the drummer and lead guitarist. *We're done-done. Time to drop my shit in the case and toss it in Red's office. He's getting everyone out of the way for...*

Hustling, her body exhilarated with the anticipation to have one more round with Jasper. Her bass and things were shut tight in the case and the lock spun. Just off stage, Rapunzel locked eyes with Jasper. He motioned with a nod of his head for her to follow, and after a crowd of women obscured the gap between them, he was gone.

Rapunzel's heart fluttered. *Fuck, where did he go?*

Jumping off stage, she beelined for the office, and tossed it in. Part of her hoped to see him there at the desk waiting for her, but no one was there. Stepping back into the now nearly empty bar, the stage was bare, the band gone, and Red cashed out a few last regulars. Her heart leapt to her throat.

Did he just bail on me? Really? With that rock hard cock... no way.

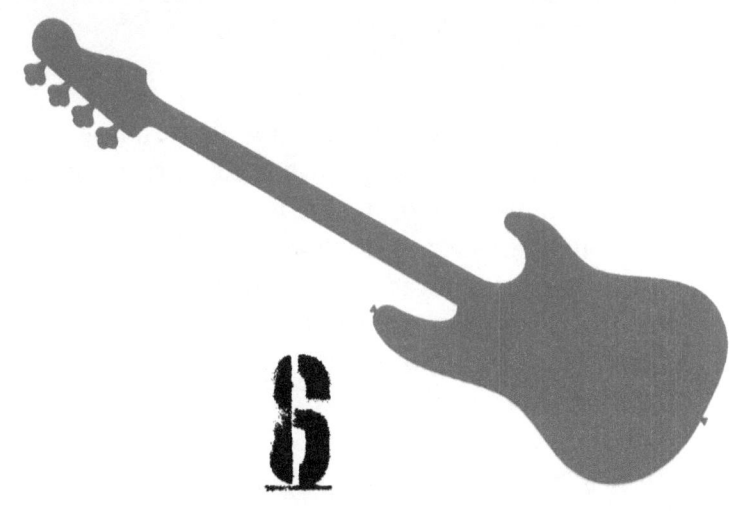

6

I Will Try My Luck

A whistle called her attention behind her where Jasper was slipping through the kitchen door. Her eyes locked with his and his smirk widened before she lost the connection. She gave chase. Weaseling through the last bit of crowd and chairs, she disregarded those who called out to her or tried to give her praise; she was going to catch her prey.

Rushing through the swinging door, ignoring the cook yelling for her to get out, she hurried through the back door. It thudded closed, the bar noise fell silent, and she found herself stumbling out into the back alley. She had lost him to the shadows of the night. Her skin pimpled as the cool air brought a round of shivers. Another whistle from a dark corner brought a smile to her face. Hips swaying, she paced herself.

Don't look desperate, don't look desperate…

"What's up with the game of chase?" she narrowed her eyes as a chill of arousal rolled through her. *I caught you!* "And all that touching and eye-play on stage… what are you hinting at, Bad Boy?" she teased.

Cheeks red, eyes lingering on her lips, he murmured, "I want to taste you so badly," before cupping his hand over his mouth as if trying to prevent anything else from slipping out. "I'm sorry, I don't usually rub up on... on female musicians. I don't know but something about you just has me all..." Holding his breath for a moment, he at last confessed, "...so fucking worked up."

Rapunzel pulled his hand down and kissed him. Lips parting, they deepened it as she pinned him between her and the brick wall. Tugging up his shirt, she wanted to feel his hard cock with her hand once more. She rubbed down the front of his tightened jeans and it throbbed. As she groped him, he moaned into her mouth, tilting his hip to press it firmer into her palm.

Pulling away, Rapunzel demanded, "Fuck me. Right now."

"Anything for her majesty." The deep coo sent an enthralling tremble through her.

Her fingers unfastened the button, and she licked her lips as she unzipped what she wanted the most. The heat of his hand slid under her tank top, shoving the cup of her bra up and off her breasts to grope her once more.

"I don't think I've ever fucked someone I barely met in a back alley." He searched her face, confusion and curiosity filling his expression.

Rapunzel laughed. "I think we're well met after the last few breaks and the way this felt against me."

Jasper wrapped his arms around her, pulling her to him and started to lick her nipple before drawing it between his lips. Her fingers were firm, stroking his length. Her pussy throbbed as her thumb slid over the tip of his cock, slick with pre-cum. Biting her lip, she arched into him, enjoying how hungry he was to taste her body.

Rapunzel lifted a knee, and he rode a hand over her thigh and held it in place. Teeth pinched her nipple and she tugged on his cock harder, squeezing her fingers tight around his solid girth.

"I want…" she panted, catching her breath and trying to speak again, "I want to taste you again."

He let go, surrendering her body as she allowed the cold air to cut between them. Jasper held his breath and watched as she knelt once more. Hot lips pulled his shaft deep into the wet warmth of her mouth, the tip of his cock riding slowly until met with the narrowing of her throat, tight as she suckled. She bobbed up and down on his shaft, and he leaned hard against the cold wall as his knees grew weak.

Gripping her hair, he pulled her off, forcing her to look up at him. Her mouth laid open, tongue like a red carpet, and he watched his dick slide back between her lips until she gagged. Another tug of her hair and the look on her face and moan told him all he needed to know. Bringing her to her feet once more, he pinned her between him and the brick wall, her ass grinding against his cock like they had done all night on stage. She landed two palms against the brick wall and bent over as his hand rode up the back of her thighs and ass cheeks, gripping them tightly before he flipped the skirt up and over her hip.

"Fuck me, Jasper," she panted, wiggling her ass.

With no panties to stop his fingers from rubbing between her swollen folds, he took his time. Slowly, he dipped a finger inside her, hot and wet, and she pushed into him. Both aching, he abandoned his initial aim to play with her. Jasper gripped Rapunzel's hips and pushed his rock-hard cock inside her dripping pussy. Both hummed with the satisfaction of getting to the main event. He took pleasure in pulling all the way out of her, his dick wet and slick from her. Again, slow and agonizing, enjoying every sensation of entering her over and over again.

Her dreads and braids swayed more as he increased the tempo of his fucking. At last, his hands glided over her hip and returned to groping her breasts. Her pussy tightened and he grunted into her ear.

"Shit, I'm…" His voice added to her arousal, her tightening cutting his words. "…Fuck."

"Cum inside me," she moaned, hands reaching back gripping fistfuls of his shirt.

"But…" his tempo faltered, "I don't have a condom."

"I'm on birth control." She rocked into him. "Now give me what I want." Her demand made his cock throb inside her.

"As you wish, my majesty." His murmur made her shiver. "You've let down your hair … and … I've entered your tower."

"Faster, harder," she moaned.

Groping her breast tightly, he pounded her. Rapunzel's skin pimpled as the heat of his breath washed over her neck and shoulder. The thought at any moment someone could discover them, goading them to the edge, until at last, he peaked. A groan escaped him as he shoved forward firm against her, trapping her between him and the brick wall. She inhaled swiftly, the knowing warmth filling her as his cock jerked with each release of cum inside her. He panted in her ear for a moment, and she let him stay there, pinning her as his lips kissed her neck and shoulder, soft and hot like petals against her skin.

Rapunzel's heart pounded and her knees were weak. *When was the last time someone gave me baby deer legs? That tour in Toronto? Or maybe that comedian in Raleigh?*

"Is this what the naughty girl wanted?" His voice was gruff in her ear as a hand slid down across her abdomen. "Are you going to be a good girl for me?"

"Y-yes." Again, he pressed himself tight against her, his cock still inside her.

A finger rolled over her clit and her pussy tightened on his cock. "Good girl, now cum for me."

He grinded into her, his circling growing more aggressive. "So… so close…"

"Be a good girl. Cum on my cock for me." The rumbling in her ear combined with the hard grope of her breast sent her over the edge.

She moaned, bucking a moment before he pounded her until she screamed in ecstasy. When her legs threatened to give out, he stopped, pulling out slowly and they caught their breaths. She flipped around, still leaning on the wall as the feeling came back to her legs.

"Come back to my place," she begged, unwilling to let this end here.

He laughed, zipping his pants. "Are you sure?"

"Fine, bad boy." She pulled off the wall, throwing her arms around his neck, kissing him before offering, "I've got keys to Bob's place."

"Bob's place?" He blinked and a grin grew on his face. "You got keys to every door in there?"

"Only one way to find out, hmm?" Rapunzel broke away from him, straightened her bra and skirt. "I think we should start with some skinny-dipping and move down to the sex dungeon for more fun?"

"You're taking me places I've never fucked before, and I can't seem to say no," he scoffed.

Honey Cummings

A passionate, award-winning author of Fantasy, Honey has turned her aim towards erotica. Blending everyday scenarios and crafting them into steamy, blood-boiling moments for every shade of audience. Whether you want something short and hot like a student-teacher hook up to the more paranormal flair where Sleep with Sasquatch has unexpected bonus, look forward to erotic short stories, novellas, and hopefully a Trilogy in the future. Honey's debut erotic short landed No. 3 in Urban Erotica and continues to satisfy readers time and time again. Be sure to leave her a review and let her know what you think!

https://www.amazon.com/Honey-Cummings/e/B07WFX5FDX
www.AuthorHoneyCummings.com
instagram.com/authorhoneycummings
twitter.com/HoneyCummings2
facebook.com/Author-Honey-Cummings-101408818012749

MORE HONEY CUMMINGS BOOKS

Sleeping with Sasquatch
Cuddling with Chupacabra
Naked with New Jersey Devil
Laying with the Lady in Blue
Wanton Woman in White
Beating it with Bloody Mary

Beau and Professor Bestialora
The Goat's Gruff
Goldie and Her Three Beards
Pied Piper's Pipe

More books from 4 Horsemen Publications

Erotica

Ali Whippe
Office Hours
Tutoring Center
Athletics
Extra Credit
Financial Aid
Bound for Release
Fetish Circuit
Now You See Him
Sexual Playground
Swingers

Chastity Veldt
Molly in Milwaukee
Irene in Indianapolis
Lydia in Louisville
Natasha in Nashville
Alyssa in Atlanta
Betty in Birmingham
Carrie on Campus

Dalia Lance
My Home on Whore Island
Slumming It on Slut Street

Training of the Tramp
The Imperfect Perfection
Spring Break
72% Match
It Was Meant To Be... Or Whatever

Nova Embers
A Game of Sales
How Marketing Beats Dick
Certified Public Alpha (CPA)
On the Job Experience
My GIF is Bigger than Your GIF
Power Play
Plugging in My USB
Hunting the White Elephant
Caution: Slippery When Wet

Shae Coon
Bound in Love
Controlling Assets
For His Own Protection
Her Broken Pieces

Discover more at
4HorsemenPublications.com